PREFACE

THIS volume of *English Short Stories of Today*, the third of the series published for the English Association, differs from its predecessors in that it includes a few stories by Commonwealth authors. Australia is represented by Dal Stivens, Canada by Morley Callaghan, India by Mrs. Jhabvala, New Zealand by Maurice Shadbolt, Nigeria by David Owoyele, South Africa, for its past place in the Commonwealth, by Nadine Gordimer, and the West Indies by George Lamming. Every year brings forth an impressive crop of short stories by accomplished writers of the Commonwealth, and it is to be regretted that room could not be found for more than a small sampling of such stories in a volume which is, as its title indicates, primarily a collection of English short stories.

CONTENTS

CONTENTS

MARY LAVIN

The Great Wave

THE Bishop was sitting in the stern of the boat. He was
in his robes, with his black overcoat thrown across his
shoulders for warmth, and over his arm he carried his vestments, turned inside out to protect them from the salt spray.
The reason he was already robed was because the distance
across to the island was only a few miles, and the island priest
was spared the embarrassment of a long delay in his small
damp sacristy.

The islanders had a visit from their Bishop only every four
years at most, when he crossed over, as now, for the Confirma-
tion ceremony, and so to have His Grace arrive thus in his
robes was only their due share: a proper prolongation of
episcopal pomp. In his alb and amice he would easily be
picked out by the small knot of islanders who would gather on
the pier the moment the boat was sighted on the tops of the
waves. Yes: it was right and proper for all that the Bishop be
thus attired. His Grace approved. The Bishop had a reason
of his own too, as it happened, but it was a small reason, and
he was hardly aware of it anywhere but in his heart.

Now, as he sat in the boat, he wrapped his white skirts
tighter around him, and looked to see that the cope and chas-
uble were well doubled over, so that the coloured silks would
not be exposed when they got away from the lee of the land
and the waves broke on the sides of the currach. The cope
above all must not be tarnished. That was why he stubbornly
carried it across his arm: the beautiful cope that came all the
way from Stansstad, in Switzerland, and was so overworked
with gilt thread that it shone like cloth of gold. The orphreys,
depicting the birth and childhood of Christ, displayed the most
elaborate work that His Grace had ever seen come from the
Paramentenwerkstätte, and yet he was far from unfamiliar
with the work of the Sisters there, in St. Klara. Ever since he

attained the bishopric he had commissioned many beautiful
vestments and altar cloths for use throughout the diocese.
He had once, at their instigation, broken a journey to Rome
to visit them. And when he was there, he asked those brilliant
women to explain to him the marvel, not of their skill, but of his
discernment of it, telling them of his birth and early life as a
simple boy, on this island towards which he was now faced.

'Mind·out!' he said, sharply, as one of the men from the
mainland who was pushing them out with the end of an oar
threw the oar into the boat, scattering the air with drops of
water from its glossy blade. 'Could nothing be done about
this?' he asked, seeing water under the bottom boards of the
boat. It was only a small sup, but it rippled up and down with
a little tide of its own, in time with the tide outside that was
already carrying them swiftly out into the bay.

'Tch, tch, tch,' said the Bishop, for some of this water had
saturated the hem of the alb, and he set about tucking it
under him upon the seat. And then, to make doubly sure of
it, he opened the knot of his cincture and re-tied it as tight
about his middle as if it were long ago and he was tying up a
sack of spuds at the neck. 'Tch, tch,' he repeated, but no one
was unduly bothered by his ejaculations because of his soft
and mild eyes, and, didn't they know him? They knew that in
his complicated, episcopal life he had to contend with a lot,
and it was known that he hated to give his old housekeeper
undue thumping with her flat iron. But there was a thing
would need to be kept dry—the crozier!

'You'd want to keep that yoke there from getting wet
though, Your Grace,' said one of the men, indicating the
crozier that had fallen on the boards. For all that they
mightn't heed his little old-womanish ways, they had a
proper sense of what was fitting for an episcopal appearance.

'I could hold the crozier perhaps,' said Father Kane, the
Bishop's secretary, who was farther up the boat. 'I still think
it would be more suitable for the children to be brought over
to you on the mainland, than for you to be traipsing over here
like this, and in those foreign vestments at that!'

He is thinking of the price that was paid for them, thought

the Bishop, and not of their beauty or their workmanship. And yet, he reflected, Father Kane was supposed to be a highly-educated man, who would have gone on for a profession if he hadn't gone for the priesthood, and who would not have had to depend on the seminary to put the only bit of gloss on him he'd ever get—Like me—he thought! And he looked down at his beautiful vestments again. A marvel, no less, he thought, savouring again the miracle of his power to appreciate such things.

'It isn't as if *they*'ll appreciate them over there,' said Father Kane, with sudden venom, looking towards the island, a thin line of green on the horizon.

'Ah, you can never say that for certain,' said the Bishop mildly, even indifferently. 'Take me, how did I come to appreciate such things?'

But he saw the answer in the secretary's hard eyes. He thinks it was parish funds that paid for my knowledge, and diocesan funds for putting it into practice! And maybe he's right! The Bishop smiled to himself. Who knows anything at all about how we're shaped, or where we're led, or how in the end we are ever brought to our rightful haven?

'How long more till we get there?' he asked, because the island was no longer a vague green mass. Its familiar shapes were coming into focus; the great high promontory throwing its purple shade over the shallow fields by the shore, the sparse white cottages, the cheap cement pier, constantly in need of repairs. And, higher up, on a ledge of the promontory itself there was the plain cement church, its spire only standing out against the sky, bleak as a crane's neck and head.

To think the full height of the promontory was four times the height of the steeple.

The Bishop gave a great shudder. One of the rowers was talking to him.

'Sure, Your Grace ought to know all about this bay. Ah, but I suppose you forget them days altogether now!'

'Not quite, not quite,' said the Bishop, quickly. He slipped his hand inside his robes and rubbed his stomach that had begun already to roll after only a few minutes of the swell.

When he was a little lad, over there on the island, he used to think he'd run away, some day, and join the crew of one of the French fishing trawlers that were always moving backwards and forwards on the rim of the sky. He used to go to a quiet place in the shade of the Point, and settling into a crevice in the rocks, out of reach of the wind, he'd spend the day long staring at the horizon; now in the direction of Liverpool, now in the direction of the Norwegian fjords.

Yet, although he knew the trawlers went from one great port to another, and up even as far as Iceland, he did not really associate them with the sea. He never thought of them as at the mercy of it in the way the little currachs were that had made his mother a widow, and that were jottled by every wave. The trawlers used to seem out of reach of the waves, away out on the black rim of the horizon.

He had in those days a penny jotter in which he put down the day and hour a trawler passed, waiting precisely to mark it down until it passed level with the pier. He put down also other facts about it which he deduced from the small vague outline discernible at that distance. And he smiled to remember the sense of satisfaction and achievement he used to get from that old jotter, which his childish imagination allowed him to believe was a full and exhaustive report. He never thought of the long nights and the early dawns, the hours when he was in the schoolroom, or the many times he was kept in the cottage by his mother, who didn't hold with his hobby.

'Ah son, aren't you all I've got! Why wouldn't I fret about you?' she'd say to him, when he chafed under the yoke of her care.

That was the worst of being an only child, and the child of a sea widow into the bargain. God be good to her! He used to have to sneak off to his cranny in the rocks when he got her gone to the shop of a morning, or up to the chapel of an afternoon to say her beads. She was in sore dread of his even looking out to sea, it seemed! And as for going out in a currach! Hadn't she every currach-crew on the island warned against taking him out?

'Your mammy would be against me, son,' they'd say, when

he'd plead with them, one after another on the shore, and they getting ready to shove their boats down the shingle and float them out on the tide.

'How will I ever get out to the trawlers if I'm not let out in the currachs?' he used to think. That was when he was a little fellow, of course, because when he got a bit older he stopped pestering them, and didn't go down near the shore at all when they were pulling out. They'd got sharp with him by then.

'We can't take any babbies out with us—a storm might come up. What would a babby like you do then?' And he couldn't blame them for their attitude because by this time he knew they could often have found a use for him out in the boats when there was a heavy catch.

'You'll never make a man of him hiding him in your petticoats,' they'd say to his mother, when they'd see him with her in the shop. And there was a special edge on the remark, because men were scarce, as could be seen anywhere on the island by the way the black frieze jackets of the men made only small patches in the big knots of women, with their flaming red petticoats.

His mother had a ready answer for them.

'And why are they scarce?' she'd cry.

'Ah, don't be bitter, Mary.'

'Well, leave me alone then. Won't he be time enough taking his life in his hands when there's more to be got for a netful of ling than there is this year!'

For the shop was always full of dried ling. When you thought to lean on the counter, it was on a long board of ling you leant. When you went to sit down on a box or a barrel it was on top of a bit of dried ling you'd be sitting. And right by the door, a greyhound bitch had dragged down a bit of ling from a hook on the wall and was chewing at it, not furtively, but to the unconcern of all, growling when it found it tough to chew, and attacking it with her back teeth and her head to one side, as she'd chew an old rind of hoof parings in the forge. The juice of it, and her own saliva mixed, was trickling out of her mouth on to the floor.

'There'll be a good price for the first mackerel,' said poor Maurya Keely, their near neighbour, whose husband was ailing, and whose son Seoineen was away in a seminary on the mainland studying to be a priest. 'The seed herring will be coming in any day now.'

'You'll have to let Jimeen out on that day if it looks to be a good catch,' she said, turning to his mother. 'We're having our currach tarred, so's to be all ready against the day.'

Everyone had sympathy with Maurya, knowing her man was nearly done, and that she was in great dread that he wouldn't be fit to go out and get their share of the new season's catch, and she counting on the money to pay for Seoineen's last year in the seminary. Seoineen wasn't only her pride, but the pride of the whole island as well, for, with the scarcity of men folk, the island hadn't given a priest to the diocese in a decade.

'And how is Seoineen? When is he coming home at all?' another woman asked, as they crowded around Maurya. 'He'll soon be facing into the straight,' they said, meaning his ordination, and thinking, as they used the expression, of the way, when Seoineen was a young fellow, he used to be the wildest lad on the island, always winning the ass-race on the shore, the first to be seen flashing into sight around the Point, and he coming up the straight, keeping the lead easily to finish at the pier-head.

'He'll be home for a last leave before the end,' said his mother, and everyone understood the apprehension she tried to keep out of her voice, but which steals into the heart of every priest's mother thinking of the staying power a man needs to reach that end. 'I'm expecting him the week after next,' she said, then suddenly her joy in the thought of having him in the home again took place over everything else.

'Ah, let's hope the mackerel will be in before then!' said several of the women at the one time, meaning there would be a jingle in everyone's pocket then, for Seoineen would have to call to every single cottage on the island, and every single cottage would want to have plenty of lemonade and shop-biscuits too, to put down before him.

Jimeen listened to this with interest and pleased anticipation. Seoineen always took him around with him, and he got a share in all that was set down for the seminarian.

But that very evening Seoineen stepped on to the pier. There was an epidemic in the college and the seminarists that were in their last year like him were let home a whole week before their time.

'Sure, it's not for what I get to eat that I come home, Mother!' he cried, when Maurya began bewailing having no feasting for him. 'If there's anything astray with the life I've chosen it's not shortage of grub! And anyway we won't have long to wait.' He went to the door and glanced up at the sky. 'The seed will be swimming inward tomorrow on the first tide!'

'Oh God forbid!' said Maurya. 'We don't want it that soon either, son, for our currach was only tarred this day!' and her face was torn with two worries now instead of one.

Jimeen had seen the twinkle in Seoineen's eye, and he thought he was only letting-on to know about such things, for how would he have any such knowledge at all, and he away at schools and colleges the best part of his life.

The seed was in on the first tide, though, the next day.

'Oh, they have curious ways of knowing things that you'd never expect them to know,' said Jimeen's own mother. It was taken all over the island to be a kind of prophecy.

'Ah, he was only letting-on, Mother,' said Jimeen, but he got a knock of her elbow over the ear.

'It's time you had more respect for him, son,' she said, as he ran out the door for the shore.

Already most of the island boats were pulling hard out into the bay. And the others were being pushed out as fast as they could be dragged down the shingle.

But the Keely boat was still upscutted in the dune grass under the promontory, and the tar wetly gleaming on it. The other women were clustered around Maurya, giving her consolation.

'Ah sure, maybe it's God's will,' she said. 'Wasn't himself doubled up with pain in the early hours, and it's in a heavy

sleep he is this minute—I wouldn't wake him up whether or
no!—He didn't get much sleep last night. It was late when he
got to his bed. Him and Seoineen stayed up talking by the fire.
Seoineen was explaining to him all about the ordination,
about the fasting they have to do beforehand, and the holy
oils and the chrism and the laying-on of hands. It beat all to
hear him! The creatureen, he didn't get much sleep himself
either, but he's young and able, thank God. But I'll have to
be going back now to call him for Mass.'

'You'll find you won't need to call Seoineen,' said one of
the women. 'Hasn't him, and the like of him, got God's
voice in their hearts all day and they ever and always listening
to it. He'll wake of himself, you'll see. He'll need no calling!'

And sure enough, as they were speaking, who came running
down the shingle but Seoineen.

'My father's not gone out without me, is he?' he cried,
not seeing his own boat, or any sign of it on the shore, a cloud
coming over his face that was all smiles and laughter when he
was running down to them. He began to scan the bay that
was blackened with boats by this time.

'He's not then,' said Maurya. 'He's above in his bed still,
but leave him be, Seoineen—leave him be—' she nodded her
head back towards the shade of the promontory. 'He tarred
the boat yesterday, not knowing the seed 'ud be in so soon, and
it would scald the heart out of him to be here and not able to
take it out. But as I was saying to these good people it's
maybe God's will the way it's happened, because he's not fit
to go out this day!'

'That's true for you, Mother,' said Seoineen, quietly.
'The poor man is nearly beat, I'm fearing.' But the next
minute he threw back his head and looked around the shore.
'Maybe I'd get an oar in one of the other boats. There's surely
a scarcity of men these days?'

'Is it you?' cried his mother, because it mortally offended
her notion of the dignity due to him that he'd be seen with his
coat off maybe—in his shirt sleeves maybe—red in the face
maybe along with that and—God forbid—sweat maybe
breaking out of him!

'To hear you, Mother, anyone would think I was a priest already. I wish you could get a look into the seminary and you'd see there's a big difference made there between the two sides of the fence!' It was clear from the light in his eyes as they swept the sea at that moment that it would take more than a suit of black clothes to stop him from having a bit of fun with an oar. He gave a sudden big laugh, but it fell away as sudden when he saw that all the boats had pulled out from the shore and he was alone with the women on the sand.

Then his face hardened.

'Tell me, Mother,' he cried. 'Is it the boat or my father that's the unfittest? For if it's only the boat then I'll make it fit! It would be going against God's plenitude to stay idle with the sea teeming like that—Look at it!'

For even from where they stood when the waves wheeled inward they could see the silver herring seed glistening in the curving wheels of water, and when those slow wheels broke on the shore they left behind them a spate of seed sticking to everything, even to people's shoes.

'And for that matter, wasn't Christ Himself a fisherman! Come, Mother—tell me the truth! Is the tar still wet or is it not?'

Maurya looked at him for a minute. She was no match for arguing with him in matters of theology, but she knew all about tarring a currach. 'Wasn't it only done yesterday, son?' she said. 'How could it be dry today?'

'We'll soon know that,' said Seoineen, and he ran over to the currach. Looking after him they saw him lay the palm of his hand flat on the upturned bottom of the boat, and then they heard him give a shout of exultation.

'It's not dry surely?' someone exclaimed, and you could tell by the faces that all were remembering the way he prophesied about the catch. Had the tar dried at the touch of his hands maybe?

But Seoineen was dragging the currach down the shingle.

'Why wouldn't it be dry?' he cried. 'Wasn't it a fine dry night. I remember going to the door after talking to my father into the small hours, and the sky was a mass of stars, and there was a fine, sharp wind blowing that you'd be in dread it would dry up the sea itself! Stand back there, Mother,' he cried, for her face was beseeching something of him, and he didn't want to be looking at it. But without looking he knew what it was trying to say. 'Isn't it towards my ordination the money is going? Isn't that argument enough for you?'

He had the boat nearly down to the water's edge. 'No, keep back there, young Jimeen,' he said. 'I'm able to manage it on my own, but let you get the nets and put them in and then be ready to skip in before I push out, because I'll need someone to help haul in the nets.'

'Is it Jimeen?' said one of the women, and she laughed, and then all the women laughed. 'Sure, he's more precious again nor you!' they said.

But they turned to his mother all the same.

'If you're ever going to let him go out at all, this is your one chance, surely? Isn't it like as if it was into the Hands of God Himself you were putting him, woman?'

'Will you let me, Ma?' It was the biggest moment in his life. He couldn't look at her for fear of a refusal.

'Come on, didn't you hear her saying yes—what are you waiting for?' cried Seoineen, giving him a push, and the next minute he was in the currach, and Seoineen had given it a great shove and he running out into the water in his fine shoes and all. He vaulted in across the keel. 'I'm destroyed already at the very start!' he cried, laughing down at his feet and trouser legs, and that itself seemed part of the sport for him. 'I'll take them off,' he cried, kicking the shoes off him, and pulling off his socks, till he was in his bare white feet. 'Give me the oars,' he cried, but as he gripped them he laughed again, and loosed his fingers for a minute, as one after the other he rubbed his hands on a bit of sacking on the seat beside him. For, like the marks left by the trawler men on the white bollard at the pier, the two bleached oars were marked with the track of his hands, palms, and fingers, in pitch black tar.

'The tar was wet!'

'And what of it?' cried Seoineen. 'Isn't it easy give it another lick of a brush?'

But he wasn't looking at Jimeen and he saying it, his eyes were lepping along the tops of the waves to see if they were pulling near the other currachs.

The other currachs were far out in the bay already: the sea was running strong. For all that, there was a strange still look about the water, unbroken by any spray. Jimeen sat still, exulting in his luck. The waves did not slap against the sides of the currach like he'd have thought they would do, and they didn't even break into spray where the oars split their surface. Instead, they seemed to go lolloping under the currach and lollop up against the far side, till it might have been on great glass rollers they were slipping along.

'God! Isn't it good to be out on the water!' cried Seoineen, and he stood up in the currach, nearly toppling them over in his exuberance, drawing in deep breaths, first with his nose, and then as if he were drinking it with his mouth, and his eyes at the same time taking big draughts of the coast-line that was getting farther and farther away. 'Ah, this is the life: this is the real life,' he cried again, but they had to look to the oars and look to the nets, then, for a while, and for a while they couldn't look up at sea or sky.

When Jimeen looked up at last, the shore was only a narrow line of green.

'There's a bit of a change, I think,' said Seoineen, and it was true.

The waves were no longer round and soft, like the little cnoceens in the fields back of the shore, but they had small sharp points on them now, like the rocks around the Point, that would rip the bottom out of a boat with one tip, the way a tip of a knife would slit the belly of a fish.

That was a venomous comparison though and for all their appearance, when they hit against the flank of the boat, it was only the waves themselves that broke and patterned the water with splotches of spray.

It was while he was looking down at these white splotches that Jimeen saw the fish.

'Oh look, Seoineen, look!' he cried, because never had he seen the like.

BESS

They were not swimming free, or separate, like you'd think they'd be, but a great mass of them together, till you'd think it was at the floor of the sea you were looking, only it nearer and shallower.

There must have been a million fish; a million, million, Jimeen reckoned wildly, and they pressed as close as the pebbles on the shore. And they might well have been motionless and only seeming to move like on a windy day you'd think the grass on the top of the promontory was running free like the waves, with the way it rippled and ran along a little with each breeze.

'Holy God, such a sight!' cried Seoineen. 'Look at them!'

But Jimeen was puzzled.

'How will we get them into the net?' he asked, because it didn't seem that there was any place for the net to slip down between them, but that it must lie on the top of that solid mass of fish, like on a floor.

'The nets: begod, I nearly forgot what we came out here for!' cried Seoineen, and at the same time they became aware of the activity in the other boats, which had drawn near without their knowing. He yelled at Jimeen. 'Catch hold of the nets there, you lazy good-for-nothing. What did I bring you with me for if it wasn't to put you to some use!' and he himself caught at a length of the brown mesh, thrown in the bottom of the boat, and began to haul it up with one hand, and with the other to feed it out over the side.

Jimeen, too, began to pull and haul, so that for a few minutes there was only a sound of the net swishing over the wood, and every now and then a bit of a curse, under his breath, from Seoineen as one of the cork floats caught in the thole pins.

At first it shocked Jimeen to hear Seoineen curse, but he reflected that Seoineen wasn't ordained yet, and that, even if he were, it must be a hard thing for a man to go against his nature.

'Come on, get it over the side, damn you,' cried Seoineen again, as Jimeen had slowed up a bit owing to thinking about the cursing. 'It isn't one net-full but thirty could be filled this

day! Sure you could fill the boat in fistfuls,' he cried, suddenly
leaning down over the side, delving his bare hand into the
water. With a shout, he brought up his hand with two fish,
held one against the other in the same grip, so that they were as
rigid as if they were dead. 'They're overlaying each other a foot
deep,' he cried, and then he opened his fist and freed them.
Immediately they writhed apart to either side of his hand in
two bright arcs and then fell, both of them, into the bottom of
the boat. But next moment they writhed into the air again,
and flashed over the side of the currach.

'Ah begorras, you'll get less elbow-room there than here,
my boys,' cried Seoineen, and he roared laughing, as he and
Jimeen leant over the side, and saw that sure enough, the two
mackerel were floundering for a place in the glut of fishes.

But a shout in one of the other currachs made them look up.

It was the same story all over the bay. The currachs were
tossing tipsily in the water with the antics of the crews, that
were standing up and shouting and feeding the nets ravenously
over the sides. In some of the boats that had got away early,
they were still more ravenously hauling them up, strained and
swollen with the biggest catch they had ever held.

There was not time for Seoineen or Jimeen to look around
either, for just then the keel of their own currach began to dip
into the water.

'Look out! Pull it up—! Catch a better grip than that,
damn you. Do you want to be pulled into the sea. Pull, damn
you, pull!' cried Seoineen.

Now every other word that broke from his throat was a
curse, or what you'd call a curse if you heard them from
another man, or in another place, but in this place, from this
man, hearing them issue wild and free, Jimeen understood that
they were a kind of psalm. They rang out over the sea in a
kind of praise to God for all his plenitude.

'Up! Pull hard—up, now, up!' he cried, and he was
pulling at his end like a madman.

Jimeen pulled too, till he thought his heart would crack,
and then suddenly the big white belly of the loaded net came
in sight over the water.

Jimeen gave a groan, though, when he saw it.

'Is it dead they are?' he cried, and there was anguish in his voice.

Up to this, the only live fish he had ever seen were the few fish tangled in the roomy nets, let down by the old men over the end of the pier, and *they* were always full of life, needling back and forth insanely in the spacious mesh till he used to swallow hard, and press his lips close together fearing one of them would dart down his gullet, and he'd have it ever after needling this way and that inside him! But there was no stir at all in the great white mass that had been hauled up now in the nets.

'Is it dead they are?' he cried again.

'Aahh, why would they be dead? It's suffocating they are, even below in the water, with the welter of them is in it,' cried Seoineen.

He dragged the net over the side where it emptied and spilled itself into the bottom of the boat. They came alive then all right! Flipping and floundering, and some of them flashing back into the sea. But it was only a few on the top that got away, the rest were kept down by the very weight and mass of them that was in it. And when, after a minute, Seoineen had freed the end of the net, he flailed them right and left till most of them fell back flat. Then, suddenly, he straightened up and swiped a hand across his face to clear it of the sweat that was pouring out of him.

'Ah sure, what harm if an odd one leps for it,' he cried. 'We'll deaden them under another netful! Throw out your end,' he cried.

As Jimeen rose up to his full height to throw the net wide out, there was a sudden terrible sound in the sky over him, and the next minute a bolt of thunder went volleying overhead, and with it, in the same instant it seemed, the sky was knifed from end to end with a lightning flash.

Were they blinded by the flash? Or had it suddenly gone as black as night over the whole sea?

'Oh God's Cross!' cried Seoineen. 'What is coming? Why didn't someone give us a shout? Where are the others? Can

you see them? Hoy there! Marteen! Seumas? Can you
hear——?'

For they could see nothing. And it was as if they were all
alone in the whole world. Then, suddenly, they made out
Marteen's currach near to them, so near that, but for Seoineen
flinging himself forward and grabbing the oars, the two
currachs would have knocked together. Yet no sooner had
they been saved from knocking together than they suddenly
seemed so far sundered again they could hardly hear each
other when they called out.

'What's happening, in Christ's name?' bawled Seoineen,
but he had to put up his hands to trumpet his voice, for the
waves were now so steep and high that even one was enough
to blot out the sight of Marteen. Angry white spume dashed in
their faces.

'It's maybe the end of the world,' said Jimeen, terror-
stricken.

'Shut up and let me hear Marteen!' said Seoineen, for
Marteen was bawling at them again.

'Let go the nets,' Marteen was bawling—'let go the nets or
they'll drag you out of the boat.'

Under them then they could feel the big pull of the net that
was filled up again in an instant with its dead weight of
suffocating fish.

'Let it go, I tell you,' bawled Marteen.

'Did you hear? He's telling us to let it go,' piped Jimeen in
terror, and he tried to free his own fingers of the brown mesh
that had closed right tight upon them with the increasing
weight. 'I can't let go,' he cried, looking to Seoineen, but he
shrank back from the strange wild look in Seoineen's eyes.
'Take care would you do anything of the kind!'

'It's cutting off my fingers!' he screamed.

Seoineen glared at him.

'A pity about them!' he cried, but when he darted a look at
them, and saw them swelling and reddening, he cursed.
'Here—wait till I take it from you,' he cried, and he went to
free his own right hand, but first he laced the laden fingers of
his left hand into the mesh above the right hand, and even

then, the blood spurted out in the air when he finally dragged it free of the mesh.

For a minute Seoineen shoved his bleeding fingers into his mouth and sucked them, then he reached out and caught the net below where Jimeen gripped it. As the weight slackened, the pain of the searing strings lessened, but next minute as the pull below got stronger, the pain tore into Jimeen's flesh again.

'Let go now, if you like, now I have a bit of a hold of it anyway—now I'm taking the weight of it off you,' said Seoineen.

Jimeen tried to drag free.

'I can't,' he screamed in terror, '—the strings are eating into my bones!'

Seoineen altered his balance and took more weight off the net at that place.

'Now!'

'I can't! I can't!' screamed Jimeen.

From far over the waves the voice of Marteen came to them again, faint, unreal, like the voices you'd hear in a shell if you held it to your ear.

'Cut free—cut free,' it cried, 'or else you'll be destroyed altogether.'

'Have they cut free themselves? That's what I'd like to know?' cried Seoineen.

'Oh, do as he says, Seoineen. Do as he says,' screamed Jimeen.

And then, as he saw a bit of ragged net, and then another and another rush past like the briery patches of foam on the water that was now almost level with the rowlocks, he knew that they had indeed all done what Marteen said; cut free.

'For the love of God, Seoineen,' he cried.

Seoineen hesitated for another instant. Then suddenly made up his mind and, reaching along the seat, he felt without looking for the knife that was kept there for slashing dogfish.

'Here goes,' he cried, and with one true cut of the knife he freed Jimeen's hands the two together at the same time, but, letting the knife drop into the water, he reached out wildly to catch the ends of the net before they slid into it, or shed any of the their precious freight.

Not a single silver fish was lost.

'What a fool I'd be,' he gasped, 'to let go. They think because of the collar I haven't a man's strength about me any more. Then I'll show them. I'll not let go this net, not if it pull me down to hell.' And he gave another wild laugh. 'And you along with me!' he cried. 'Murder?' he asked then, as if he had picked up the word from a voice in the wind. 'Is it murder? Ah sure, I often think it's all one to God what a man's sin is, as long as it's sin at all. Isn't sin poison—any sin at all, even the smallest drop of it? Isn't it death to the soul that it touches at any time? Ah then! I'll not let go!' And even when, just then, the whole sea seemed littered with tattered threads of net, he still held tight to his hold. 'Is that the way? They've all let go! Well then, I'll show them one man will not be so easy beat! Can you hear me?' he cried, because it was hard to hear him with the crazy noise of the wind and the waves.

'Oh cut free, Seoineen,' Jimeen implored, although he remembered the knife was gone now to the bottom of the sea, and although the terrible swollen fingers were beyond help in the mangling ropes of the net.

'Cut free is it? Faith now! I'll show them all,' cried Seoineen. 'We'll be the only boat'll bring back a catch this night, and the sea seething with fish.' He gave a laugh. 'Sure that was the only thing that was spoiling my pleasure in the plenty! thinking that when the boats got back the whole island would be fuller of fish than the sea itself, and it all of no more value than if it was washed of its own accord on to the dirty counters of the shop! Sure it wouldn't be worth a farthing a barrel! But it will be a different story now, I'm thinking. Oh, but I'll have the laugh on them with their hollow boats, and their nets cut to flitters! I'll show them a man is a man, no matter what vows he takes, or what way he's called to deny his manhood! I'll show them! Where are they, anyway? Can you— see them—at all?' he cried, but he had begun to gasp worse than the fishes in the bottom of the boat. 'Can you—see them

—at all? Damn you, don't sit there like that! Stand up—
there—and tell me—can—you—see—them!'

It wasn't the others Jimeen saw though, when he raised his
eyes from the torn hands in the meshes. All he saw was a
great wall, a great green wall of water. No currachs anywhere.
It was as if the whole sea had been stood up on its edge, like
a plate on a dresser. And down that wall of water there slid a
multitude of dead fish.

And then, down the same terrible wall, sliding like the dead
fish, came an oar; a solitary oar. And a moment afterwards,
but inside the glass wall, imprisoned, like under a glass dome,
he saw—oh God!—a face, looking out at him, staring out at
him through a foot of clear green water. And he saw it was the
face of Marteen. For a minute the eyes of the dead man stared
into his eyes.

With a scream he threw himself against Seoineen, and clung
to him tight as iron.

How many years ago was that? The Bishop opened his eyes.
They were so near the shore he could pick out the people by
name that stood on the pier-head. His stomach had stopped
rolling. It was mostly psychological; that feeling of nausea.
But he knew it would come back in an instant if he looked
leftward from the shore, leftwards and upwards, where, over
the little cement pier and over the crane-bill steeple of the
church, the promontory that they called the Point rose up
black with its own shadow.

For it was on that promontory—four times the height of the
steeple—they had found themselves, he and Seoineen, in the
white dawn of the day after the Wave, lying in a litter of dead
fish, with the netful of fish like an anchor sunk into the green
grass.

When he came to himself in that terrible dawn, and felt
the slippy bellies of the fish all about him, he thought he was
still in the boat, lying in the bottom among the mackerel, but
when he opened his eyes and saw a darkness as of night, over
his head, he thought it was still the darkness of the storm and
he closed them again in terror.

Just before he closed them, though, he thought he saw a

star, and he ventured to open them again, and then he saw
that the dark sky over him was a sky of skin, stretched taut
over timber laths, and the star was only a glint of light—and
the blue light of day at that—coming through a split in the
bottom of the currach. For the currach was on top of him!—
Not he in the bottom of it.

Why then was he not falling down and down and down
through the green waters? His hands rushed out to feel around
him. But even then, the most miraculous thing he thought to
grasp was a fistful of sand, the most miraculous thing he
thought to have to believe was that they were cast up safe
upon the shore.

Under his hands though, that groped through the fishes,
he came, not on sand, but on grass, and not upon the coarse
dune grass that grew back from the shore at the foot of the
Point. It was soft, sweet little grass, that was like the grass he
saw once when Seoineen and he had climbed up the face of the
Point, and stood up there, in the sun, looking down at all
below, the sea and the pier, and the shore and the fields, and
the thatch of their own houses, and on a level with them, the
grey spire of the chapel itself!

It was, when opening his eyes wide at last, he saw, out
from him a bit, the black grey tip of that same chapel-spire
that he knew where he was.

Throwing the fish to left and right he struggled to get to his
feet.

It was a miracle! And it must have been granted because
Seoineen was in the boat. He remembered how he prophesied
the seed would be on the tide, and in his mind he pictured
their currach being lifted up in the air and flown, like a bird,
to this grassy point.

But where was Seoineen?

'Oh Seoineen, Seoineen!' he cried, when he saw him
standing on the edge of the Point looking downward, like
they looked, that day, on all below. 'Oh Seoineen, was it a
miracle?' he cried, and he didn't wait for an answer, but he
began to shout and jump in the air.

'Quit, will you!' said Seoineen, and for a minute he thought

it must be modesty on Seoineen's part, it being through him
the miracle was granted, and then he thought it must be the
pain in his hands that was at him, not letting him enjoy the
miracle, because he had his two hands pressed under his
armpits.

Then suddenly he remembered the face of Marteen he had
seen under the wall of water, and his eyes flew out over the
sea that was as flat and even now, as the field of grass under
their feet. Was Marteen's currach lost? And what of the
others?

Craning over the edge of the promontory he tried to see
what currachs were back in their places, under the little wall,
dividing the sand from the dune, turned upside down and
leaning a little to one side, so you could crawl under them if
you were caught in a sudden shower.

There were no currachs under the wall: none at all.

There were no currachs on the sea.

Once, when he was still wearing a red petticoat like a
girsha, there had been a terrible storm and half a score of
currachs were lost. He remembered the night with all the
women on the island down on the shore with storm lamps,
swinging them and calling out over the noise of the waves.
And the next day they were still there, only kneeling on the
pier, praying and keening.

'Why aren't they praying and keening?' he cried then, for
he knew at last the other currachs, all but theirs, were lost.

'God help them,' said Seoineen, 'at least they were spared
that.'

And he pointed to where, stuck in the latticed shutters on
the side of the steeple, there were bits of seaweed, and—yes—
a bit of the brown mesh of a net.

'God help you,' he said then, 'how can your child's mind
take in what a grown man's mind can hardly hold—but you'll
have to know some time—we're all alone—the two of us—on
the whole island. All that was spared by that wall of water——'

'All that was on the sea, you mean?' he cried.

'And on the land too,' said Seoineen.

'Not my mother——?' he whimpered.

'Yes, and my poor mother,' said Seoineen. 'My poor mother
that tried to stop us from going out with the rest.'

But it was a grief too great to grasp, and yet, yet even in face
of it, Jimeen's mind was enslaved to the thought of their
miraculous salvation.

'Was it a miracle, Seoineen?' he whispered. 'Was it a
miracle we were spared?'

But Seoineen closed his eyes, and pushed his crossed arms
deeper under his arm-pits. The grimace of pain he made was—
even without words—a rebuke to Jimeen's exaltation. Then he
opened his eyes again.

'It was my greed that was the cause of all,' he said, and
there was such a terrible sorrow in his face that Jimeen, only
then, began to cry. 'It has cost me my two living hands,' said
Seoineen, and there was a terrible anguish in his voice.

'But it saved your life, Seoineen,' he cried, wanting to
comfort him.

Never did he forget the face Seoineen turned to him.

'For what?' he asked. 'For what?'

And there was, in his voice, such despair, that Jimeen
knew it wasn't a question but an answer; so he said no more
for a few minutes. Then he raised his voice again, timidly.

'You saved my life too, Seoineen.'

Seoineen turned dully and looked at him.

'For what?'

But as he uttered them, those same words took on a change,
and a change came over his face, too, and when he repeated
them, the change was violent.

'For what?' he demanded. 'For what?'

Just then, on the flat sea below, Jimeen saw the boats,
coming across from the mainland, not currachs like they had
on the island, but boats of wood made inland, in Athlone, and
brought down on lorries.

'Look at the boats,' he called out, four, five, six, any amount
of them; they came rowing for the island.

Less than an hour later Seoineen was on his way to the
hospital on the mainland, where he was to spend long months
before he saw the island again. Jimeen was taken across a few

hours later, but when he went it was to be for good. He was going to an aunt, far in from the sea, of whom he had never heard tell till that day.

Nor was he to see Seoineen again, in all the years that followed. On the three occasions that he was over on the island, he had not seen him. He had made enquiries, but all he could ever get out of people was that he was a bit odd.

'And why wouldn't he be?' they added.

But although he never came down to the pier to greet the Bishop like the rest of the islanders, it was said he used to slip into the church after it had filled up and he'd think he was unnoticed. And afterwards, although he never once would go down to the pier to see the boat off, he never went back into his little house until it was gone clear across to the other side of the bay. From some part of the island it was certain he'd be the last to take leave of the sight.

It had been the same on each visit the Bishop made, and it would be the same on this one.

When he would be leaving the island, there would be the same solicitous entreaties with him to put on his overcoat. Certainly he was always colder going back in the late day. But he'd never give in to do more than throw it over his shoulders, from which it would soon slip down on to the seat behind him.

'You'd do right to put it on like they told you,' said the secretary, buttoning up this own thick coat.

But there was no use trying to make him do a thing he was set against. He was a man had deep reasons for the least of his actions.

WILLIAM SANSOM

Cat up a Tree

A WILD, glassy morning—all winds and glitter . . . the sun glared low between the chimneys, through black winter branches, blinding you at a slant, dazzling white and bright straight in the eyes—it made a splintering dance of everything, it made for squints and sniggering. . . .

Winds swept from nowhere, scooping up leaves and hustling them round the corner, knocking little dogs sideways, snatching and flapping at your trouser-legs. Cold nipped at noses and pinched ears red . . . it sang with cold in the keen bright light. Under a white sky the walls, roads, people, trees shone brightly coloured, red, green, blue, grey colours, as in a folk-tale, as if everything were made of coloured glass. Behind white cloud the sun hung and fiercely glowed, a monstrous incandescent mantle. A gentleman crossing the road moved like a puppet, parts of him glittering—one feared that by his own tread he might smash to smithereens his polished boots on the brittle macadam. . . .

Gentleman? He was no gentleman, he was a fireman. A jerky, puppety fireman, in blue trousers piped red, black jogging topboots, and in his braces and white sleeves. He carried a broom. He looked like a puppet because he was then crossing the road in the light—he walked so slowly against the hustling and swirling of the leaves, the dust, the winds, the shattering light.

Hindle Rice, alias Pudden Rice, number sefenty-too-fife, going then through the big red door into the Appliance Room, white-tiled like a scrubbed lavatory for motor-cars, where big top-heavy engines stood and waited, where now Pudden Rice would sweep together over the tiled floor a few small piles of dust, leaving these neat pyramids for the officers to see as they passed in their peaked caps, while in the shelter of such evidence of work proceeding Pudden Rice would for the rest of the morning lean on his broom and think or chat or smile to the good-mornings, or break-for-tea, or perhaps if he felt brave drop the precious broom altogether and abandon his alibi to collect and break up twigs for firewood at home.

Rice soon dropped the broom. Out in front of the station the black wintry twigs cracked and snapped in his hands. That sunlight caught his eyes, so he could see nothing in front but bright light, as of a halo; and to each side things moved too quickly and glittered like glass. A cat went dashing past, its fur ruffled forward by a following gust of wind. Up the street two navvies were hitting at a metal spike with steel hammers— the blows came ringing on the wind like sharp bells distorted. An old woman in black scurried by with her veil blown fast into her teeth: she mouthed as this tickled under her nose, grimacing at Pudden Rice with her head tilted queerly to one side. Yet in a little garden opposite a girl sat reading, sheltered by a bush in a warm pocket of sunlight! A paper bag sailed like a wingless pouter suddenly out from some trees and on over her head—then disappeared abruptly over the top of a bush. The girl waved at its shadow, as if it might have been a fly, and remained throughout reading unconcerned.

Rice smiled to see the girl sitting so quietly. Then he saw a pile of leaves on the pavement in front form suddenly into a single file, trickle round in a wide circle, then run for the shelter of a tree-trunk.

A window above banged open and a voice piped: 'Rice! Rice!'

Pudden dashed for his broom and then carrying it walked slowly to the stairs. He climbed the stone steps, circling with them the black-barred well down which hung long grey hose lengths and ropes, and muttered to these shiplike hangings: 'Now what's the matter? Now what's up? I swept the tiles, didn't I? I done my job?'

He had reached the landing and was about to turn in through the green swing doors—when the whole station leapt alive with sound, sudden as a thunderclap, high-pitched and vibrating for ever, flashing off the tiles, reverberating round the brass BRNNNNNNNNG—the deafening alarm bell gripped in its electric circuit and ringing on and on for ever. . . .

Rice flung down his broom and dived through the swing doors. Across the room and into a passage—to a sudden end where two brass rails stood flanking a steel pole. Now the clatter of footsteps everywhere, and the alarm bell still jangling, Rice stamped his foot on a brass doorknob, a spring trap-door shot open upwards—and there was the hole! He jumped over it and gripping the smooth steel pole disappeared flying down. A rubber mat at the bottom, and all around suddenly the Appliance Room's white tiles again, with the engine of the Pump already roaring, men scrambling into boots, and more coming sailing down the pole, on that light-headed morning like a rain of heavy angels. But angels with funny faces— Nobby redhaired and pointed like a fox, Graetz with his comic round moon-face sprouting high up like a sunflower, Sailor with no neck and like John Bull washed white by a bad liver, Curly with his bright bald head, fairhaired Teetgen like a fresh blank Apollo with black teeth. These all came sliding down and scrambled for the Pump, Rice among them. He jumped up on to one of the high side seats and started to pull up his leggings. The automatic door flew open and the Pump clanged out into the sunshine, as into a fog of white crystal, so that as they turned and roared off down the street light struck up from each brass fitting and from the axes and silver buttons—and somehow the heaviness was washed away.

Perched high up on the side, Pudden struggled into his coat. It flapped and blew out its short tails. He was just able to see the girl in the garden smile—and then his helmet fell down over his eyes. One legging flapped loose. The engine tore along, accelerating faster and faster, until it seemed to Pudden high up above the windshields that perhaps they had left the ground and were scudding through the air itself. The officer in front clanged the clapper of the brass bell as fast as a hand could move. Up England's Lane they tore, down Downshire Hill, through the Crescent, up Flask Walk, down Well Walk, sweeping along the middle of the wide roads like an angry brass beetle, roaring up the narrow streets and scattering dogs and cats and barrows and once an old lady carrying even in November a lilac parasol.

That morning the weather had made poets of the people. It sometimes happens—an angular trick of the sun, a warmness of a wind, something stirs an exultation in the most unexpected hearts. Not in the hearts of all the people ever, but sometimes in those ready to be stirred, and sometimes also in dull hearts of which this would never have been imagined, but these people too receive a sudden jerk, a prod in the spirit, a desire for more than they usually want. Memories arise of things that have never been, tolerance arrives. They laugh— but perhaps that is only because they are nervous at the odd look of things. A trick of the weather has transformed the street, the hour, life. Perhaps this trick is a more powerful agent than the liver or even the libido. Perhaps one day it will be agreed that finally the most critical words of all are 'good morning'.

The passers-by smiled, one waved his hat, and a middle-aged butcher brandished a chop at them. Pudden still struggled with his uniform—how it eluded him! The belt and axe caught in the hooks behind him, his round helmet kept falling over an eye, an ear—and once his foot missed its support on the running-board and he nearly fell off the machine. He gripped the brass rail just in time. Yet, awkwardly as these things tugged at him—the wind, the clothes, the belt—he began to grin: 'What an odd engine—how peculiar that on most days it seems so heavy, so oiled and dully heavy with its iron extinguishers, its massive suction pipes, its hard wood ladders—yet today . . . all I can see about it is light, and how high it seems, how topheavy, and most striking of all are the brass rails and the red leather cushions! It's as upright as a queen's coach! And here we are—Nobby, Graetz, Teetgen, Sailor and me and the officer—all sitting and standing high up on top, like exuberant Boy Scouts, or tin soldiers, or travellers packed up on top of an old-fashioned coach! Ridiculous!'

But it was really so. The engine was built higher than cars are built usually, and brass rails armed the erect leather seats, vestiges of the horse days, a tradition to be surrendered unwillingly.

The bare trees skidded past. Rows of front doors approached and receded, innumerable windows winked and flashed in the fierce glare. The skyline of roofs and chimneys stood out black, giantly as against a milk-white sunset. Far off there appeared a church spire, it grew into a pointed little church, into a large grey church, and then this too was gone, veering off to the left. At last Pudden got himself straight. He then stood up and faced the wind, one leg crouched up by the ladders. This made him feel a dashing fellow. Phlegmatic usually, this pose in the wind and this clinging to a precarious rail excited him, never failing to rouse in him old postures of bravado learnt from early adventure books. Then, in the sharp sunlight, with the little houses flashing by, he thought suddenly: 'Good Lord— we're going to a fire! Perhaps to a real fire! It may possibly be a false alarm pulled by a boy or a drunk or someone. (He saw a sheet of figures—over 1,000 False Alarms Malicious last year—one of them fatal—a fireman was killed, crushed against the garage door in the rush for somebody's funny joke.) But . . . perhaps it really is a fire, this one time, by chance the real thing? Asphyxia, boiling, frying—I saw a fireman frizzled up in burning oil till he was like a little black monkey, a charred little monkey wearing a helmet several sizes too big for him. And when Sailor tripped in the molten rubber—his arm. Andy's neck after that sulphuric acid job. . . .'

Rice looked down at the two shining round helmets primping up in front of him. He laughed, and felt the corners of his mouth split and all the teeth catch in the wind, he laughed and seemed inside to shine with laughter; how could frying and falling walls happen on this kind of a glass morning? Hot smoke in this pure air? Such things happen to a rosy-cheeked crew of bright tin soldiers? The wind echoed in his ears like a sea-breeze, thrumming past as regular as telegraph wires, and still the sun shot pinpoints off the brass and glared whitely from the chimney-tops ahead. Suddenly Pudden began to hum a march, a high-pitched jigging march for dwarfs stomping off to the forest and the anvils—as joyfully repetitive as train music. . . .

They skidded round a corner and braked to a stop. They

were in a cul-de-sac made up of small white houses with painted doors. Trees growing behind showed above the roofs, an effect peculiar in a large city. These looked like country cottages, and the windows were in each case so cramped up and warped that the houses seemed to be no more than a pack of doors and windows clustered together, balancing for breath. A few trained bushes stood in tubs like sentinel birds before the black and pink and primrose doors. And there on the pavement corner stood the fire alarm post, singular and red, as bright a red as when the snow is on the ground.

They leapt off the machine, the officer ran up to the alarm and then stood by it, looking right and left, uncertain, while the broken glass twinkled beneath his polished boots. Rice thought: 'Bright as the day Teetgen went to the paint factory fire and came away with his boots varnished, bright for days!'

The officer peered into the alarm—it had certainly been pulled. But no one was there to direct him. He looked up at the windows, then behind him—searching with his eyes anxiously for smoke. 'That's the crazy people they are,' thought Rice, 'pulling the bell and then running away expecting us to find the job by magic. That's them.'

A small boy appeared from behind one of the bird-bushes. The officer frowned and strode heavily towards him in his big boots.

'Well, son—and who pulled it?' He looked like a giant wooden soldier towering above the suddenly real boy. Blue coat splashed with red, silver buttons and axe, round red face as neat as a doll's, shining black leggings stiff-legged.

Ignoring the question, the boy said: 'Is there a fire, mister?'

'How long have you been here?' the officer asked, his voice sharpening with suspicion—then turned his head so that his face shone brightly in the sunlight. He yelled over his shoulder to the firemen peering about: 'One of you—scout round the corner!'

Attracted by the sound of bells and brakes and the stamping of boots, there had by then collected a small crowd of onlookers. Half of these were boys, carrying rifles and swords, or driving small pedal cars. One wore on his head a top hat peaked with half a brim only, painted blue and labelled *La France*. Two painters in white overalls looked sadly at the fire engine. A tall man with a thin face clouded with red veins asked if he could lend a hand. A smartly dressed woman dragging a trolley laden with shopping smiled and smiled, as though she was the mother of all and 'she knew'. A man in a blue uniform winked at Teetgen, because *he* knew too—he knew it was just another bloody exercise, mate. Three Jewish exiles passed hurriedly, twisting their necks round to keep the uniforms in sight, frightened, round-eyed as owls.

By then Graetz, a tall white sunflower with his round face drooping off his long neck—Graetz was standing isolated in a circle of boys and saying aloud for their benefit: 'It's a false alarm—and from now on we've got our eye on this post. Got a policeman on it, we have, so in future . . .'

When suddenly in a garden wall between two houses a door burst open and a fat woman in a broad white apron came bustling out. She ran towards the Pump with her arms outstretched, as though the Pump might at any moment recede and vanish. She began shouting as soon as she appeared: 'Don't go! Don't go! Oh, I'm so glad you came! Milly's up a tree.' Then paused for breath as the officer went up to her. 'It's round the back, round the back,' she panted, 'and I pulled the alarm, you see. They told me it was right—you see, she's been up there since last night. She mews so.'

The officer said, 'How do we get through?' And at the same time shouted back to the men, 'Cat up a tree. Bring the ladders.'

Teetgen and Nobby jumped up to the front of the ladders on top of the Pump. Graetz and Rice began to pull at the bottom. The straps uncoiled and then the long ladder came sliding out. Once again Rice felt like a puppet, a wooden soldier clockworked with the others into an excited, pre-arranged game. The sunlight seemed to blow by in bright gusts. Now everybody was laughing—except one of the lugubrious painters, who began to grumble loudly about the

bleeding waste of petrol and men's time. But the other onlookers found it great sport, and in the laughing dazzling light
began to shout: 'Pretty Pussy!' and 'Mind it don't bite you
now!' and 'See you keep her nightdress down!'—this last
from the thin man with the bad veins.

Pulling at the ladder Nobby said: 'Last week an old girl
called us for a parrot up a tree. But we wouldn't go. Cat-up-a-
tree's legal, parrots isn't.'

Now the fat woman in the apron bolted back through the
garden door with the officer following. The four men carrying
the ladder squeezed through at the double. Rice at the rear
end nearly jammed himself between the brick wall and the
heavy wooden ladder, catching his fingers in the extension
pawl, nearly coming a cropper and laughing again. Then they
were in the garden—apple-trees and young beech saplings, a
black winter tracing of branches everywhere against the
glowing white cloud beyond. The sun glared through this
filigree, striping the litter of dry leaves, striping the air itself
with opaque lightshafts.

'There she is, lads,' shouted the doll officer, pointing upwards. The other dolls doubled up with the ladder working
like clockwork, raising their knees in a jocular movement as
they ran.

Above them, isolated at the very top of a tall sapling,
crouched on the tapering end of this thin shoot so that it
bent over under the weight like a burdened spring—sat a huge
dazed cat.

In a book of children's stories this cat would have seemed
improbable and amusing. Its position was as improbable as
that of a blue pig flying. It looked like a heavy young puma
borne by what appeared to be a tall and most resilient twig.
In real life a branch so thin would have snapped. Yet here this
was—happening on a bright November morning, a real
morning though rather light-headed. In children's books too
there are pictured with vivid meaning certain fantasies of the
weather—lowering black storms, huge golden suns, winds that
bend all the trees into weeping willows, skies of electric blue
with stars dusted on them like tinsel, moons encircled by

magical haloes. These appear highly artificial, drawn from
the inspiration of a dreamland: but they are true. These
skies and suns and winds happen quite frequently. So that on
that morning what appeared to be unreal was real, apparently
richened by association, but originally rich in its entity that
had created the fairy association. Thus this was a witches'
morning, a morning of little devils and hats popping off, of
flurry and fluster and sudden shrill laughter.

Teetgen put his weight on the foot of the ladder and
the others ran up underneath so that the ladder rose with
them until at last it was upright. It was thicker by far and
heavier than the sapling—but as its head crashed into the
tapering sprout branches they supported it easily. They swayed
precariously, then sprang back into position, while the cat,
refusing to be disturbed by these alien perplexities, looked
away scornfully—or, as animals often do, pretended to look
away, keeping an ear cocked sharply towards the new varnished ladder-head now extending towards it.

The officer began to climb at the run, stamping on the
ladder as firemen are taught to stamp, to punish the ladder
and thus to control it. More than ever he appeared to be
playing a game with this deliberate kicking of his boots.
Pudden and the others held the ladder firm at the bottom.
They were thinking: 'What if he breaks his neck? A man for a
cat? What a life . . .' Through the rungs of the ladder a line of
gaily coloured underclothes flapped and danced their strange
truncated dances. The fat woman stood a little way off,
chequered by sunlight, her hands clasped, talking all the time.
Some birds started singing, and in the middle of the city a
cock crowed.

The officer pranced to the top and picked off the cat by the
scruff of its neck. He stuck it on his shoulder and climbed
down. The crowd now jammed in the doorway cheered and
whistled. They all wanted to stroke the cat. So did Pudden.
But as the officer reached the bottom rung the cat jumped
from his shoulder to the ground. It was a black cat, fully
grown, with white whiskers and paws. As it collected itself on
the ground, several of the firemen stretched down their free

hands to stroke it, somehow to congratulate it also upon its narrow escape.

However, the cat never even looked at them. With deliberation it stiffened its legs, so that it seemed to stand on its toes, flung up its tail straight as a poker—and walked disdainfully away from the firemen, leaving only the bright adieu beneath its tail.

By the time they had reached the station again, the cloud had thickened. Beneath this new low blanket the winds had died and the air had grown dull.

Pudden jumped off the machine and looked across to the girl in the garden, ready to smile and perhaps shout across to her what they had done. But she had gone indoors.

As they backed the Pump into the Appliance Room an officer walked through and said that no coal had been delivered—it would be a cold day inside, no fire in the messroom, an empty grate littered with cigarette ends as after some night before. Nobby said: 'Firemen! And not even a bleeding fire we can call our own.'

The white tiles looked dull, clean, solid and efficient. This was again an engine-room for engines, smelling of petrol, decked with ladders and drums of oil. The fire engines again assumed their weight—their massive tyres appeared again hard and heavy to touch, slugging and relentless, heavily set in duplicate on thick oiled axles. The ladders and hooks and ropes and hose all appeared dull and intractable, bruising to the fingers.

Pudden Rice looked over at Teetgen taking off his jacket, at the braces and the soiled striped shirt emerging, at the man peeled of the doll. 'Well,' he thought, and for a moment hesitated standing there, thinking he was thinking. Suddenly he looked up, in surprise—there seemed nothing to think about—and walked slowly over into the boothole, where under the bare electric light he took up the blacking brush and looked round, without success, for something to polish.

DAL STIVENS

The Pepper-Tree

M Y father often spoke about the pepper-tree when we were kids, and it was clear it meant a lot to him. It stood for something—like the Rolls-Royce he was always going to buy. It wasn't what he said about the pepper-tree— my father had no great gift for words—but how he said it that counted. When he spoke of the pepper-tree at Tullama where he had been brought up you saw it clearly; a monster of a tree with long shawls of olive-green leaves in a big generous country-town backyard. 'A decent backyard—none of your city pocket-handkerchief lots,' my father said. There were berries on the tree that turned from green to pink with wax-like covers which you could unpick and get the sticky smell of them all over your fingers. In this spanking tree there was always, too, a noisy traffic of sparrows and starlings fluttering and hopping from branch to branch.

When we lived at Newtown, Sydney, I used to look for pepper-trees when my father took me for a walk on Sunday afternoons. 'Look, there's a pepper-tree,' I'd say to him when I saw one with its herring-bone leaves.

'By golly, boy, that's only a little runt of a tree,' my old man would say. 'They don't do so well in the city. Too much smoke, by golly. You ought to see them out west where I come from.'

My father was a tall, thin man with melancholy brown eyes and the soul of a poet. It was the poet in him that wanted to own a Rolls-Royce one day.

'First our own house and then some day, when my ship comes home, I'll buy a Rolls-Royce,' he'd say.

Some of his friends thought my old man was a little crazy to have such an ambition.

'What would you do with one of those flash cars, Peter?' they'd tease him. 'Go and live among the swells?'

My father would stroke his long brown moustache, which had only a few bits of white in it, and try to explain, but he couldn't make them understand. He couldn't even get his ideas across to my mother. Only now do I think I understand what a Rolls-Royce meant to him.

'I don't want to swank it, as you put it, Emily,' he'd say to my mother. 'No, by golly. I want to own a Rolls-Royce because it is the most perfect piece of machinery made in this world. Why, a Rolls-Royce——'

And then he'd stop and you could feel him groping for the right words to describe what he felt, and then go on blunderingly with the caress of a lover in his voice, talking about how beautiful the engine was. . . .

'What would a garage mechanic do with a Rolls-Royce, I ask you!' my mother would say. 'I'd feel silly sitting up in it.'

At such times my mother would give the wood stove in the kitchen a good shove with the poker, or swish her broom vigorously. My mother was a small plump woman with brown hair which she wore drawn tight back from her forehead.

Like the pepper-tree, the Rolls-Royce symbolized something for my father. He had been born in Tullama in the mallee. His father was a bricklayer and wanted his son to follow him. But my father had had his mind set on becoming an engineer. When he was eighteen he had left Tullama and come to the city and got himself apprenticed to a mechanical engineer. He went to technical classes in the evening. After two years his eyes had given out on him.

'If I had had some money things might have been different, by golly,' my father told me once. 'I could have gone to the university and learnt things properly. I could have become a civil engineer. I didn't give my eyes a fair go—I went to classes five nights a week and studied after I came home.'

After his eyes went, my father had to take unskilled jobs but always near machinery. 'I like tinkering but I had no proper schooling,' he said once.

He knew a lot and in spite of his eyes he could only have learnt most of it from books. He knew all about rocks and how they were formed. He could talk for hours, if you got him started, about fossils and the story of evolution. My mother didn't like to hear him talking about such things because she thought such talk was irreligious. Looking back now I'd say that in spite of his lack of orthodox schooling my father was a learned man. He taught me more than all the teachers I ever had at high school. He was a keen naturalist, too.

Just before the depression came when we were living at Newtown, my father had paid one hundred pounds off the house. He was forty-seven years old then. I was twelve.

'By golly, we'll own the house before we know where we are,' he said.

'Will we?' said my mother. 'At a pound a week we have twelve years to go—unless we win Tatts.'

'You never know what may turn up,' said my old man cheerfully.

'I have a good idea what with people losing their jobs every day.'

'I haven't lost mine,' my father said, 'and what's more, if I do, I have a way of making some money.'

'I suppose it's another of your inventions, Peter? What is it this time, I ask you?'

'Never you mind,' said my father. But he said it gently.

One of my mother's complaints was that my father was always losing money on the things he tried to invent. Another was that he was always filling the backyard up with junk.

'What can you do with these pocket-handkerchief lots?' my father would say. 'Now, when I was a nipper at Tullama we had a decent backyard—why it was immense—it was as big——'

He'd stop there not being able to get the right word.

Auction sales, according to my mother, were one of my father's weaknesses. He could never resist anything if it looked cheap, even if he had no use for it, she'd say. Soon after my old man had told my mother he had something in mind to make some money, he went away early one Sunday morning. He came back about lunch-time in a motor lorry. On the back of the Ford was a two-stroke kerosene engine. I came running out.

'I've bought it, Joe, by golly,' he told me.

He had, too. Both engine and lorry.

'Dirt cheap. Forty quid the lot,' he said. 'Ten quid down, boy, and ten bob a week.'

My mother cut up when she heard.

'Wasting money when it could have gone into the house, Peter.'

'This'll pay the house off in no time, by golly,' my father said. 'And buy a lot of other things, too.'

I knew by the way he looked up and over my mother's head he was thinking of the Rolls-Royce which to him was like a fine poem or a great symphony of Beethoven.

All that day he was very excited, walking round the engine, standing back to admire it, and then peering closely at it. He started it running and stopped it continually all the afternoon. Every night when he came home from the garage during the next week, he'd go first thing and look at the engine. He had some plan in his mind but wouldn't say what it was at first.

'Wait and see, Joe,' he'd said. 'You'll see all right.'

He didn't let me into his secret for over a week, although I knew he was bursting to tell someone. In the end, he drew me aside mysteriously in the kitchen one night, when my mother was in the bedroom, and whispered, 'It's an invention for cleaning out underground wells, boy.'

'For cleaning out wells?'

'Underground wells.'

He listened to hear if my mother was coming back.

'I'm rigging a light out there tonight, boy,' he whispered. 'Come out later and I'll show you.'

My father's idea, he explained later, was to clean underground wells in country towns by suction. You pushed a stiff brush on the end of the pipe down the sides and along the bottom of underground wells. The pipe sucked up the silt and you didn't lose much water from the well.

'Every country town has half a dozen underground wells, boy,' he said. 'The banks and one or two of the wealthier blokes in the town. Just like it was in Tullama. There's

money in it because you can clean the well out without losing
too much water. It's a gold-mine.'

It sounded good to me.

'When do you start?' I asked.

'Soon, by golly,' he said. 'The job at the garage won't
spin out much longer.'

He was right about that, but until the day she died my
mother always had a sneaking idea that the old man had
helped to give himself the sack. It was early in 1930 when
the old man set out in the lorry, heading out west.

'You've got to go to the low-rainfall districts,' he said.

'Like Tullama?' I said.

'Yes, like Tullama, by golly.'

I started thinking of the pepper-tree then.

'Will you go to Tullama and see the pepper-tree?'

My father stroked his long straggling moustache. Into his
eyes came that look like when he was thinking or talking about
the Rolls. He didn't answer me for a bit.

'By golly, yes, boy, if I go there.'

Soon after this he started off. Every week brought a letter
from him. He did well too. He was heading almost due west
from Sydney and I followed the towns he spoke of in my school
atlas. It took him nearly a day on a well, so in the larger
towns he might stay over a week, in the smaller a day or a day
and a half.

After he had been away for two months he still had a good
few wells to go before he reached Tullama. You could see that
he was heading that way.

'Him and that silly pepper-tree!' said my mother, but she
didn't say it angrily. My father was sending her as much
money as he used to bring home when he worked at the
garage.

But in spite of what my mother said about the pepper-
tree, she became a bit keen as my father got only two weeks
off Tullama. She made a small pin-flag for me to stick on
the map. About this time a change came in the old man's
letters home. At first they had been elated, but now they
were quieter. He didn't boast so much about the money he

was making, or say anything about the Rolls. Perhaps excitement was making him quieter as he got nearer to the pepper-
tree, I thought.

'I know what it is,' my mother said. 'He's not getting his
proper meals. He's too old to be gallivanting off on his own. I
bet he's not cooking proper meals for himself. And without a
decent bed to sleep in—only the back of that lorry.'

I thought the day would never come, but soon enough my
dad had only one town to do before he would reach Tullama.
His letters usually arrived on a Tuesday—he wrote home on
the Sundays—but round this time I watched for the mail every
day and was late for school three mornings running. When a
letter did come I grabbed it from the postman's hand and
hurried inside with it, reading the post-mark on the run. It
was from Tullama.

'All right, all right, don't rush me, Joe,' my mother said.
'You and your pepper-tree.'

I read over her elbow. There was only one page. There was
nothing about the pepper-tree. Dad was well and making
money, but he was thinking of returning soon. Only a few
lines.

I couldn't understand it.

On the next Tuesday there was no letter. Nor on the
Wednesday. On the Thursday my father came home. He
turned up at breakfast-time. He gave us a surprise walking
in like that. He said that he had sold the truck and engine
and come home by train. He looked tired and shamefaced
and somehow a lot older. I saw a lot more white in his
moustache.

'The engine was no good,' he said. 'It kept breaking down.
It cost me nearly all I earned and it was hungry on petrol. I
had to sell it to pay back what I borrowed and get my fare
home.'

'Oh, Peter,' my mother said, putting her arms round him.
'You poor darling. I knew something was wrong.'

'Mother reckoned it was the food,' I said. 'She reckoned
you weren't getting your proper meals.'

'I'll make you a cup of tea, Peter,' my mother said, bustling over to the stove and pushing another piece of wood into it. 'Then I'll get you some breakfast.'

'By golly, that sounds a bit of all right,' my father said then. This was the first time since he had walked in that he had sounded like his old self.

My mother hurried about the kitchen and my father talked a bit more. 'I thought I was going to do well at first,' he said. 'But the engine was too old. It was always spare parts. It ate up all I earned.'

He talked on about the trip. I had got over my surprise at seeing him walk in and now wanted to know all about the pepper-tree.

'Did you see the pepper-tree, dad?'

'Yes, I saw it all right.'

I stood directly in front of him as he sat at the table, but he was not looking at me but at something far away. He didn't answer for what seemed a long time.

'It was a little runt of a tree, boy—and a little backyard.'

He wouldn't say any more than that and he never spoke of the pepper-tree—or the Rolls—again.

VIOLA MEYNELL

The Size of a Pocket Handkerchief

I F Hale had learnt it from anyone else—if a third person had come to him and said: Have you heard Simpson has bought that bit of land? he would have said: That's a lie—or if it isn't he's the dirtiest scoundrel unhung. But Simpson had himself told him: 'By the by, I've bought that field of Short's,' hoping no doubt to make it sound the most natural thing in the world; and what with the surprise and the unlikelihood of face-to-face abuse between two friends, there had been a few moments' time-lag before Hale's reaction got under way. Those moments had lost him his chance. He had only uttered an ominous: 'So that's what you've done is it?' when they were interrupted. Fortune had favoured Simspon—an additional injustice, and he must be thanking his lucky stars. Or—yes, there was no doubt of it, Simpson had chosen a moment when interruption was secure. But let him wait.

It riled Hale beyond words that Simpson probably thought that he, Hale, having said those few words, would now let it go at that, would let them stand for all the resentment which the situation was worth. The thought of Simpson congratulating himself on the ease with which the thing had been carried off gave Hale no respite from planning just how he would be undeceived. Perhaps he thought that injuries sometimes merely fade away. Well, he would quickly be hearing some home-truths, deadly to any false hopes on the subject. And the facts, when they would be recapitulated to Simpson that evening, would need no doctoring; they were completely damning.

'In the first place you wouldn't be here at all, would you, but for me. Directly I heard of a good holding coming up for sale I wrote and told you, didn't I, because I remembered our talks when we were prisoners together. I knew it was the thing for you, and I was as keen on your getting it as you were yourself, wasn't I?'

He'd say yes to that.

'And in these three years I've smoothed out a few things for you, or done my best to. And I thought we were on a decent footing as between neighbours and friends.'

He might mumble: Well, aren't we?

'Then a few weeks ago I said in your hearing that that bit of land between yours and mine was coming into the market and it would suit me well enough and I intended to buy it. And you've gone behind my back and bought it. I've come across some unscrupulous customers in my time, but this is as nasty a bit of work as I've met with.'

Simpson wouldn't answer that because he couldn't; it was the exact truth.

But that evening, by another stroke of ill-luck, Hale had the exasperation of still being unable to speak his mind. He saw Simpson at the Club and waited for an opportunity when they should not be overheard or disturbed. The Club was full; the two men were always at some distance. When the company thinned a little and there was likely to be more chance of a private exchange, their eyes met across the room for a moment which gave time to develop the grim purposeful look of the one man and the unmistakably hangdog look of the other. Hale was held in conversation; when he freed himself Simpson was gone.

Hale pushed his way angrily to the door and opened it in the hope that Simpson had but just sneaked out. Closing the door behind him to shut in the noise of the club-room, he listened in the darkness for the sound of retreating footsteps, but all was quiet. Like someone just missing a train it was essential he should catch, he stood there so baffled that it seemed some miraculous happening must defeat the logic of Simpson's escape.

He thought of following him to his house, but would not care to say what he had to say in front of his wife. He turned on his heel and went back into the club-room.

Galling as the delay was, it yet served to allow of mature consideration of the form of the indictment. Protests made in a hurry can leave out telling points. And a man may commit a

treacherous act and just because the right words of accusation
are not found, may think his infamy is not fully realized, and
may even become only half-convinced of it himself. Hale
did not waste the time of waiting; he got on to more familiar
terms with the injury done him, and would have more to say
than he would have had in the first place.

'Perhaps you think I'm the only one to know you for what
you are—that I'm sore because I lost it, but that no one else is
taking any notice. All right, take Chadwick, a man you like to
stand well with. I saw you and him talking and having a
drink just as usual, and I daresay you're feeling set up because
his manner didn't show a bit of difference. Nor it might—to
you. Now I'll tell you what he said to me. He said "It's an
eye-opener." He said "What a low-down thing to go and do."
That's in case you think it's just me kicking up a fuss.'

He'd probably say, Well, I didn't think you'd mind all
that much (which would be a lie) and anyway it's done now.

Whether by good luck or good management Simpson's
movements were untraceable the next day. Certainly good
luck played its part, for on Hale going to Simpson's yard at a
time when he would normally have found him feeding his
calves, only the fact that Simpson had received an emergency
summons from his wife prevented his being found. Good management, on the other hand, was not absent. To avoid Hale
consistently, considering that they lived so much along the
same lines, would not have been a reasonable ambition; but
Simpson could induce circumstances favourable to a post-
ponement. He should have driven past Hale's farm on his
way home that afternoon; on many a day Hale was about
when he did so, and he stopped and they chatted. But today,
uneasily aware that Hale might be on the look-out for him, he
remembered an errand he had some time to perform, and chose
to do it today, thus taking another way home—while Hale
was actually waiting.

Simpson was not a man who had gone into hiding, but
while not making avoidance of Hale his main object, if he
could reasonably apply himself to do a job that took him out of
Hale's way he did so.

Hale could hardly believe that twenty-four hours after hearing of Simpson's act he should still not have spoken his mind. His indignation boiled up in him. The offence should have been stigmatized from the very start. But as things were, he could at least rehearse his interview with Simpson, and if he could not deliver his oration he could at any rate add to it.

'It's not such a wonderful bit of land, there's only nine acres of it, but that's not the question. You not only heard from me that I was going to buy it, but you heard me say that I wanted it for some grass. You trod on me and on my needs. I wonder where you'd stop. I don't see why you don't pinch the corn out of my barn, or the money out of my pocket if it comes to that.'

He'd say that he too wanted the field, that it's handy for him too, and what about him wanting some grass.

'So you might need some, but I happened to be in on this first, and you knew nothing of it but what I told you. And when I told you I was going to buy you didn't say a word, you only crept off on the sly.'

He might say Why did you tell me?

'I told you because I didn't know you had it in you to do what you did. I told you as one man talks to another he believes is a decent fellow.'

The next morning Hale had unfortunately to be away taking calves to market, but whatever he did his mind ran on the talk with Simpson which the afternoon would bring about.

'The last thing I would remember in an ordinary way is the help I've tried to be to you since your wife was ill. But how you've behaved serves to put me in mind of it. I suppose that in an ordinary neighbourly manner I've done your work for you twenty times since poor Mrs. Simpson started having her fits—I couldn't do any other. I took her to hospital when you weren't there. God knows it isn't my idea to bring up a thing like that, I only mean I thought we were neighbours one to another.'

He'd probably say You know I was grateful to you. He'd say Until I did this I never acted in an unneighbourly manner.

There wasn't much someone like me could do for you because trouble doesn't seem to come your way. Still when you had that bad go of pneumonia twelve months ago last January I did some of your jobs for you and was glad to.

'That's my point. We were neighbours and friends. That's what makes this a damned low-down way to behave.'

So Hale was well-primed for the talk. He had an infallible scheme for trapping Simpson this afternoon. As regular as clockwork Simpson went to his bank at two-thirty on Friday afternoons. On his road home Simpson in his car would meet Hale in his. Hale would stop him and say his piece at last.

'You're no doubt very pleased with yourself for pulling this thing off, but you know it won't do you much good. I met Short this morning. He said when you turned up to buy the field he concluded I was off it—and you let him think so, or else he'd never have dreamed of selling to you. You'll find it doesn't pay in the long run to get that kind of reputation.'

He might say Yes, Short would rather sell it to you than to me—and why? Because you've made a success of things and that always goes down well. You're in with more people than I am because you've got more time and more money. To him that hath . . . that's the kind of thing.

'There's an excuse for everything nowadays. But if you think you can make excuses for what you've done you won't deceive anyone except yourself.'

But Simpson was to achieve yet one more lucky escape before the actual encounter took place.

Hale drove slowly along the road at the time when Simpson's car was nearing on its way from the town. They could not avoid passing, and soon they were aware of each other's approach. Both realized that the show-down was now inevitable.

Simpson put on his brake; but the charabanc immediately behind him could not overtake him until he and Hale had passed each other; they therefore passed. It would still be the natural thing for himself and Hale to draw up at the roadside. On the other hand acceptance of the charabanc incident as a reason for continuing on their way would also be normal, especially if the two occupants had nothing particular to say to each other. Either course was open. When Hale looked back it was to see that Simpson had driven on.

As if Hale's pursuit of his quarry were closing in and narrowing down, it assuredly seemed that this, the most fortuitous of his escapes, must be the last—and so it proved.

By now one thing was certain: the occasion was not going to find Hale unprepared.

'I'm not grasping, that I know of. You can ask who you like. If this bit of ground had been put up to auction and it had fallen to you, I wouldn't have had anything to say except good luck to you. I've got a use for it certainly, but it's all in the fortunes of war, and if I'd lost it fairly and squarely that would have been all right by me. What I don't like is what no man likes—and that's a stab in the back.'

He'd say If it had been put up to auction a fat chance I'd have had if you'd wanted it. As for your having a use for it, I daresay you have, but for me it'll make just that difference of being able to milk a cow or two to help my business along. That's what I need, something to help me along. I've not been one of you lucky ones, and it's not for want of hard work. I lost my pigs the year before last, didn't I, and this year my bit of barley has failed. My home's in a muddle with my wife in and out of hospital, and I have to pay someone to come and do her work. I've had a good deal against me. What I want is to get properly on my feet, and once I'd done that I could carry on.

'I don't doubt all that. So could I improve my business if I played a shabby trick or two. So could any man, you're not the only one. It's just a matter of what you're willing to do. And what you'll do once you'll do again. It doesn't make for good feeling, does it, if you're ready to knock anyone down and stand on them to make yourself taller.'

Up till now Hale had mostly calculated to catch Simpson in the ordinary coming and going of every day, to fall in with him in the same circumstances as those in which they were used to meet and speak. Thwarted in that, he now set out to pin him down on his home-ground.

He walked out into the pearly dawn of the March morning, along field-paths well known to his feet, cutting corners, scrambling through a hedge; he was a born time-saver. Not that he was a quick walker—perhaps because his eyes had plenty to do; for at the end of a walk like this he had an exact knowledge of the condition of every bit of cultivated ground, hedge, ditch or wild life, as far as the eye could see; also perhaps because he was built on the heavy side. (But in some emergency, such as a driven heifer to be headed-off from escape down a side-track, or a sheep to be pounced on for examination, the slow heavy walk could be turned in an instant into a run of amazing agility.)

At length he reached the fence bordering Simpson's holding, and there he stood and waited. He was not used to seeing Simpson at this hour of the morning, but Hale knew that his assignment in his yard for the first jobs of the day was as inflexible as that of a soldier on parade.

Hale stood with his legs slightly apart, as if his stoutness made them be so; the firm wide planting of his feet always made whatever ground, pavement or floor he stood on seem to belong to him.

He had not been there for five minutes when he saw Simpson. He was emerging from the paddock into his yard, a bucket in either hand. He did not see Hale until he heard his name called sharply.

'Simpson!'

He started, stared, put down the buckets and commenced the slow approach from which there was no escape. He had some way to come, across the width of the yard and the corner of an untidy orchard in which the hens were pecking at their early feed. If this meeting had been a sporting contest Hale was certainly in the position of the player who had won the toss, for while he stood immovable at the fence Simpson had to cover the distance under his eye.

Hale had time to observe his man from head to toe. There was no mistaking the general demeanour of that figure as it approached—it was an incongruous mixture of sheepishness and defiance.

Simpson was a lanky type. He gave the impression that all the tasks he did were more irksome on account of his having to stoop further to them than another man would; his loose-limbed figure was not typical of his calling. Hale realized, as he watched him, that he was a man rarely to be seen without his sporting a sign of some minor physical disability (changing according to the season as if by the vagaries of some fashion), which decorated him with a bit of bandage or a finger-stall or a scab or a scar. Today's demonstration of distress was a square inch of plaster affixed to the side of his neck but standing out a half-inch from it, while he carried his head a bit stiffly. Shaving, it seemed, took place later in the day, or perhaps he sometimes gave it a miss. His clothes were the rough and grubby ones of anyone doing the like kind of chores, except for the almost indefinable difference of their non-country origin and of their having received their first layer of shabbiness in town-wear. (When Simpson spoke, too, his voice had a remotely cockney sound not otherwise to be heard for many a mile around.)

The fact that he had to make his approach while Hale was held at the fence could not do otherwise than make him seem like an accused person coming up for judgement; and every step he took had the subtle reluctance of someone drawing near to punishment. He had no cover. Offenders being apt to carry off their misdeeds, a grown man does not often have to cut so sorry a figure before his friend, and an attempt at jauntiness on Simpson's part carried no conviction. One would not have wished to be in his shoes. Hale may have had to wait for his feast, but it was served to him on a gold plate now.

'Well I daresay I know what you're here for,' Simpson said, coming to a standstill, and perhaps having a blustering hope that there was an advantage in taking the initiative. 'You want to have a word with me about me buying that bit of ground.'

'Wa—al, that's the kind of idea,' said Hale in the drawling voice he sometimes used, with unconscious artistry, at the start of a subject which was going to work up to high words.

'All right. I suppose I did know when I did it that you'd

cut up rough, but I've got something to say for myself all the same.'

'You would have. And you'd need to.'

Simpson had a defeated look for a moment, which imparted an unlikely dignity to him. But he rallied to his own defence.

'Can't you take the luck of the draw? I mean to say——'

'I wouldn't say much if I was you. You'll only get deeper in.'

Having checked him again, Hale saw him painfully at a loss, and surprisingly now felt no pleasure on that account. It seemed too easy.

'What you can't do,' said Simpson, 'you can't put yourself in my place. I've had some bad luck. I——'

'Hold on a minute,' drawled Hale. 'Who says I can't put myself in your place?' He was temporizing. 'But you can't turn black into white, you know.'

This was a favourite oft-repeated axiom, but he found himself saying it now automatically, without the usual relish. He was not comfortable. He felt unaccountably small. He had become less conscious of himself than of the lanky man in front of him, complete with warts, scabs, cotton-woolled neck, shifty eye and spluttering mouth so ready for its job of self-defence. Somehow that figure had stolen the morning. The importance had shifted away from himself and lay with Simpson standing there, the perfect illustration to his own hard-luck story.

'If you want to try and make me pass the sale over to you I don't see what right——'

But Hale drowned the rest with the weighty emphasis which he made use of for silencing people.

'I wasn't aware of that being my intention——'

But what *was* his intention? He no longer felt sure. It wasn't what it had been. He knew he had a lot of things to say, but they seemed remote and unreal now. But his voice took on the soft persuasive tone he used when things were going his way.

'What's there in that bit of field to make a lot of fuss about anyway?' he said. 'It's only the size of a pocket handkerchief. Still I daresay you can make some use of it. How's the wife?'

'She's on the mend.'

'Present my compliments to her,' said Hale in the formal stilted voice he used for society manners. 'As to that bit of ground, put it down to clover if I were you,' he told Simpson, for he always liked to give advice. They chatted about the day's weather and parted, Simpson returning to his chores, and Hale sauntering back through the delicious morning of spring.

MAURICE SHADBOLT

The People Before

I

M Y father took on that farm not long after he came
back from the first war. It was pretty well the last farm
up the river. Behind our farm, and up the river, there was all
kind of wild country. Scrub and jagged black stumps on the
hills, bush in gullies where fire hadn't reached; hills and more
hills, deep valleys with caves and twisting rivers, and mountains white with winter in the distance. We had the last piece
of really flat land up the river. It wasn't the first farm my
father'd taken on—and it certainly wasn't to be the last—but
it was the most remote. He always said that was why he'd got
the place for a song. This puzzled me as a child. For I'd heard,
of course, of having to sing for your supper. I wondered what
words, to what tune, he was obliged to sing for the farm; and
where, and why? Had he travelled up the river, singing a
strange song, charming his way into possession of the land?
It always perplexed me.

And it perplexed me because there wasn't much room for
singing in my father's life. I can't remember ever having heard
him sing. There was room for plodding his paddocks in all
weathers, milking cows and sending cream down river to the
dairy factory, and cursing the bloody government; there was
room in his life for all these things and more, but not for
singing.

In time, of course, I understood that he only meant he'd
bought the place cheaply. Cheaply meant for a song. I
couldn't, even then, quite make the connexion. It remained for
a long while one of those adult mysteries. And it was no use
puzzling over it, no use asking my father for a more coherent
explanation.

'Don't be difficult,' he'd say. 'Don't ask so many damn

questions. Life's difficult enough, boy, without all your damn questions.'

He didn't mean to be unkind; it was just his way. His life was committed to winning order from wilderness. Questions were a disorderly intrusion, like gorse or weed springing up on good pasture. The best way was to hack them down, grub out the roots, before they could spread. And in the same way as he checked incipient anarchy on his land he hoped, perhaps, to check it in his son.

By that time I was old enough to understand a good many of the things that were to be understood. One of them, for example, was that we weren't the first people on that particular stretch of land. Thirty or forty years before, when white men first came into our part of the country, it was mostly forest. Those first people fired the forest, right back into the hills, and ran sheep. The sheep grazed not only the flat, but the hills which rose sharply behind our farm; the hills which, in our time, had become stubbly with manuka and fern. The flatland had been pretty much scrub too, the day my father first saw it; and the original people had been gone twenty years—they'd given up, or been ruined by the land; we never quite knew the story. The farmhouse stood derelict among the returning wilderness.

Well, my father saw right away that the land—the flat land—was a reasonable proposition for a dairy farm. There was a new launch service down to the nearest dairy factory, in the township ten miles away; only in the event of flood, or a launch breakdown, would he have to dispose of his cream by carrying it on a sledge across country, three miles, to the nearest road.

So he moved in, cleared the scrub, sowed new grass, and brought in cows. Strictly speaking, the hills at the back of the farm were his too, but he had no use for them. They made good shelter from the westerlies. Otherwise he never gave the hills a thought, since he had all the land he could safely manage; he roamed across them after wild pig, and that was about all. There were bones up there, scattered skeletons of lost sheep, in and about the scrub and burnt stumps.

Everything went well; he had the place almost paid off by the time of the depression. 'I never looked back, those years,' he said long afterwards. It was characteristic of him not to look back. He was not interested in who had the farm before him. He had never troubled to inquire. So far as he was concerned, history only began the day he first set foot on the land. It was his, by sweat and legal title: that was all that mattered. That was all that could matter.

He had two boys; I was the eldest son. 'You and Jim will take this place over one day,' he often told me. 'You'll run it when I get tired.'

But he didn't look like getting tired. He wasn't a big man, but he was wiry and thin with a lean face and cool blue eyes; he was one of those people who can't keep still. When neighbours called he couldn't ever keep comfortable in a chair, just sitting and sipping tea, but had to start walking them round the farm—or at least the male neighbours—pointing out things here and there. Usually work he'd done, improvements he'd made: the new milking-shed, the new water-pump on the river. He didn't strut or boast, though; he just pointed them out quietly, these jobs well done. He wanted others to share his satisfaction. There was talk of electricity coming through to the farm, the telephone; a road up the river was scheduled. It would all put the value of the property up. The risk he'd taken on the remote and abandoned land seemed justified in every way.

He didn't ever look like getting tired. It was as if he'd been wound up years before, like something clockwork, and set going: first fighting in the war, then fighting with the land; now most of the fighting was done, he sometimes found it quite an effort to keep busy. He never took a holiday. There was talk of taking a holiday, one winter when the cows dried off; talk of us all going down to the sea, and leaving a neighbour to look after the place. But I don't think he could have trusted anyone to look after his land, not even for a week or two in winter when the cows were dried off. Perhaps, when Jim and I were grown, it would be different. But not until. He always found some reason for us not to get away. Like our schooling.

'I don't want to interfere with their schooling,' he said once. 'They only get it once in their lives. And they might as well get it while they can. I didn't get much. And, by God, I regret it now. I don't know much, and I might have got along all right, but I might have got along a damn sight better if I'd had more schooling. And I'm not going to interfere with theirs by carting them off for a holiday in the middle of the year.'

Yet even then I wondered if he meant a word of it, if he really wasn't just saying that for something to say. He was wrangling at the time with my mother, who held opinions on a dwindling number of subjects. She never surrendered any of these opinions, exactly; she just kept them more and more to herself until, presumably, they lapsed quietly and died. As she herself, much later, was to lapse quietly from life, without much complaint.

For if he'd really been concerned about our schooling, he might have been more concerned about the way we fell asleep in afternoon classes. Not that we were the only ones. Others started getting pretty ragged in the afternoons too. A lot of us had been up helping our fathers since early in the morning. Jim and I were up at half-past four most mornings to help with the milking and working the separators. My father increased his herd year after year, right up to the depression. After school we rode home just in time for the evening milking. And by the time we finished it was getting dark; in winter it was dark by the time we were half-way through the herd.

I sometimes worried about Jim looking worn in the evenings, and I often chased him off inside before milking was finished. I thought Jim needed looking after; he wasn't anywhere near as big as me. I'd hear him scamper off to the house, and then I'd set about stripping the cows he had left. Father sometimes complained.

'You'll make that brother of yours a softy,' he said. 'The boy's got to learn what work means.'

'Jim's all right,' I answered. 'He's not a softy. He's just not very big. That's all.'

He detested softies, even the accomplices of softies. My mother, in a way, was such an accomplice. She'd never been keen about first me, then Jim, helping with work on the farm. But my father said he couldn't afford to hire a man to help with the herd. And he certainly couldn't manage by himself, without Jim and me.

'Besides,' he said, 'my Dad and me used to milk two hundred cows'—sometimes, when he became heated, the number rose to three hundred—'when I was eight years old. And thin as a rake too, I was. Eight years old and thin as a rake. It didn't do me no harm. You boys don't know what work is, let me tell you.'

So there all argument finished. My mother kept one more opinion to herself.

And I suppose that, when I chased Jim off inside, I was only taking my mother's side in the argument, and was only another accomplice of softies. Anyway, it would give me a good feeling afterwards—despite anything my father would have to say—when we tramped back to the house, through the night smelling of frost or rain, to find Jim sitting up at the table beside my mother while she ladled out soup under the warm yellow lamplight. He looked as if he belonged there, beside her; and she always looked, at those times, a little triumphant. Her look seemed to say that one child of hers, at least, was going to be saved from the muck of the cowshed. And I suppose that was the beginning of how Jim became his mother's boy.

I remained my father's. I wouldn't have exchanged him for another father. I liked seeing him with people, a man among men. This happened on winter Saturdays when we rode to the township for the football. We usually left Jim behind to look after my mother. We tethered our horses near the football field and went off to join the crowd. Football was one of the few things which interested my father outside the farm. He'd been a fine rugby forward in his day and people respected what he had to say about the game. He could out-argue most people; probably out-fight them too, if it ever came to that. He often talked about the fights he'd had when young. For he'd done a bit of boxing too, only he couldn't spare the time from his father's farm to train properly. He knocked me down once, with his bare fists, in the cowshed; and I was careful never to let it happen again. I just kept my head down for days afterwards, so that he wouldn't see the bruises on my face or the swelling round my eye.

At the football he barracked with the best of them in the thick of the crowd. Sometimes he called out when the rest of the crowd was silent and tense; he could be very sarcastic about poor players, softies who were afraid to tackle properly.

After the game he often called in, on the way home, to have a few beers with friends in the township's sly-grog shop—we didn't have a proper pub in the township—while I looked after the horses ouside. Usually he'd find time, while he gossiped with friends, to bring me out a glass of lemonade. At times it could be very cold out there, holding the horses while the winter wind swept round, but it would be nice to know that I was remembered. When he finished we rode home together for a late milking. He would grow talkative, as we cantered towards dark, and even give me the impression he was glad of my company. He told me about the time he was young, what the world looked like when he was my age. His father was a sharemilker, travelling from place to place; that is, he owned no land of his own and did other people's work.

'So I made up my mind, boy,' he told me as we rode along together, 'I made up my mind I'd never be like that. I'd bend my head to no man. And you know what the secret of that is, boy? Land. Land of your own. You're independent, boy. You can say no to the world. That's if you got your own little kingdom. I reckon it was what kept me alive, down there on the beach at Gallipoli, knowing I'd have some land I could call my own.' This final declaration seemed to dismay him for some reason or other, perhaps because he feared he'd given too much of himself away. So he added half-apologetically, 'I had to think of something, you know, while all that shooting was going on. They say it's best to fix your mind on something if you don't want to be afraid. That's what I fixed my mind on, anyhow. Maybe it did keep me alive.'

In late winter or spring we sometimes arrived back, on Saturdays, to see the last trembling light of sunset fade from the hills and land. We'd canter along a straight stretch, coast up a rise, rein in the horses, and there it was—his green kingdom, his tight tamed acres beneath the hills and beside the river, a thick spread of fenced grass from the dark fringe of hill-scrub down to the ragged willows above the water. And at the centre was his castle, the farmhouse, with the sheds scattered round, and the pine trees.

Reining in on that rise, I knew, gave him a good feeling. It would also be the time when he remembered all the jobs he'd neglected, all the work he should have done instead of going to the football. His conscience would keep him busy all day Sunday.

At times he wondered—it was a conversation out loud with himself—why he didn't sell up and buy another place. There were, after all, more comfortable farms, in more convenient locations nearer towns or cities. 'I've built this place up from nothing,' he said. 'I've made it pay, and pay well. I've made this land worth something. I could sell out for a packet. Why don't I?'

He never really—in my presence anyway—offered himself a convincing explanation. Why didn't he? He'd hardly have said he loved the land: loved, in any case, would have been an extravagance. Part of whatever it was, I suppose, was the knowledge that he'd built where someone else had failed; part was that he'd given too much of himself there, to be really free anywhere else. It wouldn't be the same, walking on to another successful farm, a going concern, everything in order. No, this place—this land from the river back up to the hills— was his. In a sense it had only ever been his. That was why he felt so secure.

If Sunday was often the day when he worked hardest, it was also the best day for Jim and me, our free day. After morning milking, and breakfast, we did more or less what we liked. In summer we swam down under the river-willows; we also had a canoe tied there and sometimes we paddled up-river, under great limestone bluffs shaggy with toi toi, into country which grew wilder and wilder. There were huge bearded caves in the bush above the water which we explored from time to time. There were also big eels to be fished from the pools of the river.

As he grew older Jim turned more into himself, and became still quieter. You could never guess exactly what he was thinking. It wasn't that he didn't enjoy life; he just had his own way of enjoying it. He didn't like being with his father, as I did; I don't even know that he always enjoyed being with me. He just tagged along with me: we were, after all, brothers. When I was old enough, my father presented me with a ·22 rifle; Jim never showed great enthusiasm for shooting. He came along with me, all right, but he never seemed interested in the rabbits or wild goat I shot, or just missed. He wandered around the hills, way behind me, entertaining himself and collecting things. He gathered leaves, and tried to identify the plants from which the leaves came. He also collected stones, those of some interesting shape or texture; he had a big collection of stones. He tramped along, in his slow, quiet way, poking into everything, adding to his collections. He wasn't too slow and quiet at school, though; he was faster than most of us with an answer. He borrowed books from the teacher, and took them home. So in time he became even smarter with his answers. I grew to accept his difference from most people. It didn't disturb me particularly: on the farm he was still quiet, small Jim. He was never too busy with his books to come along with me on Sundays.

There was a night when Jim was going through some new stones he'd gathered. Usually, in the house, my father didn't take much notice of Jim, his reading or his hobbies. He'd fought a losing battle for Jim, through the years, and now accepted his defeat. Jim still helped us with the herd, night and morning, but in the house he was ignored. But this night my father went across to the table and picked up a couple of new stones. They were greenish, both the same triangular shape.

'Where'd you get these?' he asked.

Jim thought for a moment; he seemed pleased by the interest taken in him. 'One was back in the hills,' he said. 'The other was in a cave up the river. I just picked them up.'

'You mean you didn't find them together?'

'No,' Jim said.

'Funny,' my father said. 'They look like greenstone. I seen some greenstone once. A joker found it, picked it up in the bush. Jade, it is; same thing. This joker sold it in the city for a packet. Maori stuff. Some people'll buy anything.'

We all crossed to the table and looked down at the greenish stones. Jim's eyes were bright with excitement.

'You mean these used to belong to the Maoris?' he said. 'These stones?'

'Must have,' my father said. 'Greenstone doesn't come natural round here. You look it up in your books and you'll see. Comes from way down south, near the mountains and glaciers. Had to come up here all the way by canoe. They used to fight about greenstone, once.' He paused and looked at the stones again. 'Yes,' he added. 'I reckon that's greenstone, all right. You never know, might be some money in that stuff.'

Money was a very important subject in our house at that time. It was in a lot of households, since that time was the depression. In the cities they were marching in the streets and breaking shop windows. Here on the farm it wasn't anywhere near so dramatic. The grass looked much the same as it had always looked; so did the hills and river. All that had happened, really, was that the farm had lost its value. Prices had fallen; my father sometimes wondered if it was worth while sending cream to the factory. Some of the people on poorer land, down the river, had walked off their properties. Everything was tighter. We had to do without new clothes, and there wasn't much variety in our eating. We ran a bigger garden, and my father went out more frequently shooting wild pig for meat. He had nothing but contempt for the noisy people in the city, the idlers and wasters who preferred to go shouting in the streets rather than fetch a square meal for their families, as he did with his rifle. He thought they, in some way, were to blame for the failure of things. Even so, he became gripped by

the idea that he might have failed himself, somehow; he tried
to talk himself out of this idea—in my presence—but without
much success. Now he had the land solid beneath his feet,
owned it entirely, it wasn't much help at all. If it wasn't for our
garden and the wild pig, we might starve. The land didn't
bring him any money; he might even have to leave it. He had
failed, perhaps much as the land's former owners had failed;
why? He might have answered the question for himself satis-
factorily, while he grubbed away at the scrub encroaching on
our pasture; but I doubt it.

'Yes,' he said. 'Might be some money in that stuff.'

But Jim didn't seem to hear, or understand. His eyes were
still bright. 'That means there must have been Maoris here in
the old days,' he said.

'I suppose there must have,' my father agreed. He didn't
seem much interested. Maoris were Maoris. There weren't
many around our part of the river; they were mostly down
towards the coast. (Shortly after this, Jim did some research
and told me the reason why. It turned out that the land about
our part of the river had been confiscated from them after the
Maori wars.) 'They were most places, weren't they?' he
added.

'Yes,' Jim said. 'But I mean they must have been here. On
our place.'

'Well, yes. They could of been. Like I said, they were most
places.' It didn't seem to register as particularly important.
He picked up the greenstones again. 'We ought to find out
about this,' he continued. 'There might be a bit of money
in it.'

Later Jim took the stones to school and had them identified as
Maori adzes. My father said once again that perhaps there was
money in them. But the thing was, where to find a buyer?
It mightn't be as easy as it used to be. So somehow it was all
forgotten. Jim kept the adzes.

Jim and I did try to find again that cave in which he had
picked up an adze. We found a lot of caves, but none of them
seemed the right one. Anyway we didn't pick up another adze.

We did wander down one long dripping cave, striking matches, and in the dark tripped on something. I struck another match and saw some brownish-looking bones. 'A sheep,' I said. 'It must have come in here and got lost.'

Jim was silent; I wondered why. Then I saw he wasn't looking at the bones, but at a human skull propped on a ledge of the cave. It just sat there sightless, shadows dancing in its sockets.

We got out of that cave quickly. We didn't even talk about it when we reached home. On the whole I preferred going out with my ·22 after rabbits.

2

It was near the end of the depression. But we didn't know that then, of course. It might have been just the beginning, for all we knew. My father didn't have as much interest in finishing jobs as he used to have. He tired easily. He'd given his best to the land, and yet his best still wasn't good enough. There wasn't much sense in anything, and his dash was done. He kept going out of habit.

I'd been pulled out of school to help with the farm. Jim still more or less went to school. I say more or less because he went irregularly. This was because of sickness. Once he was away in hospital two months. And of course it cost money; my father said we were to blame, we who allowed Jim to become soft and sickly. But the doctor thought otherwise; he thought Jim had been worked hard enough already. And when Jim returned to the farm he no longer helped with the herd. And this was why I had to leave school: if he couldn't have both of us working with him part-time, my father wanted one full-time. Jim was entirely surrendered at last, to the house and his books, to school and my mother. I didn't mind working on the farm all day, with my father; it was, after all, what I'd always wanted. All the same, I would have been happier if he had been: his doubts about himself, more and more frequently expressed, disturbed me. It wasn't like my father at all. He was convinced now he'd done the wrong thing, somewhere. He went back through the years, levering each year up like a stone, to see what lay beneath; he never seemed to find anything. It was worst of all in winter, when the land looked bleak, the hills were grey with low cloud, and the rain swirled out of the sky. All life vanished from his face and I knew he detested everything: the land which had promised him independence was now only a muddy snare; he was bogged here, between hills and river, and couldn't escape. He had no pride left in him for the place. If he could have got a price for the farm he would have gone. But there was no longer any question of a price. He could walk off if he liked. Only the bush would claim it back.

It was my mother who told us there were people coming. She had taken the telephone message while we were out of the house, and Jim was at school.

'Who are they?' my father said.

'I couldn't understand very well. It was a bad connexion. I think they said they were the people who were here before.'

'The people who were here before? What the hell do they want here?' His eyes became suspicious under his frown.

'I think they said they just wanted to have a look around.'

'What the hell do they want here?' my father repeated, baffled. 'Nothing for them to see. This farm's not like it was when they were here. Everything's different. I've made a lot of changes. They wouldn't know the place. What do they want to come back for?'

'Well,' my mother sighed, 'I'm sure I don't know.'

'Perhaps they want to buy it,' he said abruptly; the words seemed simultaneous with his thought, and he stiffened with astonishment. 'By God, yes. They might want to buy the place back again. I hadn't thought of that. Wouldn't that be a joke? I'd sell, all right—for just about as much as I paid for the place. I tell you, I'd let it go for a song, for a bloody song. They're welcome.'

'But where would we go?' she said, alarmed.

'Somewhere,' he said. 'Somewhere new. Anywhere.'

'But there's nowhere,' she protested. 'Nowhere any better. You know that.'

'And there's nowhere any worse,' he answered. 'I'd start again somewhere. Make a better go of things.'

'You're too old to start again,' my mother observed softly.

There was a silence. And in the silence I knew that what my mother said was true. We all knew it was true.

'So we just stay here,' he said. 'And rot. Is that it?' But he really wished to change the subject. 'When are these people coming?'

'Tomorrow, I think. They're staying the night down in the township. Then they're coming up by launch.'

'They didn't say why they were interested in the place?'

'No. And they certainly didn't say they wanted to buy it. You might as well get that straight now. They said they just wanted a look around.'

'I don't get it. I just don't get it. If I walked off this place I wouldn't ever want to see it again.'

'Perhaps they're different,' my mother said. 'Perhaps they've got happy memories of this place.'

'Perhaps they have. God knows.'

It was early summer, with warm lengthening days. That sunny Saturday morning I loitered about the house with Jim, waiting for the people to arrive. Eventually, as the sun climbed higher in the sky, I grew impatient and went across the paddocks to help my father. We were working together when we heard the sound of the launch coming up the river.

'That's them,' he said briefly. He dropped his slasher for a moment, and spat on his hands. Then he took up the slasher again and chopped into a new patch of unruly gorse.

I was perplexed. 'Well,' I said, 'aren't you going down to meet them?'

'I'll see them soon enough. Don't worry.' He seemed to be conducting an argument with himself as he hacked into the gorse. 'I'm in no hurry. No, I'm in no hurry to see them.'

I just kept silent beside him.

'Who are they, anyway?' he went on. 'What do they want to

come traipsing round my property for? They've got a bloody cheek.'

The sound of the launch grew. It was probably travelling round the last bend in the river now, past the swamp of raupo, and banks prickly with flax and toi toi. They were almost at the farm. Still chopping jerkily, my father tried to conceal his unease.

'What do they want?' he asked for the last time. 'By God, if they've come to gloat, they've got another think coming. I've made something decent out of this place, and I don't care who knows it.'

He had tried everything in his mind and it was no use: he was empty of explanation. Now we could see the launch white on the gleaming river. It was coasting up to the bank. We could also see people clustered on board.

'Looks like a few of them,' I observed. If I could have done so without upsetting my father, I would have run down to meet the launch, eager with curiosity. But I kept my distance until he finished arguing with himself.

'Well,' he said, as if he'd never suggested otherwise, 'we'd better go down to meet them, now they're here.' He dug his slasher into the earth and began to stalk off down to the river. I followed him. His quick strides soon took him well ahead of me; I had to run to keep up.

.   .   .   .   .

Then we had our surprise. My father's step faltered; I blundered up alongside him. We saw the people climbing off the launch. And we saw who they were, at last. My father stopped perfectly still and silent. They were Maoris. We were still a hundred yards or more away, but there was no mistaking their clothing and colour. They were Maoris, all right.

'There's something wrong somewhere,' he said at last. 'It doesn't make sense. No Maori ever owned this place. I'd have known. Who the hell do they think they are, coming here?'

I couldn't answer him. He strode on down to the river. There were young men, and two old women with black headscarves. And last of all there was something the young men carried. As we drew nearer we saw it was an old man in a rough litter. The whole party of them fussed over making the old man comfortable. The old women, particularly; they had tattoos on their chins and wore shark-tooth necklaces. They straightened the old man's blankets and fixed the pillow behind his head. He had a sunken, withered face and he didn't look so much sick, as tired. His eyes were only half-open as everyone fussed around. It looked as if it were a great effort to keep them that much open. His hair was mostly grey, and his dry flesh sagged in thin folds about his ancient neck. I reckoned that he must have been near enough to a hundred years old. The young men talked quickly among themselves as they saw my father approaching. One came forward, apparently as spokesman. He looked about the oldest of them, perhaps thirty. He had a fat, shiny face.

'Here,' said my father. 'What's all this about?' I knew his opinion of Maoris: they were lazy, drank too much, and caused trouble. They just rode on the backs of the men on the land, like the loafers in the cities. He always said we were lucky there were so few in our district. 'What do you people think you're doing here?' he demanded.

'We rang up yesterday,' the spokesman said. 'We told your missus we might be coming today.'

'I don't know about that. She said someone else was coming. The people who were here before.'

'Well,' said the young man, smiling. 'We were the people before.'

'I don't get you. You trying to tell me you owned this place?'

'That's right. We owned all the land round this end of the river. Our tribe.'

'That must have been a hell of a long time ago.'

'Yes,' agreed the stranger. 'A long time.' He was pleasantly spoken and patient. His round face, which I could imagine looking jolly, was very solemn just then.

I looked around and saw my mother and Jim coming slowly down from the house.

'I still don't get it,' my father said. 'What do you want?'

'We just want to go across your land, if that's all right. Look, we better introduce ourselves. My name's Tom Taikaka. And this is——'

My father was lost in a confusion of introductions. But he still didn't shake anyone's hand. He just stood his ground, aloof and faintly hostile. Finally there was the old man. He looked as though he had gone to sleep again.

'You see he's old,' Tom explained. 'And has not so long to live. He is the last great man of our tribe, the oldest. He wishes to see again where he was born. The land over which his father was chief. He wishes to see this before his spirit departs for Rerengawairua.'

By this time my mother and Jim had joined us. They were as confused as we were.

'You mean you've come just to——' my father began.

'We've come a long way,' Tom said. 'Nearly a hundred miles, from up the coast. That's where we live now.'

'All this way. Just so——'

'Yes,' Tom said. 'That's right.'

'Well,' said my father. 'What do you know? What do you know about that?' Baffled, he looked at me, at my mother, and even finally at Jim. None of us had anything to say.

'I hope we're not troubling you,' Tom said politely. 'We don't want to be any trouble. We just want to go across your land, if that's all right. We got our own tucker and everything.'

We saw this was true. The two old women had large flax kits of food.

'No liquor?' my father said suspiciously. 'I don't want any drinking round my place.'

'No,' Tom replied. His face was still patient. 'No liquor. We don't plan on any drinking.'

The other young men shyly agreed in the background. It was not, they seemed to say, an occasion for drinking.

'Well,' said my father stiffly, 'I suppose it's all right. Where are you going to take him?' He nodded towards the old sleeping man.

'Just across your land. And up to the old *pa*.'

'I didn't know there used to be any *pa* round here.'

'Well,' said Tom. 'It used to be up there.' He pointed out the largest hill behind our farm, one that stood well apart and above the others. We called it Craggy Hill, because of limestone outcrops. Its flanks and summit were patchy with tall scrub. We seldom went near it, except perhaps when out shooting; then we circled its steep slopes rather than climbed it. 'You'd see the terraces,' Tom said, 'if it wasn't for the scrub. It's all hidden now.'

Now my father looked strangely at Tom. 'Hey,' he said, 'you sure you aren't having me on? How come you know that hill straight off? You ever been here before?'

'No,' Tom said. His face shone as he sweated with the effort of trying to explain everything. 'I never been here before. I never been in this part of the country before.'

'Then how do you know that's the hill, eh?'

'Because,' Tom said simply, 'the old men told me. They described it so well I could find the place blindfold. All the stories of our tribe are connected with that hill. That's where we lived, up there, for hundreds of years.'

'Well, I'll be damned. What do you know about that?' My father blinked, and looked up at the hill again. 'Just up there, eh? And for hundreds of years.'

'That's right.'

'And I never knew. Well, I'll be damned.'

'There's lots of stories about that hill,' Tom said. 'And a lot of battles fought round here. Over your place.'

'Right over my land?'

'That's right. Up and down here, along the river.'

My father was so astonished he forgot to be aloof. He was trying to fit everything into his mind at once—the hill where they'd lived hundreds of years, the battles fought across his land—and it was too much.

'The war canoes would come up here,' Tom went on. 'I reckon they'd drag them up somewhere here'—he indicated the grassy bank on which we were standing—'in the night, and go on up to attack the *pa* before sunrise. That's if we hadn't sprung a trap for them down here. There'd be a lot of blood soaked into this soil.' He kicked at the earth beneath our feet. 'We had to fight a long while to keep this land here, a lot of battles. Until there was a day when it was no use fighting any more. That was when we left.'

We knew, without him having to say it, what he meant. He meant the day when the European took the land. So we all stood quietly for a moment. Then my mother spoke.

'You'd better come up to the house,' she said. 'I'll make you all a cup of tea.'

A cup of tea was her solution to most problems.

We went up to the house slowly. The young men followed behind, carrying the litter. They put the old man in the shade of a tree, outside the house. Since it seemed the best thing to do, we all sat around him; there wouldn't have been room for everyone in our small kitchen anyway. We waited for my mother to bring out the tea.

Then the old man woke. He seemed to shiver, his eyes opened wide, and he said something in Maori. 'He wonders where he is.' Tom explained. He turned back to the old man and spoke in Maori.

He gestured, he pointed. Then the old man knew. We all saw it the moment the old man knew. It was as if we were all willing him towards that moment of knowledge. He quivered and tried to lift himself weakly; the old women rushed forward to help him. His eyes had a faint glitter as he looked up to the place we called Craggy Hill. He did not see us, the house, or anything else. Some more Maori words escaped him in a long, sighing rush. '*Te Wahiokoahoki*,' he said.

'It is the name,' Tom said, repeating it. 'The name of the place.'

The old man lay back against the women, but his eyes were still bright and trembling. They seemed to have a life independent of his wrinkled flesh. Then the lids came down, and they were gone again. We could all relax.

'*Te Wahiokoahoki*,' Tom said. 'It means the place of happy return. It got the name when we returned there after our victories against other tribes.'

My father nodded. 'Well, I'll be damned,' he said. 'That

place there. And I never knew.' He appeared quite affable now.

My mother brought out tea. The hot cups passed from hand to hand, steaming and sweet.

'But not so happy now, eh?' Tom said. 'Not for us.'

'No. I don't suppose so.'

Tom nodded towards the old man. 'I reckon he was just about the last child born up there. Before we had to leave. Soon there'll be nobody left who lived there. That's why they wanted young men to come back. So we'd remember too.'

Jim went into the house and soon returned. I saw he carried the greenstone adzes he'd found. He approached Tom shyly.

'I think these are really yours,' he said, the words an effort.

Tom turned the adzes over in his hand. Jim had polished them until they were a vivid green. 'Where'd you get these, eh?' he asked.

Jim explained how and where he'd found them. 'I think they're really yours,' he repeated.

There was a brief silence. Jim stood with his eyes downcast, his treasure surrendered. My father watched anxiously; he plainly thought Jim a fool.

'You see,' Jim added apologetically, 'I didn't think they really belonged to anyone. That's why I kept them.'

'Well,' Tom said, embarrassed. 'That's real nice of you. Real nice of you, son. But you better keep them, eh? They're yours now. You find, you keep. We got no claims here any more. This is your father's land now.'

Then it was my father who seemed embarrassed. 'Leave me out of this,' he said sharply. 'You two settle it between you. It's none of my business.'

'I think you better keep them all the same,' Tom said to Jim.

Jim was glad to keep the greenstone, yet a little hurt by rejection of his gift. He received the adzes back silently.

'I tell you what,' Tom went on cheerfully, 'you ever find another one, you send it to me, eh? Like a present. But you keep those two.'

'All right,' Jim answered, clutching the adzes. He seemed

much happier. 'I promise if I find any more, I'll send them to you.'

'Fair enough,' Tom smiled, his face jolly. Yet I could see that he too really wanted the greenstone.

After a while they got up to leave. They made the old man comfortable again and lifted him. 'We'll see you again to-morrow,' Tom said. 'The launch will be back to pick us up.'

'Tomorrow?' my father said. It hadn't occurred to him that they might be staying overnight on his land.

'We'll make ourselves a bit of a camp up there tonight,' Tom said, pointing to Craggy Hill. 'We ought to be comfortable up there. Like home, eh?' The jest fell mildly from his lips.

'Well, I suppose that's all right.' My father didn't know quite what to say. 'Nothing you want?'

'No,' Tom said. 'We got all we want, thanks. We'll be all right. We got ourselves. That's the important thing, eh?'

We watched them move away, the women followed by the young men with the litter. Tom went last, Jim trotting along beside him. They seemed, since the business of the greenstone, to have made friends quickly. Tom appeared to be telling Jim a story.

I thought for a moment that my father might call Jim back. But he didn't. He let him go.

The old women now, I noticed, carried green foliage. They beat it about them as they walked across our paddocks and up towards Craggy Hill; they were chanting or singing, and their wailing sound came back to us. Their figures grew smaller with distance. Soon they were clear of the paddocks and beginning to climb.

My father thumbed back his hat and rubbed a handker-chief across his brow. 'Well, I'll be damned,' he said.

.   .   .   .   .

We sat together on the porch that evening, as we often did in summer after milking and our meal. Yet that evening was very different from any other. The sun had set, and in the dusk we saw faint smoke rising from their campfire on Craggy Hill, the place of happy return. Sometimes I thought I heard the wailing sound of the women again, but I couldn't quite be sure.

What were they doing up there, what did they hope to find? We both wondered and puzzled, yet didn't speak to each other.

Jim had returned long before, with stories. It seemed he had learned, one way and another, just about all there was to be learned about the tribe that had once lived on Craggy Hill. At the dinner table he told the stories breathlessly. My father affected to be not much interested; and so, my father's son, did I. Yet we listened, all the same.

'Then there was the first musket,' Jim said. 'The first musket in this part of the country. Someone bought it from a trader down south and carried it back to the *pa*. Another tribe, one of their old enemies, came seeking *uta*—*uta* means revenge—for something that had been done to them the year before. And when they started climbing up the hill they were knocked off one by one, with the musket. They'd never seen anything like it before. So the chief of the tribe on Craggy Hill made a sign of peace and called up his enemies. It wasn't a fair fight, he said, only one tribe with a musket. So he'd let his enemies have the musket for a while. They would have turns with the musket, each tribe. He taught the other tribe how to fire and point the musket. Then they separated and started the battle again. And the next man to be killed by the musket was the chief's eldest son. That was the old man's uncle—the old man who was here today.'

'Well, I don't know,' said my father. 'Sounds bloody queer to me. That's no way to fight a battle.'

'That's the way they fought,' Jim maintained.

So we left Jim, still telling stories to my mother, and went out on the porch.

The evening thickened. Soon the smoke of the campfire was lost. The hills grew dark against the pale sky. And at last my father, looking up at the largest hill of all, spoke softly...

'I suppose a man's a fool,' he said. 'I should never have let that land go. Shouldn't ever have let it go back to scrub. I could of run a few sheep up there. But I just let it go. Perhaps

I'll burn it off one day, run a few sheep. Sheep might pay better too, the way things are now.'

But it wasn't, somehow, quite what I expected him to say. I suppose he was just trying to make sense of things in his own fashion.

3

They came down off Craggy Hill the next day. The launch had been waiting for them in the river some time.

When we saw the cluster of tiny figures, moving at a fair pace down the hills, we sensed there was something wrong. Then, as they drew nearer, approaching us across the paddocks, we saw what was wrong. There was no litter, no old man. They all walked freely, separately. They were no longer burdened.

Astonished, my father strode up to Tom. 'Where is he?' he demanded.

'We left him back up there,' Tom said. He smiled sadly and I had a queer feeling that I knew exactly what he would say.

'Left him up there?'

'He died last night, or this morning. When we went to wake him he was cold. So we left him up there. That's where he wanted to be.'

'You can't do that,' my father protested. 'You can't just leave a dead man like that. Leave him anywhere. And, besides, it's my land you've leaving him on.'

'Yes,' Tom said. 'Your land.'

'Don't you understand? You can't just leave dead people around. Not like that.'

'But we didn't just leave him around. We didn't just leave him anywhere. We made him all safe and comfortable. He's all right. You needn't worry.'

'Christ, man,' my father said. 'Don't you see?'

But he might have been asking a blind man to see. Tom just smiled patiently and said not to worry. Also he said they'd better be catching the launch. They had a long way to go home, a tiring journey ahead,

And as he walked off, my father still arguing beside him, the old women clashed their dry greenery, wailing, and their shark-tooth necklaces danced under their heaving throats.

In a little while the launch went noisily off down the river. My father stood on the bank, still yelling after them. When he returned to the house, his voice was hoarse.

He had a police party out, a health officer too. They scoured the hills, and most of the caves they could find. They discovered no trace of a burial, nor did they find anything in the caves. At one stage someone foolishly suggested we might have imagined it all. So my father produced the launchman and people from the township as witness to the fact that an old Maori, dying, had actually been brought to our farm.

That convinced them. But it didn't take them anywhere near finding the body. They traced the remnants of the tribe, living up the coast, and found that indeed an old man of the tribe was missing. No one denied that there had been a visit to our farm. But they maintained that they knew nothing about a body. The old man, they said, had just wandered off into the bush; they hadn't found him again.

He might, they added, even still be alive. Just to be on the safe side, in case there was any truth in their story, the police put the old man on the missing persons register, for all the good that might have done.

But we knew. We knew every night we looked up at the hills that he was there, somewhere.

So he was still alive, in a way. Certainly it was a long time before he let us alone.

And by then my father had lost all taste for the farm. It seemed the land itself had heaped some final indignity upon him, made a fool of him. He never talked again, anyway, about running sheep on the hills.

When butter prices rose and land values improved, a year or two afterwards, he had no hesitation in selling out. We shifted into another part of the country entirely, for a year or two, and then into another. Finally we found ourselves milking a small herd for town supply, not far from the city.

We're still on that farm, though there's talk of the place being purchased soon for a city sub-division. We think we might sell, but we'll face the issue when it arises.

Now and then Jim comes to see us, smart in a city suit, a lecturer at the university. My father always found it difficult to talk to Jim, and very often now he goes off to bed and leaves us to it. One thing I must say about Jim: he has no objection to helping with the milking. He insists that he enjoys it; perhaps he does. It's all flat-land round our present farm, with one farm much like another, green grass and square farmhouses and pine shelter belts, and it's not exactly the place to sit out on a summer evening and watch shadows gathering on the hills. Because there aren't hills within sight; or shadows either, for that matter. It's all very tame and quiet, apart from cars speeding on the highway.

I get on reasonably well with Jim. We read much the same books, have much the same opinions on a great many subjects. The city hadn't made a great deal of difference to him. We're both married, with young families. We also have something else in common: we were both in the war, fighting in the desert. One evening after milking, when we stood smoking and yarning in the cool, I remembered something and decided I might put a question to Jim.

'You know,' I began, 'they say it's best, when you're under fire in the war, to fix your mind on something remote. So you won't be afraid. I remember Dad telling me that. I used to try. But it never seemed any good. I couldn't think of anything. I was still as scared as hell.'

'I was too. Who wasn't?'

'But, I mean, did you ever think of anything?'

'Funny thing,' he said. 'Now I come to think of it, I did. I thought of the old place—you know, the old place by the river. Where,' he added, and his face puckered into a grin, 'where they buried that old Maori. And where I found those greenstones. I've still got them at home, you know, up on the mantelpiece. I seem to remember trying to give them away once, to those Maoris. Now I'm glad I didn't. It's my only souvenir from there, the only thing that makes that place still live for me.' He paused. 'Well, anyway, that's what I thought about. That old place of ours.'

I had a sharp pain. I felt the dismay of a long-distance runner who, coasting confidently to victory, imagining himself well ahead of the field, finds himself overtaken and the tape snapped at the very moment he leans forward to breast it. For one black moment it seemed I had been robbed of something which was rightfully mine.

I don't think I'll ever forgive him.

H. E. BATES

Great Uncle Crow

ONCE in the summer-time, when the water-lilies were in bloom and the wheat was new in ear, his grandfather took him on a long walk up the river, to see his Uncle Crow. He had heard so much of Uncle Crow, so much that was wonderful and to be marvelled at, and for such a long time, that he knew him to be, even before that, the most remarkable fisherman in the world.

'Masterpiece of a man, your Uncle Crow,' his grandfather said. 'He could git a clothes-line any day and tie a brick on it and a mossel of cake and go out and catch a pike as long as your arm.'

When he asked what kind of cake his grandfather seemed irritated and said it was just like a boy to ask questions of that sort.

'Any kind o' cake,' he said. 'Plum cake. Does it matter? Carraway cake. Christmas cake if you like. Anything. I shouldn't wonder if he could catch a pretty fair pike with a cold baked tater.'

'Only a pike?'

'Times,' his grandfather said, 'I've seen him sittin' on the bank on a sweltering hot day like a furnace, when nobody was gettin' a bite not even off a blood-sucker. And there your Uncle Crow'd be a-pullin' 'em out by the dozen, like a man shellin' harvest beans.'

'And how does he come to be my Uncle Crow?' he said, 'if my mother hasn't got a brother? Nor my father.'

'Well,' his grandfather said, 'he's really your mother's own cousin, if everybody had their rights. But all on us call him Uncle Crow.'

'And where does he live?'

'You'll see,' his grandfather said. 'All by hisself. In a little titty bit of a house by the river.'

The little titty bit of a house, when he first saw it, surprised him very much. It was not at all unlike a black tarred
boat that had either slipped down a slope and stuck there on
its way to launching or one that had been washed up and left
there in a flood. The roof of brown tiles had a warp in it and
the sides were mostly built, he thought, of tarred beer-barrels.

The two windows with their tiny panes were about as large
as chessboards and Uncle Crow had nailed underneath each
of them a sill of sheet tin that was still a brilliant blue, each
with the words 'Backache Pills' in white lettering on it, upside
down.

On all sides of the house grew tall feathered reeds. They
enveloped it like gigantic whispering corn. Some distance
beyond the great reeds the river went past in a broad slow arc,
on magnificent kingly currents, full of long white islands of
water-lilies, as big as china breakfast cups, shining and yellow-
hearted in the sun.

He thought, on the whole, that that place, the river with the
water-lilies, the little titty bit of a house, and the great forest
of reeds talking between soft brown beards, was the nicest he
had ever seen.

'Anybody about?' his grandfather called. 'Crow!—anybody at home?'

The door of the house was partly open, but at first there was
no answer. His grandfather pushed open the door still farther
with his foot. The reeds whispered down by the river and were
answered, in the house, by a sound like the creak of bed springs.

'Who is't?'

'It's me, Crow,' his grandfather called. 'Lukey. Brought
the boy over to have a look at you.'

A big gangling red-faced man with rusty hair came to the
door. His trousers were black and very tight. His eyes were a
smeary vivid blue, the same colour as the stripes of his shirt,
and his trousers were kept up by a leather belt with brass
escutcheons on it, like those on horses' harness.

'Thought very like you'd be out a-pikin',' his grandfather
said.

'Too hot. How's Lukey boy? Ain't seed y'lately, Lukey boy.'

His lips were thick and very pink and wet, like cow's lips. He made a wonderful erupting jolly sound somewhat between a belch and a laugh.

'Comin' in it a minute?'

In the one room of the house was an iron bed with an old red check horse-rug spread over it and a stone copper in one corner and a bare wooden table with dirty plates and cups and a tin kettle on it. Two osier baskets and a scythe stood in another corner.

Uncle Crow stretched himself full length on the bed as if he was very tired. He put his knees in the air. His belly was tight as a bladder of lard in his black trousers, which were mossy green on the knees and seat.

'How's the fishin'?' his grandfather said. 'I bin tellin' the boy——'

Uncle Crow belched deeply. From where the sun struck full on the tarred wall of the house there was a hot whiff of baking tar. But when Uncle Crow belched there was a smell like the smell of yeast in the air.

'It ain't bin all that much of a summer yit,' Uncle Crow said. 'Ain't had the rain.'

'Not like that summer you catched the big 'un down at Archer's Mill. I recollect you a-tellin' on me——'

'Too hot and dry by half,' Uncle Crow said. 'Gits in your gullet like chaff.'

'You recollect that summer?' his grandfather said. 'Nobody else a-fetching on 'em out only you——'

'Have a drop o' neck-oil,' Uncle Crow said.

The boy wondered what neck-oil was and presently, to his surprise, Uncle Crow and his grandfather were drinking it. It came out of a dark-green bottle and it was a clear bright amber, like cold tea, in the two glasses.

'The medder were yeller with 'em,' Uncle Crow said. 'Yeller as a guinea.'

He smacked his lips with a marvellously juicy, fruity sound. The boy's grandfather gazed at the neck-oil and said he thought it would be a corker if it was kept a year or two, but Uncle Crow said:

'Trouble is, Lukey boy, it's a terrible job to keep it. You start tastin' on it to see if it'll keep and then you taste on it again and you go on tastin' on it until they ain't a drop left as 'll keep.'

Uncle Crow laughed so much that the bed springs cackled underneath his bouncing trousers.

'Why is it called neck-oil?' the boy said.

'Boy,' Uncle Crow said, 'when you git older, when you git growed-up, you know what'll happen to your gullet?'

'No.'

'It'll git sort o' rusted up inside. Like a old gutter pipe. So's you can't swaller very easy. Rusty as old Harry it'll git. You know that, boy?'

'No.'

'Well, it will. I'm tellin' on y'. And you know what y' got to do then?'

'No.'

'Every now and then you gotta git a drop o' neck-oil down it. So's to ease it. A drop o' neck-oil every once in a while —that's what you gotta do to keep the rust out.'

The boy was still contemplating the curious prospect of his neck rusting up inside in later years when Uncle Crow said: 'Boy, you go outside and jis' round the corner you'll see a bucket. You bring handful o' cresses out on it. I'll bet you're hungry, ain't you?'

'A little bit.'

He found the watercresses in the bucket, cool in the shadow of the little house, and when he got back inside with them Uncle Crow said:

'Now you put the cresses on that there plate there and then put your nose inside that there basin and see what's inside. What is't, eh?'

'Eggs.'

'Ought to be fourteen on 'em. Four-apiece and two over. What sort are they, boy?'

'Moor-hens'.'

'You got a knowin' boy here, Lukey,' Uncle Crow said. He dropped the scaly red lid of one eye like an old cockerel going to sleep. He took another drop of neck-oil and gave another fruity, juicy laugh as he heaved his body from the bed. 'A very knowin' boy.'

Presently he was carving slices of thick brown bread with a great horn-handled shut-knife and pasting each slice with summery golden butter. Now and then he took another drink of neck-oil and once he said:

'You get the salt pot, boy, and empty a bit out on that there saucer, so's we can all dip in.'

Uncle Crow slapped the last slice of bread on to the buttered pile and then said:

'Boy, you take that there jug there and go a step or two up the path and dip yourself a drop o' spring water. You'll see it. It comes out of a little bit of a wall, jist by a doddle-willer.'

When the boy got back with the jug of spring water Uncle Crow was opening another bottle of neck-oil and his grandfather was saying: 'God a-mussy man, goo steady. You'll have me agoin' one way and another——'

'Man alive,' Uncle Crow said, 'and what's wrong with that?'

Then the watercress, the salt, the moor-hens' eggs, the spring water, and the neck-oil were all ready. The moor-hens' eggs were hard-boiled. Uncle Crow lay on the bed and cracked them with his teeth, just like big brown nuts, and said he thought the watercress was just about as nice and tender as a young lady.

'I'm sorry we ain't got the gold plate out though. I had it out a-Sunday.' He closed his old cockerel-lidded eye again and licked his tongue backwards and forwards across his lips and dipped another peeled egg in salt. 'You know what I had for my dinner a-Sunday, boy?'

'No.'

'A pussy-cat on a gold plate. Roasted with broad-beans and new taters. Did you ever heerd talk of anybody eatin' a roasted pussy-cat, boy?'

'Yes.'

'You did?'

'Yes,' he said, 'that's a hare.'

'You got a very knowin' boy here, Lukey,' Uncle Crow said. 'A very knowin' boy.'

Then he screwed up a big dark-green bouquet of watercress and dipped it in salt until it was entirely frosted and then crammed it in one neat wholesale bite into his soft pink mouth.

'But not on a gold plate?' he said.

He had to admit that.

'No, not on a gold plate,' he said.

All that time he thought the fresh watercress, the moor-hens' eggs, the brown bread-and-butter, and the spring water were the most delicious, wonderful things he had ever eaten in the world. He felt that only one thing was missing. It was that whenever his grandfather spoke of fishing Uncle Crow simply took another draught of neck-oil.

'When are you goin' to take us fishing?' he said.

'You et up that there egg,' Uncle Crow said. 'That's the last one. You et that there egg up and I'll tell you what.'

'What about gooin' as far as that big deep hole where the chub lay?' grandfather said. 'Up by the back-brook——'

'I'll tell you what, boy,' Uncle Crow said, 'you git your grandfather to bring you over September time, of a morning, afore the steam's off the winders. Mushroomin' time. You come over and we'll have a bit o' bacon and mushroom for breakfast and then set into the pike. You see, boy, it ain't the pikin' season now. It's too hot. Too bright. It's too bright of afternoon, and they ain't a-bitin'.'

He took a long rich swig of neck-oil.

'Ain't that it, Lukey? That's the time, ain't it, mushroom time?'

'Thass it,' his grandfather said.

'Tot out,' Uncle Crow said. 'Drink up. My throat's jist easin' orf a bit.'

He gave another wonderful belching laugh and told the boy to be sure to finish up the last of the watercress and the bread-and-butter. The little room was rich with the smell of neck-oil, and the tarry sun-baked odour of the beer-barrels that formed its walls. And through the door came, always, the sound of reeds talking in their beards, and the scent of summer meadows drifting in from beyond the great curl of the river with its kingly currents and its islands of full blown lilies, white and yellow in the sun.

'I see the wheat's in ear,' his grandfather said. 'Ain't that the time for tench, when the wheat's in ear?'

'Mushroom time,' Uncle Crow said. 'That's the time. You git mushroom time here, and I'll fetch you a tench out as big as a cricket bat.'

He fixed the boy with an eye of wonderful, watery, glassy blue and licked his lips with a lazy tongue, and said:

'You know what colour a tench is, boy?'

'Yes,' he said.

'What colour?'

'The colour of the neck-oil.'

'Lukey,' Uncle Crow said, 'you got a very knowin' boy here. A very knowin' boy.'

After that, when there were no more cresses or moor-hens' eggs, or bread-and-butter to eat, and his grandfather said he'd get hung if he touched another drop of neck-oil, he and his grandfather walked home across the meadows.

'What work does Uncle Crow do?' he said.

'Uncle Crow? Work?—well, he ain't—Uncle Crow? Well, he works, but he ain't what you'd call a reg'lar worker——'

All the way home he could hear the reeds talking in their beards. He could see the water-lilies that reminded him so much of the gold and white inside the moor-hens' eggs. He could hear the happy sound of Uncle Crow laughing and sucking at the neck-oil, and crunching the fresh salty cresses into his mouth in the tarry little room.

He felt happy, too, and the sun was a gold plate in the sky.

BILL NAUGHTON

Late Night on Watling Street

IT WAS after midnight when I drew my lorry on to the parking ground in front of 'Lew's' caff. I switched off the engine and lights, got out of the cab, knew it would be safe without locking it up, and stretched my limbs and looked up at the sky. It was all starry. The air had a nice fresh rinsed taste to it. I walked round the wagon and kicked my tyres, testing the ropes round my load, and with that nice week-end feeling you get on a Friday night, I went inside.

It was nearly empty. I went up to the counter. Ethel, Lew's young wife, was making a fresh pot of tea, and Lew was watching her. I heard him say: 'Make it any stronger an' you'll hatta serve it with knives and forks.'

'I can't stand the sight of weak tea,' said Ethel.

'You can get it a good colour without putting all that much in,' said Lew.

'It's not colour a man wants,' said Ethel, 'it's body.' She winked at me. 'Eh, Bolton?'

Lew hadn't seen me listening, and he tried to laugh it off. I didn't take much notice of him. I never do. He's turned fifty, has a thin face with red cheeks and sandy hair. He always wears a big jersey with a polo collar, a check cap, and sandals, and he always has a fag in his mouth. Box? You could blow him over. But during the war, with all the shortage of food and fags, he suddenly found himself important, like most little shopkeepers and café owners, and he started giving orders, and took to wearing this boxer's rig-out. I hate fakes and show-offs, and Lew's one. But maybe he's not a bad bloke at heart, for they say he's good for a touch if you're short of cash. But I can never forget that he used to put soda in his tea urn, and I blame that for the guts' ache I used to get. That was before he married Ethel.

I said nothing to Ethel except to give her my usual warm

nod and wink, and then I ordered a large tea, and asked could I have some egg and chips.

'Yes,' said Lew. 'She's got the chip pan all ready.'

'I'll bring your tea over,' said Ethel.

I knew he was getting at her over something. And I'd a good idea what it was—a driver called Jackson. Ethel wouldn't shut shop until he'd been. I said nothing because I reckoned I was lucky to get my egg and chips. Practically the only spot in the British Isles you could get them on a Friday night at that hour. I walked across to the big table where Taff and Ned were sitting, and sat at one end.

'I see old Babyface is out on the scout again,' said Taff.

'That dirty little bleeder,' said Ned. 'I've known many a speed cop in my day, but never one like him, an' his mate. The way they creep up on your tail and hang there.'

'He's done that man Jackson three times,' said Taff.

'Once more,' said Ned, 'an' his licence will go for a walk for six months.'

Ethel brought my tea. She came up behind me and put it on the table. I saw her brown arm and strong woman's fingers. I like a healthy woman. Especially when she's just on thirty. A woman's best age. I could have made her for myself until Jackson came on the scene. Our feeling had been warming up nicely in looks. But at forty-two you don't compete with a bloke of twenty-eight. But if she had known it, I was better than I'd ever been in my life. Outside a lorry drew on to the parking ground and the engine revved up and then shut off. Taff said, 'That'll be Jackson.' I could see Lew looking a bit tense.

'It's not Jackson,' said Ethel. She smiled at me, and went back to the counter. The door opened and in came Walter, a driver from St. Helens, and behind him his trailer-mate, Willie.

Walter, a short little stiff chap, carrying his lunch basket, and Willie, one of these artistic lads you see around these days, with a silk scarf round his neck. He always followed Walter like a faithful poodle. Walter let out a shout and when he came up to Lew he got up on his toes and began boxing. This just suited Lew who began throwing in what he thought were snappy lefts. Old Walter could have let him have one and knocked him out for good. But he always liked to gee old Lew up a bit. He went up and kissed Ethel on the cheek. Those cheery blokes, I thought, can get away with murder.

'Love me as much as ever, love?' said Walter to Ethel.

'You know me, Walter,' said Ethel.

'That's why I'm asking,' said Walter.

Old Lew said, 'Lay off mate, in front of the husband.'

'You can always rely on a chap as does it under your nose, Lew,' said Walter.

It was a lively little entrance and it brightened the place up.

Taff called out, 'Did you see old Babyface on your way down?'

'Did we see him, Willie!' said Walter. 'Ethel, double eggs and chips for my mate. I'm treating him.' Walter came over to the table and cocked his leg across a chair. 'We were just coming down the Long Hill there, we had the stick out, doing a nice forty-five, and old Willie here crooning away, when he suddenly broke off like he'd been shot. "What's up, Willie?" I says. "Sum'dy on our tail," says Willie. I revved up and put the old stick in and got into tear. I looked through the mirror. Not a thing in sight. I watched closely, not a thing. And I think the lad must be seeing something. I get the old speed down to a bit of a crawl, and still nothing in sight. "Are you sure, Willie?" I says. "I am that an' all," says Willie here. Well, I'm crawling along and still can't see nothing and I comes to thinking that old Willie's psychic bump has let him down. So I tells him to lean out of the cab at his side while I give a chancy swerve and switch off my own lights for better seeing. Right enough it was that damn great mardarse, Babyface. Him and his mate had been stuck on our tail.'

'What happened then?' said Ned.

'They knew they'd been rumbled,' said Walter. 'So the next thing they drew ahead and went into a side road. And there they're stuck this minute, waiting for the next poor sod that comes down.'

Ethel came across with my egg and chips. A minute later she was back with Willie's.

'Ee, were you expectin' me, Ethel?' said Willie, all smiles.

'Not *you*,' said Lew, looking at the door.

I was wiping my plate clean with bread when a lorry came belting off the road on to the parking ground outside. It hammered along and stopped with a loud brake squeal right at the door. Nobody looked up.

'That's Jackson now,' said Willie.

'And a good job his anchors are all right,' said Taff, 'or else——'

'Curse the bloody man,' said Lew. 'He'll drive up to the blasted counter one of these fine days.' He turned what he must have thought was a tough face to the door. We all gave a look that way. It was Jackson all right. Lew quickly dropped his stare and started wiping a table.

'Has he got the rats in him!' said Ned.

'He's not in the best of moods surely,' said Taff.

Jackson came striding up slowly. He had a dark chin, pale face, black hair. As he was passing our table he saw Willie still eating his egg and chips. The sight of the plate seemed to stop him dead. His face went even darker. Willie looked dead nervous. Walter picked up the sauce bottle.

'Here y'are, Willie boy,' he said in a loud easy-going way, 'have a shake of the old bottle.'

Willie smiled at Walter. Jackson went to the next table, an empty one. When Lew saw that Walter had got one over Jackson, he seemed to take heart. He went up to the table.

'What is it?' he said.

'What's what?' said Jackson, looking for Ethel.

'Have you ordered?' said Lew.

'Ordered?' said Jackson. 'I'm not getting measured for a suit. Small tea.'

'That's all?' said Lew.

'That an' a bit of peace,' said Jackson.

'You're supposed to bring your own,' said Lew, walking away.

When he went up to the counter I could see he said something to Ethel, and I heard her say: 'There's times when your
funny stuff just isn't funny, Lew. I'll serve him.'

'You're welcome,' said Lew.

He looked hurt. She took his arm and smiled at him. He
smiled back.

'Sorry,' said Ethel.

'We've had eighteen hours of it,' said Lew, looking at the
clock. 'Another half-hour and we're through. What about a
tune?'

Ethel takes the tea across to Jackson. He gives one tight
grip over her wrist.

'You want your egg an' chips, don't you, Jack?' she says.

Jackson shakes his head. Lew dropped his coin into the juke-
box, and the next thing you can hear a woman singing
something about 'Waltzing with her darling'. It's called *The
Tennessee Waltz*. Jackson kissed Ethel's arm. Then Ethel moved
slowly away from his table, looking like a woman with a
dream on her mind.

As it happens, old Lew is just moving away from the juke-
box, and this music and woman's voice is filling the place,
and Ethel comes up facing Lew with that faraway walk, and
the next thing Lew has got hold of her and is dancing her
gently around to a slow foxtrot or something.

Although I don't like him I had to admit to myself that he
handled it nicely. And he danced nicely too, with a nice skilful
movement. They all began calling out, 'Life in the old dog yet',
and 'Go on', but there was no doubt they all liked to see the
dance. All except Jackson. His face went dead poisonous. He
kept himself sitting there for a time and then he got to his feet.
He went across to the juke-box, half turned his back on it, and
gave it a back-heeler. It was a dead sharp kick, and the next
thing there was a groan and the tune died away in the middle
of the woman singing something about 'remembering the
night'.

I looked up and saw old Lew's face. One second it had that
look that comes over a chap's face when he's enjoying a dance.
The next it had the look of a child that's had its dummy

snatched out of its mouth in the middle of a good suck. Ethel gave Jackson a sharp sort of look and went behind the counter. Willie looked towards Lew, his big eyes soft and wide open with sympathy. Lew stood there in a daze for a couple of ticks, then he went across to Jackson.

'You did that,' he said.

'What about it?' said Jackson.

'You'd no right,' said Lew. 'Didn't you see us dancin'?'

'I saw you,' said Jackson.

'I won't bloody stand for it,' said Lew.

'What'll you do?' said Jackson.

'I'll show you what I'll do,' said Lew. Then he weakened. 'I mean, we were doin' no harm.'

'I told you I wanted some peace,' said Jackson. 'I've had enough din in my ears for the last five hours.'

'But you'd no right,' said Lew. He went across to the juke-box and shook it. You could hear the record whirring round but missing the needle or something. He came hurrying back to Jackson. 'You had no right to do what you did,' he said, talking legal like. 'I'd put my money in that box.'

Jackson leant back in his chair. 'Why didn't you say it was the money was troubling you?' he said. He put his hand in his pocket and drew out a fistful of silver and copper. 'Here y'are,' he said, holding out his hand. 'You can take it outa that.'

Lew being a money-mean sort of bloke, couldn't help being caught off guard. The sight of money carelessly handled seems to make some people so that they can't think for a minute. He just stared at Jackson and at the money and didn't know what to do. Then Ethel came walking up behind Lew. She went round him in a gentle way, until she was facing Jackson, and before he knew what was happening she brought up her hand with a swift smack under his. The money went right up in the air and flew all over the place.

'And you,' she said, 'can take it out of that!'

Then she turned to Lew like a mother who has gone out into the street to help her lad who is being challenged by a bigger lad. 'Come on, Lew,' she said and led him back to the counter.

We drivers said nothing. After all, Jackson himself was a driver. Jackson didn't know where to look or what to do. Then another lorry stopped outside.

The door opened with a quick jerk and in came Clive. A real spiv kid, the clothes, the walk, the lot, even to the old rub of the hands, as though he's going to sell you something. He comes whistling along.

'What you all bleedin' talkin' at once for?' he says, everything being dead silent. 'Large tea, Ethel, two of toast and drip. Don't be tight with the jelly—m'back's bad.'

Clive eyes everybody.

'Howzit goin', Bolton?' he says to me.

'Not bad,' I says.

Suddenly he makes a dive for something on the floor.

'Coo, I'm in bleedin' luck,' he says, picking up half a crown. I beckon with my thumb to where Jackson is sitting. Clive catches on. He goes across and puts it on the table in front of Jackson.

'I wouldn't rob you, Jackson,' he says. 'You might need it. I see old Babyface did you again—back up the road there on the Long Hill.'

As soon as Clive said that, the atmosphere changed.

'Bloody hard luck, Jackson,' said Ned.

'I hope they don't scrub your licence,' said Taff.

I gave him a look. He didn't seem to have Babyface on his mind. A lot had happened to him since that.

'He must have nailed you just after he left us,' said Walter. He took out his fags, handed them round, hesitated, then held the packet out to Jackson. Jackson thought it over for a moment, and then took one. The matey feeling came up then, the feeling of all being drivers and the law always after you.

Clive leant over the table and looked at Jackson: 'I was stuck in a lay-by up the road, mate, with a floozie, when you came whamming past. You was goin' like the clappers of hell. *Whoof* . . . "Wot's that?" she says. She went dead cold on me.'

Ethel came up with Clive's tea and toast and drip.

'You was goin' at a hell of a lick, Jackson,' went on Clive. 'What was on your bleedin' mind?'

Ethel was leaning over the table. I saw Jackson give her a long and hungry look. Ethel looked at him. She picked up his cup. 'Piece of my apple pie?' she said. He nodded. Then he looked at Clive. 'What did you say?' he said.

'Let it pass,' said Clive, his eye following Ethel. He didn't miss much.

The atmosphere had come on matey, and even Lew came up and hung around.

'I wouldn't like to say what I'd do to a cop like that,' said Taff.

'Babyface?' said Lew. 'Got his job to do, ain't he? That's what he's paid for—bookin' you! Well, ain't it?'

'He ain't paid bleedin' bonus on the job,' said Ned. 'He don't have to creep on your tail. None of the others do it.'

'It's legal, ain't it?' said Lew. 'You keep to the law too, then nob'dy can touch you.'

They went on yapping about the law then, about loads, log sheets, brakes, licences, and all the rest of it, with old Lew sticking his motty in at every chance.

Then Walter said: 'Has it ever struck you, Lew, what a dangerous caper it is—tailing a lorry?'

I saw Jackson suddenly take an interest.

Clive said: 'Suppose you didn't know this geezer was on your tail! Say you was doin' a nice fifty-five, when you spotted something just ahead of you?'

'Yeh,' said Ned, 'an' down on the bleedin' anchors.'

'Pull up with a jerk,' said Clive, 'and where's Babyface?'

'Over the bloody top,' said Taff.

'No, he ain't,' said Ned, 'he's *under* the back. You get out an' run around the back, and there's the bleedin' bogeymen an' their car, practically buried under the back axle. "Wot wuz you a-doin' of?" said Babyface. So you says, "Testin' my bleedin' brakes for efficiency. Why, officah, you've scratched your radiator—not to mention bashin' in your National 'Ealth dentures!"'

'Come on, Ned,' said Taff, rising, 'you'd talk all night.'

'It's about time you was all off,' said Lew. 'We want to get to bed.'

Ethel came over with Jackson's tea and apple pie. 'You go off, Lew,' she said. She looked at Jackson as she put the piece of pie in front of him, but he was staring down at the table. He didn't seem to notice the pie, or, come to that, Ethel herself.

'Can I trust you to lock up properly if I go off?' said Lew to Ethel.

'I'll help her,' said Walter.

'Then I think I'll go off to bed,' said Lew.

'That's right,' said Clive, 'let your bleedin' brains cool down. "Keep to the law." Never heard such bull in all my life.'

'Come on, Taff,' said Ned.

They went off.

'I think I'll go,' said Lew.

'All right,' said Walter, 'go, but stop natterin' about it.'

'Don't be long, Ethel,' said Lew. 'Turf 'em out.'

'It's too late to hurry,' said Ethel.

'Goodnight, Lew,' said Willie.

'Goodnight, Willie lad,' said Lew.

When Lew had gone off, Clive turned to me: 'Fancy a game of darts, Lofthouse?'

They either call me by the town I come from or its best-known footballer.

'I'm getting down for ten minutes,' I said.

'I'll give you a game, Bermondsey,' said Walter.

They went off, up beside the counter for their darts game. I put my cap on the table and rested my forehead on it, and shut out all the light with my arms. Even if you don't sleep the eyes and head get rested. You need some relief when you've been driving a ten-tonner through the night. Ethel must have come up and sat at Jackson's table, because after a bit I could hear their voices.

'What made you blow your top?' he said.

'I won't stand by and see a young chap taking the micky out of an older one,' she said. 'I don't like you being that way, Jacky.'

'Before I forget,' said Jackson. 'I've something here for you.

Hope they're not too squashed. I had to keep 'em out of sight.'

There was a bit of rustling and then Ethel whispered: 'Roses! how lovely, Jacky! Well, I never expected roses!'

Even with my head down I could smell roses.

Ethel must have given him a hand squeeze. He went on: 'Come off with me tonight. I'll wait for you outside in my tub. We'll drive off together. Don't worry about clothes— look, see, I've enough money in that book to buy you all the clothes you want.'

Post Office savings book. But I knew how he felt. The thought of having a woman in the warm cab there beside you, as you drive through the night, is the most tempting thought a driver can get. At least, that I can get. It's so cosy in the cab of your own lorry, with the faint warm smell of diesel oil, but it gets lonely. If only you had a woman beside you. For part of the time anyway.

Ethel went on about Lew. 'When I first came in that door,' I heard her say, 'I wasn't much to look at. I'd had things rough, I can tell you that, Jacky. And Lew is the first man I've ever met who has treated me with respect. He never tried anything on. And that's what I liked about him.'

'Am I trying anything on?' said Jackson. 'I'm asking you to come off with me.'

'And the day we got back after the marriage,' went on Ethel, 'he already had a new sign up outside. It said, *"Lew's and Ethel's"*.'

'Come off it,' said Jackson. 'He made the ropiest cup of tea between here and Gretna Green. The place was fallin' apart, an' so was he. You've pulled it all together. You're straight with him.'

'Another thing Lew gave me,' said Ethel, 'was security.'

Jackson seemed to fly off the handle at that. 'Security? What the hell are you talking about? I come bashing down Watling Street tonight—never a bloody stop except to snatch your roses. One thought on my mind—will I see you? How do you think that rat Babyface caught me again?—and you talk to me about security.'

GESS

'Sorry, Jacky,' said Ethel. 'What happens if they take your licence?'

'No licence, no job,' said Jackson. 'But we'll see about that. They won't get me working under a roof that easily.'

Just then the juke-box let go *The Tennessee Waltz* again. I looked up with a start, as though I'd been asleep. Willie was standing beside it. He called across to Walter: 'That's not the record I picked, Walter.' It was just then I looked towards Jackson. He looked real poisonous. He got up and walked slowly towards Willie at the juke-box.

'Jacky!' whispered Ethel. He took no notice.

Walter had spotted him. He left the darts game and hurried casually across to Willie beside the juke-box. Willie had seen Jackson, and he looked white.

'Enjoy yourself, lad,' said Walter. Then he turned and faced Jackson. I got up and walked across. Same as they used to say, Lancashire helps Lancashire. Walter was only a bantam; Jackson was on the big side and tough.

'Move over, Scouse,' said Jackson.

'What d'you want?' said Walter.

'I'm going to stop that bloody thing,' said Jackson.

'I don't think you are,' said Walter. His eyes never left Jackson as he handed the darts to Willie. I could see what Walter had in mind. He'd grab Jackson's coat lapels in a tick and pull him down and tup him with his head. And Jackson wouldn't be able to see for blood. I could almost hear the crack of Jackson's nose in my ears, even before it happened.

Ethel slipped round.

'What's up?' she said.

'Willie's paid to hear a tune,' said Walter, 'and he's goin' to hear one.'

'Yeh, but it might not be the one he's paid for,' said Jackson.

Jackson had a savage look on his face. But Walter was determined, and on the aware.

'Don't make any trouble,' said Ethel. 'Please go, and let me lock up.'

Jackson turned and looked at her. Walter was ready to make his grab. I stepped in.

'Come on, Walt,' I said.

'Not till the bloody tune's up,' he said.

So we all stood there for half a minute until the woman on the record stopped singing.

'You can all go now,' said Ethel.

'Ee, but we haven't paid yet, Ethel,' said Willie.

'Ee, lad, so you haven't,' said Ethel, taking him off a bit.

That seemed to break up the tension.

'What about the old darts?' said Clive.

Walter took the darts off Willie.

'Is it me?' he said.

'Yip,' said Clive. 'You want seventy-nine for game. Not be a minute, Ethel.'

Walter toed the line. He threw a nineteen, then a twenty, and a double-top with the last dart.

'Who'd 'ave bleedin' thought it!' said Clive, putting down his darts.

We all paid and walked to the door. 'Have you a minute, Bolton?' said Jackson. I nodded. He slipped back and had a last word with Ethel. Maybe a hug. I went up beside Walter.

'I was right there behind you, Walter,' I said, 'but I reckoned you didn't need me.'

Walter took off his cap and patted his head: 'I had this ready for him,' he said.

I went across to my tub. Then Jackson came up.

'I was going to ask you,' he said; 'you ain't got an old driving mirror, have you?'

As soon as he said it I remembered I had one in my tool-box. And it struck me that he must have seen it when I once lent him a spanner. He took out his fags and handed me one. Then he shone the torch in my tool-box. I got the driving mirror out. It was one that had been wrenched away when I drew too close to a wagon at the sidings one day. The metal arm had been ripped from the bracket.

'That do you?' I said.

'It might,' he said.

I didn't ask him what he wanted it for. If he wants me to know, I reckoned, he'll tell me.

'You've been done for speeding?' he said.

'More'n once,' I said.

'The cop who charges you has got to have a witness— that so?' he said.

'His mate,' I said, 'that's all.'

'There's got to be two of 'em in court?' he said.

'If you plead "not guilty" an' make a case of it,' I said. 'But how many drivers do? You know damn well you're guilty.'

'But they've *both* got to be there,' he said. 'Haven't they?'

'Look here, Jackson,' I said, 'if you're goin' on about Babyface doin' you tonight, forget it. You——'

'Look here,' cut in Jackson, 'if you want to question his witness and his witness fails to appear, or either one of them fails to appear——'

'Then it's "failure to produce witnesses",' I said, 'and you get "Case Dismissed".'

'That's what I wanted to know,' said Jackson.

'But I'll tell you one thing you're sufferin' from, Jackson,' I said, 'that's a bad dose of *copitis*.'

'You said it,' he said. 'I could murder the bleedin' lot of 'em.'

'It won't get you nowhere,' I said. 'We've all had it some time or other. Anyway, they won't take your licence just for speedin'.'

'It's not speedin'. He's doin' me for dangerous drivin',' said Jackson.

'That's a bit more serious,' I said.

'An' not only that,' said Jackson.

'What else?' I said.

'I'd a fiver folded up in my licence when I handed it over,' he said.

'A fiver! You must be crazy,' I said. 'It should be a quid. An' you get the licence back with a caution an' no quid. What's wrong with that? I'd sooner give a cop a quid than a magistrate a fiver.'

'I'd sooner cut their bleedin' throats,' said Jackson, 'the lot of 'em. Babyface is trying to make out I wanted to bribe him.'

'I suppose you said you kept it in your licence for safety?' I said.

Jackson nodded.

'Then,' I said, 'it's your word against his.'

'Against his and his mate's, and I know whose they'll take,' he said. Then he picked up the mirror and had a good look at it. 'We'll see,' he said. 'They ain't heard the charge yet. There's another three weeks to go. Anything could happen in that time.' He waved the mirror and went off.

It was a fortnight later, about two o'clock in the morning, a pitch black night, and I was belting along Watling Street, hoping I might make 'Lew's' in time, have a bite to eat and get a look at Ethel. She'd begun to get into my thoughts a lot. I was going at a fair lick, because you can see better on a dark night, since your headlights carve out the road for you, and you don't get those dicey shadows the moon makes. I had my eye watching out for Babyface, for I knew I was on his beat.

Suddenly, ahead down the road, I saw a lorry's headlights flashing on and off, giving me the danger signal. I flashed back, braked, and watched the road behind me and the road ahead. You can't be too careful on a trunk road at night. I once knew a young driver called Sam who got out to mend his tail light on the road. It was the last ever seen of him. Another wagon was belting down the road behind him. The driver, a Geordie, not seeing any light, came hammering along. It was too late to do anything about it when he saw the lorry. He went clean into the back of it as Sam was fixing his tail light.

I drew up in a safe clear spot. In the beam of my headlight I could see a lorry skew-whiff across the road. There was a black car that had crashed into the back of it and with such force that it seemed to be buried under the chassis. I lit a fag. As I was getting out a driver came running up to me.

'Leave your headlights on, Bolton,' he called. 'They need all the light they can get.'

'That you, Ned?' I said. 'What's happened?'

'A right bleeding smash up,' said Ned. He whispered. 'It's old Jackson. Police car run into the back of him. They're trying to get the bodies out.'

We walked down together to the smash up. The police and ambulance men were on the job. They were trying to jack up the back axle of the lorry so that they could get the car out. The police car hooter was going all the time. The blue plate on the back of the car with the word 'POLICE' on it was intact, but that was about all that was. Nobody would ever drive that car again. As for the two blokes inside, well, one glimpse was enough.

'Babyface?' I said to Ned.

'It was,' said Ned. 'Poor old sod. His mate, too.' He gave me a knowing look, but said no more.

I heard someone talking in a husky voice and I turned and saw Jackson. He was talking to a young patrol cop who was making notes in his book.

'Well, I'll tell you all I know,' said Jackson. 'I'm coming along at a fair crack. No use wrapping it up, I had my toe down, because I wanted to get to the caff down the road before they close. I usually have egg and chips about this time. But I was keeping my eyes open and the road was dead clear in front and behind me—so far as I could see. I could have sworn to it. And I was just coming along there, when on the bend here, dead in front of me, I saw what looked like a body curled in the roadway.'

'A body?' said the cop. 'Where is it now?'

'I looked after,' said Jackson. 'See—under there.'

He pointed under his lorry. We all looked.

'That old overcoat?' said the cop.

'I can see what it is *now*,' said Jackson. 'But catch it in your headlights an' it looks different.'

The cop nodded.

'I've known many an old geezer get drunk and go to sleep in the middle of the road,' went on Jackson. 'Anyway, I slammed on my brakes at once. Then I got the shock of my life. *Something hit me from behind*. I couldn't think what had happened. It wasn't a tap, it was a real bash. Even with my brakes on it knocked me across the road.'

The patrol cop looked sympathetic.

'What did you do then?' he asked.

'It took me a minute or two to come round,' said Jackson. 'The shock and one thing and another. Then I got out of the cab and walked round to the back. It's dark, see, and for a bit I couldn't make out what had happened. I could hear this horn blowing away in my ears, but I didn't know where it was coming from, not at first. Then suddenly I began to make it out. I looked inside the car and saw 'em. It was a shock, mate, I can tell you that. How are they? Will they be all right?'

'Take it easy,' said the cop. 'We're doing all we can.'

Jackson wiped his face with his hand: 'Is it all right if I walk down the road and get myself a cup of tea?' he asked. 'I feel all out.'

The cop said: 'Just a minute, I'll see.' He went up to a police sergeant and one of the ambulance men. Jackson turned and winked at me, then he went on wiping his forehead. The patrol cop came back and said, 'So long as you are not too far away.'

Jackson said, 'I'll be in the caff.'

'Better let me have your licence,' said the cop.

'I'll get it out of my coat pocket,' said Jackson, 'in the cab.' He turned to me. 'You'll give me a lift down the road, Lofty?'

The cop warmed up: 'Come on,' he said, 'let's get the road clear, or we'll be having another smash up. Tell the other drivers not to line up along there.'

Jackson got into my cab. I drove round by his lorry and down the road to Lew's. He was thinking about something and he said nothing as we went down the road, and I didn't feel like talking either. When I drew up to a halt outside Lew's he turned to me and digging his hand inside his coat he carefully pulled something out.

' 'Ere you are, mate,' he said.

I looked. In his hand was the driving mirror I had lent him. The glass was broken.

'It came in handy,' he said.

I didn't say anything. He looked like a man at peace with himself.

'I had it planted down below the floorboards,' he said.

'Oh, aye?' I said.

I wasn't as surprised as I made it sound.

'It was there waiting for Babyface,' he said. 'I knew whenever he crept on my tail, even if he had all his lights out, I'd spot him down in that mirror. Half an hour ago I caught him creeping up behind me. Right, I thought to myself, I'll draw you on, Charlie. I stuck in the booster gear and put my toe down. They fell for it and crept right up behind me. I was coming down Long Hill and I knew the exact spot he'd overtake me, just near the bend at the bottom. So as we were drawing near to it I got every ounce I could out of the old tub. We were fair cracking along, I can tell you. *Right mate*, I thought, *you're trying to do me, but I'm going to do you instead.* So, I steeled myself for the shock, then I slammed both feet down at once and swung on the handbrake at the same time.'

Jackson scratched his nose:

'I've got some lovely anchors on the old wagon. They drew me up like that. They'd have had to be bloody good drivers to stop that quick. They didn't have a chance. They crashed right clean in the back.'

I felt I needed a bit of fresh air after that lot, so I got out of the cab. Jackson got out at the other side and walked round to me.

'First thing I did, when I stopped,' he said, 'was to take that old mirror out and put the floorboard back straight. Breaking that mirror brought 'em bad luck all right. Then I took that old topcoat that I had specially for the job and planted it on the road under the lorry. It's not mine.'

He followed me round as I kicked at my tyres, and tested my loading ropes.

'Well, here's your mirror, mate,' he said.

I could hardly bear to look at it, let alone take hold of it.

'If you don't want it, I can soon lose it for you,' said Jackson. He was back in a minute. 'Take a bloody good detective to find it now,' he said.

'Jackson,' I said, 'what's the idea telling me all this?'

He smiled softly at me and then he said, 'A bloke don't want to walk round with a basinful of that on his mind. I know I'm safe with an old driver. Come on, let's see if Ethel has the egg and chips ready.'

I followed him. At the door he turned and said to me, 'Nothing I like better than getting one across the law. Y'know what it means for my dangerous drivin' charge?—*Case dismissed.*'

I went in after him. There were half a dozen drivers in. Walter and Willie, young Clive, a driver and his mate from Glasgow, and an old driver from Hull. They all gave nods and waves to me. But as for Jackson, not a word was spoken. Not a sign was made. You felt everything going dead quiet. Lew was wiping the tables and kept right away from where Jackson sat. Ethel was behind the counter and she never gave him so much as a glance. She looked across to me and waved her hand. Jackson looked at her but she didn't seem to see him. I knew then the word had gone round. It doesn't take long. He might have got one across the law, but he hadn't got one across Watling Street. Nobody would split, but already, North and South, they were putting the poison in for him. Within a week he'd be lucky to get a civil cup of tea anywhere along the A.5. And I could see by the look on Jackson's face, he knew one thing at least—no matter what the police found or didn't find—he'd never get anywhere with Ethel now. And his driving days on Watling Street were over. And, looking across to the counter, where Ethel was working with her sleeves rolled up, I couldn't help thinking to myself, *Bolton, this is where you might move in.*

L. P. HARTLEY

A High Dive

THE circus-manager was worried. Attendances had been
falling off and such people as did come—children they
were, mostly—sat about listlessly, munching sweets or sucking
ices, sometimes talking to each other without so much as
glancing at the show. Only the young or little girls, who came
to see the ponies, betrayed any real interest. The clowns'
jokes fell flat, for they were the kind of jokes that used to raise
a laugh before 1939, after which critical date people's sense
of humour seemed to have changed, along with many other
things about them. The circus-manager had heard the word
'corny' flung about and didn't like it. What did they want?
Something that was, in his opinion, sillier and more pointless
than the old jokes; not a bull's-eye on the target of humour,
but an outer or even a near-miss—something that brought in
the element of futility and that could be laughed at as well as
with: an unintentional joke against the joker. The clowns
were quick enough with their patter but it just didn't go down:
there was too much sense in their nonsense for an up-to-date
audience, too much articulateness. They would do better to
talk gibberish, perhaps. Now they must change their style, and
find out what really did make people laugh, if people could be
made to; but he, the manager, was over fifty and never good
himself at making jokes, even the old-fashioned kind. What
was this word that everyone was using—'sophisticated'?
The audiences were too sophisticated, even the children were:
they seemed to have seen or heard all this before, even when
they were too young to have seen and heard it.

'What shall we do?' he asked his wife. They were standing
under the Big Top, which had just been put up, and wondering
how many of the empty seats would still be empty when they
gave their first performance. 'We shall have to do something,
or it's a bad look-out.'

'I don't see what we can do about the comic side,' she said. 'It may come right by itself. Fashions change, all sorts of old things have returned to favour, like old-time dances. But there's something we could do.'

'What's that?'

'Put on an act that's dangerous, really dangerous. Audiences are never bored by that. I know you don't like it, and no more do I, but when we had the Wall of Death——'

Her husband's big chest-muscles twitched under his thin shirt.

'You know what happened then.'

'Yes, but it wasn't our fault, we were in the clear.'

He shook his head.

'Those things upset everyone. I know the public came after it happened—they came in shoals, they came to see the place where someone had been killed. But our people got the needle and didn't give a good performance for I don't know how long. If you're proposing another Wall of Death I wouldn't stand for it—besides, where will you find a man to do it?—especially with a lion on his bike, which is the great attraction.'

'But other turns are dangerous too, as well as dangerous-looking. It's *being* dangerous that is the draw.'

'Then what do you suggest?'

Before she had time to answer a man came up to them.

'I hope I don't butt in,' he said, 'but there's a man outside who wants to speak to you.'

'What about?'

'I think he's looking for a job.'

'Bring him in,' said the manager.

The man appeared, led by his escort, who then went away. He was a tall, sandy-haired fellow with tawny leonine eyes and a straggling moustache. It wasn't easy to tell his age—he might have been about thirty-five. He pulled off his old brown corduroy cap and waited.

'I hear you want to take a job with us,' the manager said, while his wife tried to size up the newcomer. 'We're pretty full up, you know. We don't take on strangers as a rule. Have you any references?'

'No, sir.'

'Then I'm afraid we can't help you. But just for form's sake, what can you do?'

As if measuring its height the man cast up his eyes to the point where one of the two poles of the Big Top was embedded in the canvas.

'I can dive sixty feet into a tank eight foot long by four foot wide by four foot deep.'

The manager stared at him.

'Can you now?' he said. 'If so, you're the very man we want. Are you prepared to let us see you do it?'

'Yes,' the man said.

'And would you do it with petrol burning on the water?'

'Yes.'

'But have we got a tank?' the manager's wife asked.

'There's the old Mermaid's tank. It's just the thing. Get somebody to fetch it.'

While the tank was being brought the stranger looked about him.

'Thinking better of it?' said the manager.

'No, sir,' the man replied. 'I was thinking I should want some bathing-trunks.'

'We can soon fix you up with those,' the manager said. 'I'll show you where to change.'

Leaving the stranger somewhere out of sight, he came back to his wife.

'Do you think we ought to let him do it?' she asked.

'Well, it's his funeral. You wanted us to have a dangerous act, and now we've got it.'

'Yes, I know, but——' The rest was drowned by the rattle of the trolley bringing in the tank—a hollow, double cube like a sarcophagus. Mermaids in low relief sported on its leaden flanks. Grunting and muttering to each other the men slid it into position, a few feet from the pole. Then a length of hosepipe was fastened to a faucet, and soon they heard the sound of water swishing and gurgling in the tank.

'He's a long time changing,' said the manager's wife.

'Perhaps he's looking for a place to hide his money,' laughed her husband, and added, 'I think we'll give the petrol a miss.'

At length the man emerged from behind a screen, and slowly walked towards them. How tall he was, lanky and muscular. The hair on his body stuck out as if it had been combed. Hands on hips he stood beside them, his skin pimpled by goose-flesh. A fit of yawning overtook him.

'How do I get up?' he asked.

The manager was surprised, and pointed to the ladder. 'Unless you'd rather climb up, or be hauled up! You'll find a platform just below the top, to give you a foot-hold.'

He had started to go up the chromium-plated ladder when the manager's wife called after him: 'Are you still sure you want to do it?'

'Quite sure, madam.'

He was too tall to stand upright on the platform, the awning brushed his head. Crouching and swaying forty feet above them he swung his arms as though to test the air's resistance. Then he pitched forward into space, unseen by the manager's wife who looked the other way until she heard a splash and saw a thin sheet of bright water shooting up.

The man was standing breast-high in the tank. He swung himself over the edge and crossed the ring towards them, his body dripping, his wet feet caked with sawdust, his tawny eyes a little bloodshot.

'Bravo!' said the manager, taking his shiny hand. 'It's a first-rate act, that, and will put money in our pockets. What do you want for it, fifteen quid a week?'

The man shook his head. The water trickled from his matted hair on to his shoulders, oozed from his borrowed bathing-suit and made runnels down his sinewy thighs. A fine figure of a man: the women would like him.

'Well, twenty then.'

Still the man shook his head.

'Let's make it twenty-five. That's the most we give anyone.'

Except for the slow shaking of his head the man might not have heard. The circus-manager and his wife exchanged a rapid glance.

'Look here,' he said. 'Taking into account the draw your

act is likely to be, we're going to make you a special offer—thirty pounds a week. All right?'

Had the man understood? He put his finger in his mouth and went on shaking his head slowly, more to himself than at them, and seemingly unconscious of the bargain that was being held out to him. When he still didn't answer, the knot of tension broke, and the manager said, in his ordinary, brisk voice.

'Then I'm afraid we can't do business. But just as a matter of interest, tell us why you turned down our excellent offer.'

The man drew a long breath and breaking his long silence said, 'It's the first time I done it and I didn't like it.'

With that he turned on his heel and straddling his long legs walked off unsteadily in the direction of the dressing-room.

The circus-manager and his wife stared at each other.

'It was the first time he'd done it,' she muttered. 'The first time.' Not knowing what to say to him, whether to praise, blame, scold or sympathize, they waited for him to come back, but he didn't come.

'I'll go and see if he's all right,' the circus-manager said. But in two minutes he was back again. 'He's not there,' he said. 'He must have slipped out the other way, the crack-brained fellow!'

R. PRAWER JHABVALA

The Interview

I AM always very careful of my appearance, so you could not say that I spent much more time than usual over myself that morning. It is true, I trimmed and oiled my moustache, but then I often do that; I always like it to look very neat, like Raj Kapoor's, the film star's. But I knew my sister-in-law and my wife were watching me. My sister-in-law was smiling, and she had one hand on her hip; my wife only looked anxious. I knew she was anxious. All night she had been whispering to me. She had whispered, 'Get this job and take me away to live somewhere alone, only you and I and our children.' I had answered, 'Yes,' because I wanted to go to sleep. I don't know where and why she has taken this notion that we should go and live alone.

When I had finished combing my hair, I sat on the floor and my sister-in-law brought me my food on a tray. It may sound strange that my sister-in-law should serve me, and not my wife, but it is so in our house. It used to be my mother who brought me my food, even after I was married; she would never allow my wife to do this for me, though my wife wanted to very much. Then, when my mother got so old, my sister-in-law began to serve me. I know that my wife feels deeply hurt by this, but she doesn't dare to say anything. My mother doesn't notice many things any more, otherwise she certainly would not allow my sister-in-law to bring me my food; she has always been very jealous of this privilege herself, though she never cared who served my brother. Now she has become so old that she can hardly see anything, and most of the time she sits in the corner by the family trunks and folds and strokes her pieces of cloth. For years now she has been collecting pieces of cloth. Some of them are very old and dirty, but she doesn't care, she loves them all equally. Nobody is allowed to touch them. Once there was a great quarrel, because my wife

had taken one of them to make a dress for our child. My
mother shouted at her—it was terrible to hear her: but then,
she has never liked my wife—and my wife was very much
afraid and cried and tried to excuse herself. I hit her across the
face, not very hard and not because I wanted to, but only to
satisfy my mother. The old woman kept quiet then and went
back to folding and stroking her pieces of cloth.

All the time I was eating, I could feel my sister-in-law
looking at me and smiling. It made me uncomfortable. I
thought she might be smiling because she knew I wouldn't
get the job for which I had to go and be interviewed. I also
knew I wouldn't get it, but I didn't like her to smile like
that. It was as if she were saying, 'You see, you will always
have to be dependent on us.' It is clearly my brother's duty
to keep me and my family until I can get work and contribute
my own earnings to the family household. There is no need for
her to smile about it. But it is true that I am more dependent
on her now than on anyone else. Since my mother has got so
old, my sister-in-law has become more and more the most
important person in the house, so that she even keeps the keys
and the household stores. At first I didn't like this. As long as
my mother managed the household, I was sure of getting many
extra tit-bits. But now I find that my sister-in-law is also very
kind to me—much more kind than she is to her husband. It is
not for him that she saves the tit-bits, nor for her children, but
for me; and when she gives them to me, she never says anything and I never say anything, but she smiles and then I feel
confused and rather embarrassed. My wife has noticed what
she does for me.

I have found that women are usually kind to me. I think
they realize that I am a rather sensitive person and that
therefore I must be treated very gently. My mother has
always treated me very gently. I am her youngest child, and
I am fifteen years younger than my brother who is next to
me (she did have several children in between us, but they all
died). Right from the time when I was a tiny baby, she
understood that I needed greater care and tenderness than
other children. She always made me sleep close beside her in

the night, and in the day I usually sat with her and my grandmother and my widowed aunt, who were also very fond of me.
When I got bigger, my father sometimes wanted to take me to
help in his stall (he had a little grocer's stall, where he sold
lentils and rice and cheap cigarettes and coloured drinks in
bottles) but my mother and grandmother and aunt never liked
to let me go. Once he did take me with him, and he made me
pour some lentils out of paper bags into a tin. I rather liked
pouring the lentils—they made such a nice noise as they
landed in the tin—but suddenly my mother came and was
very angry with my father for making me do this work. She
took me home at once, and when she told my grandmother and
aunt what had happened, they stroked me and kissed me
and then they gave me a hot fritter to eat. The fact is, right
from childhood I have been a person who needs a lot of peace
and rest, and my food too has to be rather more delicate than
that of other people. I have often tried to explain this to my
wife, but as she is not very intelligent, she doesn't seem to
understand.

Now my wife was watching me while I ate. She was squatting on the floor, washing our youngest baby; the baby's
head was in her lap, and all one could see of it was the back of
its legs and its naked bottom. My wife did not watch me as
openly as my sister-in-law did; only from time to time she
raised her eyes to me, I could feel it, and they were very
worried and troubled. She too was thinking about the job
for which I was going to be interviewed, but she was anxious
that I should get it. 'We will go and live somewhere alone,'
she had said. Why did she say it? When she knows that it is
not possible and never will be.

And even if it were possible, I would not like it. I can't
live away from my mother; and I don't think I would like
to live away from my sister-in-law. I often look at her and it
makes me happy. Even though she is not young any more
she is still beautiful. She is tall, with big hips and big breasts
and eyes that flash; she often gets angry, and when she is
angry, she is the most beautiful of all. Then her eyes are like
fire and she shows all her teeth which are very strong and

white, and her head is proud with the black hair flying loose. My wife is not beautiful at all. I was very disappointed in her when they first married me to her. Now I have got used to her and I even like her, because she is so good and quiet and never troubles me at all. I don't think anybody else in our house likes her. My sister-in-law always calls her 'that beauty', but she does not mean it; and she makes her do all the most difficult household tasks, and often she shouts at her and even beats her. This is not right; my wife has never done anything to her —on the contrary, she always treats her with respect. But I cannot interfere in their quarrels.

Then I was ready to go, though I didn't want to go. I knew only too well what would happen at the interview. My mother blessed me, and my sister-in-law looked at me over her shoulder and her great eyes flashed with laughter. I didn't look at my wife, who still sat squatting on the floor, but I knew she was pleading with me to get the job like she had pleaded in the night. As I walked down the stairs, the daughter of the carpenter, who lives in one of the rooms on the lower floor, came out of her door and she walked up the stairs as I walked down, and she passed very close beside me, with her eyes lowered but her arm just touching my sleeve. She always waits for me to come out and then she passes me on the stairs. We have never spoken together. She is a very young girl, her breasts are only just forming; her blouse has short sleeves and her arms are beautiful, long and slender. I think soon she is to be married, I have heard my sister-in-law say so. My sister-in-law laughed when she told me, she said, 'It is high time' and then she said something coarse. Perhaps she has noticed that the girl waits for me to pass on the stairs.

No, I did not want to go to the interview. I had been to so many during the last few months, and always the same things happened. I know I have to work, in order to earn money and give it to my mother or my sister-in-law for the household, but there is no pleasure for me in the work. Last time I had work it was in an insurance office and all day they made me sit at a desk and write figures. What pleasure could there be for me in that? I am a very thoughtful person, and I like always to sit and think my own thoughts; but while I thought my own thoughts in the office, I sometimes made mistakes over the figures and then my superiors were very angry with me. I was always afraid of their anger, and I begged their forgiveness and admitted that I was much at fault. When they forgave me, I was no longer afraid and I continued doing my work and thinking my thoughts. But the last time they would not forgive me again, though I begged and begged and cried what a faulty, bad man I was and what good men they were, and how they were my mother and my father and how I looked only to them for my life and the lives of my children. But when they still said I must go, I saw that the work there was really finished and I stopped crying. I went into the washroom and combed my hair and folded my soap in my towel, and then I took my money from the accountant without a word and I left the office with my eyes lowered. But I was no longer afraid, because what is finished is finished, and my brother still had work and probably one day I would get another job.

Ever since then my brother has been trying to get me into government service. He himself is a clerk in government service and enjoys many advantages: every five years he gets an increase of ten rupees in his salary and he has ten days sick-leave in the year and when he retires he will get a pension. It would be good for me also to have such a job; but it is difficult to get, because first there is an interview at which important people sit at a desk and ask many questions. I am afraid of them, and I cannot understand properly what they are saying, so I answer what I think they want me to answer. But it seems that my answers are not after all the right ones, because up till now they have not given me a job.

On my way to this interview, I thought how much nicer it would be to go to the cinema instead. If I had had ten annas, perhaps I would have gone; it was just time for the morning show. The young clerks and the students would be collecting in a queue outside the cinema now. They would be standing and not talking much, holding their ten annas and waiting for the box-office to open. I enjoy these morning shows, perhaps because the people who come to them are all young men like myself, all silent and rather sad. I am often sad; it would even be right to say that I am sad most of the time. But when the film begins, I am happy. I love to see the beautiful women, dressed in golden clothes with heavy ear-rings and necklaces and bracelets covering their arms, and their handsome lovers who are all the things I would like to be. And when they sing their love-songs, so full of deep feelings, the tears sometimes come into my eyes; but not because I am sad, no, on the contrary, because I am so happy. After the film is over, I never go home straight away, but I walk around the streets and think about how wonderful life could be.

When I arrived at the place where the interview was, I had to walk down many corridors and ask directions from many peons before I could find the right room. The peons were all rude to me, because they knew what I had come for. They lounged on benches outside the offices, and when I asked them, they looked me up and down before answering, and sometimes they made jokes about me with one another. I was very polite to them, for even though they were only peons, they had uniforms and jobs and belonged here, and they knew the right way whereas I did not. At last I came to the room where I had to wait. Many others were already sitting there, on chairs which were drawn up all round the room against the wall. No one was talking. I also sat on a chair, and after a while an official came in with a list and he asked if anyone else had come. I got up and he asked my name, and then he looked down the list and made a tick with a pencil. He said to me very sternly, 'Why are you late?' I begged pardon and told him the bus in which I had come had had an accident. He said, 'When you are called for interview, you have to be here exactly on time, otherwise your name is crossed off the list.' I begged pardon again and asked him very humbly please not to cross me off this time. I knew that all the others were listening, though none of them looked at us. He was very stern with me and even scornful, but in the end he said, 'Wait here, and when your name is called, you must go in at once.'

I did not count the number of people waiting in the room, but there were many. Perhaps there was one job free, perhaps two or three. I knew that all the others were very worried and anxious to get the job, so I became worried and anxious too. The walls of the room were painted green halfway up and white above that and were quite bare. There was a fan turning from the ceiling, but it was not turning fast enough to give much breeze. Behind the big door the interview was going on; one by one we would all be called in behind this closed door.

I began to worry desperately. It always happens like this. When I come to an interview, I don't want the job at all, but when I see all the others waiting and worrying, I want it terribly. Yet at the same time I know that I don't want it. It would only be the same thing over again: writing figures and making mistakes and then being afraid when they found out. And there would be a superior officer to whom I would have to be very deferential, and every time I saw him or heard his voice I would begin to be afraid that he had found out something against me. For weeks and months I would sit and write figures, getting wearier of it and wearier, so that more and more I would be thinking my own thoughts. Then the mistakes would come, and my superior officer would be angry and I afraid.

My brother never makes mistakes. For years he has been sitting in the same office, writing figures and being deferential to his superior officer; he concentrates very hard on his work, and so he doesn't make mistakes. But all the same he is afraid; that is why he concentrates so hard—because he is afraid that he will make a mistake and they will be angry with him and take away his job. He is afraid of this all the time. And he is right: what would become of us all if he also lost his job? It is not the same with me. I think I am afraid to lose my job only because that is a thing of which one is expected to be afraid. When I have actually lost it, I am really relieved. But I am very different from my brother; even in appearance I am

very different. It is true, he is fifteen years older than I am,
but even when he was my age, he never looked like I do. My
appearance has always attracted others, and up to the time I
was married, my mother used to stroke my hair and my face
and say many tender things to me. Once, when I was walking
on my way to school through the bazaar, a man called to me,
very softly, and when I came he gave me a ripe mango, and
then he took me into a dark passage which led to a disused
mosque, and he touched me under my clothes and he said,
'You are so nice, so nice.' He was very kind to me. I love
wearing fine clothes, very thin white muslin kurtas which have
been freshly washed and starched and are embroidered at the
shoulders. Sometimes I also use scent, a fine khas smell; my
hair-oil also smells of khas. Some years ago, when the carpenter's daughter was still a small child and did not yet wait
for me on the stairs, there was a girl living in the tailor's shop
opposite our house and she used to follow me when I went out.
But it is my brother who is married to a beautiful wife, and
my wife is not beautiful at all. He is not happy with his wife;
when she talks to him, she talks in a hard scornful way; and it
is not for him that she saves the best food, but for me, even
though I have not brought money home for many months.

The big closed door opened and the man who had been
in there for interview came out. We all looked at him, but he
walked out in a great hurry, with a preoccupied expression
on his face; probably he was going over in his mind all that
had been said at the interview. I could feel the anxiety in
the other men getting stronger, so mine got stronger too. The
official with the list came and we all looked at him. He read
out another name and the man whose name was called
jumped up from his chair; he did not notice that his dhoti
had got caught on a nail in the chair and he wondered why
he could not go farther. When he realized what had happened,
he tried to disentangle himself, but his fingers shook so much
that he could not get the dhoti off the nail. The official
watched him and said, 'Hurry, now, do you think the gentlemen will wait for you for as long as you please?' Then the
man also dropped the umbrella he was carrying and now he

was trying both to disentangle the dhoti and to pick up the umbrella. When he could not get the dhoti loose, he became so desperate that he tore at the cloth and ripped it free. It was a pity to see the dhoti torn because it was a new one, which he was probably wearing for the first time and had put on specially for the interview. He clasped his umbrella to his chest and walked in a great hurry to the interviewing room, with his dhoti hanging about his legs and his face swollen with embarrassment and confusion.

We all sat and waited. The fan, which seemed to be a very old one, made a creaking noise. One man kept cracking his finger-joints—*tik*, we heard, *tik* (it made my own finger-joints long to be cracked too). All the rest of us kept very still. From time to time the official with the list came in, he walked round the room very slowly, tapping his list, and then we all looked down at our feet and the man who had been cracking his finger-joints stopped doing it. A faint and muffled sound of voices came from behind the closed door. Sometimes a voice was raised, but even then I could not make out what was being said, though I strained very hard.

The last time I had an interview, it was very unpleasant for me. One of the people who was interviewing took a dislike to me and shouted at me very loudly. He was a large fat man and he wore an English suit; his teeth were quite yellow, and when he became angry and shouted, he showed them all, and even though I was very upset, I couldn't help looking at them and wondering how they had become so yellow. I don't know why he was angry. He shouted: 'Good God, man, can't you understand what's said to you?' It was true, I could not understand, but I had been trying so hard to answer well. What more did he expect of me? Probably there was something in my appearance which he did not like. It happens that way sometimes—they take a dislike to you, and then of course there is nothing you can do.

When I thought of the man with the yellow teeth, I became more anxious than ever. I need great calm in my life. Whenever anything worries me too much, I have to cast the thoughts of it off immediately, otherwise there is a danger that I may become very ill. All my limbs were itching so that it was diffi-cult for me to sit still, and I could feel blood rushing into my brain. It was this room that was doing me so much harm: all the other men waiting, anxious and silent, and the noise from the fan and the official with the list walking round, tapping his list or striking it against his thigh, and the big closed door behind which the interview was going on. I felt great need to get up and go away. I didn't *want* the job. I wasn't even thinking about it any more—I was thinking only about how to avoid having to sit here and wait.

Now the door opened again and the man with the torn new dhoti came out. He was biting his lip and scratching the back of his neck, and he too walked straight out without looking at us at all. The big door was left slightly open for a moment, and I could see a man's arm in a white shirt-sleeve and part of the back of his head. His shirt was very white and of good material, and his ears stood away from his head so that one could see how his spectacles fitted into the back of his ears. I realized at once that this man would be my enemy and that he would make things very difficult for me and perhaps even shout at me. Then I knew it was no use for me to stay there. The official with the list came back and great panic seized me that he would read out my name. I got up quickly, murmuring, 'Please excuse me—bathroom,' and went out. The official with the list called after me, 'Hey mister, where are you going?' so I lowered my head and walked faster. I would have started to run, but that might have caused sus-picion, so I just walked as fast as I could, down the long corridors and right out of the building. There at last I was able to stop and take a deep breath, and I felt much better.

I stood still for only a little while, then I moved on though not in any particular direction. There were many clerks and peons moving around in the street, hurrying from one office building to another and carrying files and papers. Everyone seemed to have something to do. I was glad when I had moved out of this block and on to the open space where people like myself, who had nothing to do, sat under the trees or in any other patch of shade they could find. But I couldn't sit there; it was too close to the office blocks, and any moment someone might come and say to me, 'Why did you go away?' So I walked farther. I was feeling quite light-hearted; it was such a relief for me not to have to be interviewed.

I came to a row of eating-stalls, and I sat down on a wooden bench outside one of them, which was called the Paris Hotel, and asked for tea. I felt badly in need of tea, and since I intended to walk part of the way home, I was in a position to pay for it. There were two Sikhs sitting at the end of my bench, who were eating with great appetite, dipping their hands very rapidly into brass bowls. In between eating they exchanged remarks with the proprietor of the Paris Hotel, who sat high up inside his stall, stirring in a big brass pot in which he was cooking the day's food. He was chewing a betel leaf, and from time to time he spat out the red betel juice far over the cooking-pot and on to the ground between the wooden benches and tables.

I sat quietly at my end of the bench and drank my tea. The food smelt very good, and it made me realize that I was hungry. I decided that if I walked all the way home, I could afford a little cake (I am very fond of sweet things). The cake was not new, but it had a beautiful piece of bright-green peel inside it. On reaching home I would lie down at once to sleep and not wake up again till tomorrow morning. That way no one would be able to ask me any questions. I would not look at my wife at all, so I would be able to avoid her eyes. I would not look at my sister-in-law either; but she would be smiling, that I knew already—leaning against the wall with her hand on her hip, looking at me and smiling. She would know that I had run away, but she would not say anything.

Let her know! What does it matter? It is true I have no job and no immediate prospect of getting one. It is true that I am dependent on my brother. Everybody knows that. There is no shame in it: there are many people without jobs. And she has been so kind to me up till now, there is no reason why she should not continue to be kind to me. Though I know she is not by nature a kind woman, she speaks mostly with a very harsh tongue and her actions also are harsh. Only to me she has been kind.

The Sikhs at the end of the bench had finished eating. They licked their fingers and belched deeply, the way one does after a good meal. They started to laugh and joke with the proprietor. I sat quiet and alone at my end of the bench. Of course they did not laugh and joke with me. They knew that I was superior to them, for whereas they worked with their hands, I am a lettered man who does not have to sweat for a living but sits on a chair in an office and writes figures and can speak in English. My brother is very proud of his superiority, and he has great contempt for carpenters and mechanics and such people who work with their hands. I am also proud of being a lettered man, but when I listened to the Sikhs laughing and joking, the thought came to me that perhaps their life was happier than mine. It was a thought that had come to me before. There is the carpenter who lives downstairs in our house, the one whose daughter waits for me on the stairs, and though he is poor, there is always great eating in his house and many people come and I hear them laughing and singing and even dancing. The carpenter is a big strong man and he always looks happy, never anxious and sick with worry the way my brother does. He doesn't wear shoes and clean white clothes like my brother and I do, nor does he speak any English, but all the same he is happy. Even though his work is inferior, I don't think he gets as weary of it as I do of mine, and he has no superior officer to make him afraid.

Then I thought again about my sister-in-law and I thought that if I were kind to her, she would continue to be kind to me. I became quite excited when I thought of being kind to her. I would know then how her big breasts felt under the blouse, how warm they were and how soft. And I would know about the inside of her mouth with the big strong teeth. Her tongue and palate are very pink, like the pink satin blouse she wears on festive occasions, and I had often wondered whether they felt as soft as the blouse too. Her eyes would be shut and perhaps there would be tears on the lashes; and she would be making warm animal sounds and her big body too would be warm like an animal's. I became very excited when I thought of it; but when the excitement had passed, I was sad. Because then I thought of my wife, who is thin and not beautiful and there is no excitement in her body. But she does whatever I want and always tries to please me. I remembered her whispering to me in the night, 'Take me away, let us go and live somewhere alone, only you and I and our children.' That can never be, and so always she will have to be unhappy.

I was very sad when I thought of her being unhappy; because it is not only she who is unhappy but I also and many others. Everywhere there is unhappiness. I thought of the man whose new dhoti had been torn and who would now have to go home and sew it carefully so that the tear would not be seen. I thought of all the other men sitting and waiting to be interviewed, all but one or two of whom would not get the job for which they had come to be interviewed, and so again they would have to go to another interview and another and another, to sit and wait and be anxious. And my brother who has a job, but is frightened that he will lose it; and my mother so old that she can only sit on the floor and stroke her pieces of cloth; and my sister-in-law who does not care for her husband; and the carpenter's daughter who is to be married and perhaps she also will not be happy. Yet life could be so different. When I go to the cinema and hear the beautiful songs they sing, I know how different it could be; and also sometimes when I sit alone and think my thoughts, then I have a feeling that everything could be so beautiful. But now my tea was finished and also my cake, and I wished I had not bought them, because it was a long way to walk home and I was tired.

JOHN WAIN

A Message from the Pig-man

HE was never called Ekky now, because he was getting to be a real boy, nearly six, with grey flannel trousers that had a separate belt, and weren't kept up by elastic, and his name was Eric. But this was just one of those changes brought about naturally, by time, not a disturbing alteration; he understood that. His mother hadn't meant that kind of change when she had promised, 'Nothing will be changed.' It was all going to go on as before, except that Dad wouldn't be there, and Donald would be there instead. He knew Donald, of course, and felt all right about his being in the house, though it seemed, when he lay in bed and thought about it, mad and pointless that Donald's coming should mean that Dad had to go. Why should it mean that? The house was quite big. He hadn't any brothers and sisters, and if he *had* had any he wouldn't have minded sharing his bedroom, even with a baby that wanted a lot of looking after, so long as it left the spare room free for Dad to sleep in. If he did that, they wouldn't have a spare room, it was true, but then, the spare room was nearly always empty; the last time anybody had used the spare room was *years* ago, when he had been much smaller— last winter, in fact. And, even then, the visitor, the lady with the funny teeth who laughed as she breathed in, instead of as she breathed out like everyone else, had only stayed two or three nights. *Why* did grown-ups do everything in such a mad, silly way? They often told him not to be silly, but they were silly themselves in a useless way, not laughing or singing or anything, just being silly and sad.

It was so hard to read the signs; that was another thing. When they did give you something to go on, it was impossible to know how to take it. Dad had bought him a train, just a few weeks ago, and taught him how to fit the lines together.

That ought to have meant that he would stay; what sensible person would buy a train, and fit it all up ready to run, even as a present for another person—*and then leave*? Donald had been quite good about the train, Eric had to admit that; he had bought a bridge for it and a lot of rolling-stock. At first he had got the wrong kind of rolling-stock, with wheels too close together to fit on to the rails; but instead of playing the usual grown-ups' trick of pulling a face and then not doing anything about it, he had gone back to the shop, straight away that same afternoon, and got the right kind. Perhaps that meant *he* was going to leave. But that didn't seem likely. Not the way Mum held on to him all the time, even holding him round the middle as if he needed keeping in one piece.

All the same, he was not Ekky now, he was Eric, and he was sensible and grown-up. Probably it was his own fault that everything seemed strange. He was not living up to his grey flannel trousers—perhaps that was it; being afraid of too many things, not asking questions that would probably turn out to have quite simple answers.

The Pig-man, for instance. He had let the Pig-man worry him far too much. None of the grown-ups acted as if the Pig-man was anything to be afraid of. He probably just *looked* funny, that was all. If, instead of avoiding him so carefully, he went outside one evening and looked at him, took a good long, unafraid look, leaving the back door open behind him so that he could dart in to the safety and warmth of the house . . . no! It was better, after all, not to see the Pig-man; not till he was bigger, anyway; nearly six was quite big but it wasn't really *very* big. . . .

And yet it was one of those puzzling things. No one ever told him to be careful not to let the Pig-man get hold of him, or warned him in any way; so the Pig-man *must* be harmless, because when it came to anything that *could* hurt you, like the traffic on the main road, people were always ramming it into you that you must look both ways, and all that stuff. And yet when it came to the Pig-man, no one ever mentioned him; he seemed beneath the notice of grown-ups. His mother would say, now and then, 'Let me see, it's to-day the Pig-man comes, isn't it?' or, 'Oh dear, the Pig-man will be coming round soon, and I haven't put anything out.' If she talked like this, Eric's spine would tingle and go cold; he would keep very still and wait, because quite often her next words would be, 'Eric, just take these peelings', or whatever it was, 'out to the bucket, dear, will you?' The bucket was about fifty yards away from the back door; it was shared by the people in the two next-door houses. None of *them* was afraid of the Pig-man, either. What was their attitude, he wondered? Were they sorry for him, having to eat damp old stuff out of a bucket— tea-leaves and eggshells and that sort of thing? Perhaps he cooked it when he got home, and made it a bit nicer. Certainly, it didn't look too nice when you lifted the lid of the bucket and saw it all lying there. It sometimes smelt, too. Was the Pig-man very poor? Was he sorry for himself, or did he feel all right about being like that? *Like what?* What did the Pig-man look like? He would have little eyes, and a snout with a flat end; but would he have trotters, or hands and feet like a person's?

Lying on his back, Eric worked soberly at the problem. The Pig-man's bucket had a handle; so he must carry it in the ordinary way, in his hand—unless, of course, he walked on all fours and carried it in his mouth. But that wasn't very likely, because if he walked on all fours, what difference would there be between him and an ordinary pig? To be called the Pig-man, rather than the Man-pig, surely implied that he was upright, and dressed. Could he talk? Probably, in a kind of grunting way, or else how would he tell the people what kind of food he wanted them to put in his bucket? *Why hadn't he asked Dad about the Pig-man?* That had been his mistake; Dad would have told him exactly all about it. But he had gone. Eric fell asleep, and in his sleep he saw Dad and the Pig-man going in a train together; he called, but they did not hear him and the train carried them away. 'Dad!' he shouted desperately after it. 'Don't bring the Pig-man when you come back! Don't bring the Pig-man!' Then his mother was in the room, kissing him and smelling nice; she felt soft, and the softness ducked him into sleep, this time without dreams; but the next day his questions returned.

Still, there was school in the morning, and going down to the swings in the afternoon, and altogether a lot of different things to crowd out the figure of the Pig-man and the questions connected with it. And he was never further from worrying about it all than that moment, a few evenings later, when it suddenly came to a crisis.

Eric had been allowed, 'just for once', to bring his train into the dining-room after tea, because there was a fire there that made it nicer than the room where he usually played. It was warm and bright, and the carpet in front of the fireplace was smooth and firm, exactly right for laying out the rails on. Donald had come home and was sitting—in Dad's chair, but never mind—reading the paper and smoking. Mum was in the kitchen, clattering gently about, and both doors were open so that she and Donald could call out remarks to each other. Only a short passage lay between. It was just the part of the day Eric liked best, and bed-time was comfortably far off. He fitted the sections of rail together, glancing in anticipation at the engine as it stood proudly waiting to haul the carriages round and round, tremendously fast.

Then his mother called, 'Eric! Do be a sweet, good boy, and take this stuff out to the Pig-man. My hands are covered with cake mixture. I'll let you scrape out the basin when you come in.'

For a moment he kept quite still, hoping he hadn't really heard her say it, that it was just a voice inside his head. But Donald looked over at him and said, 'Go along, old man. You don't mind, do you?'

Eric said, 'But tonight's when the Pig-man *comes*.'

Surely, *surely* they weren't asking him to go out, in the deep twilight, just at the time when there was the greatest danger of actually *meeting* the Pig-man

'All the better,' said Donald, turning back to his paper.

Why was it better? Did they *want* him to meet the Pig-man?

Slowly, wondering why his feet and legs didn't refuse to

move, Eric went through into the kitchen. 'There it is,' his mother said, pointing to a brown-paper carrier full of potato-peelings and scraps.

He took it up and opened the back door. If he was quick, and darted along to the bucket *at once*, he would be able to lift the lid, throw the stuff in quickly, and be back in the house in about the time it took to count ten.

One—two—three—four—five—six. He stopped. The bucket wasn't there.

It had gone. Eric peered round, but the light, though faint, was not as faint as *that*. He could see that the bucket had gone. *The Pig-man had already been.*

Seven—eight—nine—ten, his steps were joyous and light. Back in the house, where it was warm and bright and his train was waiting.

'The Pig-man's gone, Mum. The bucket's not there.'

She frowned, hands deep in the pudding-basin. 'Oh, yes, I do believe I heard him. But it was only a moment ago. Yes, it was just before I called you, darling. It must have been that that made me think of it.'

'Yes?' he said politely, putting down the carrier.

'So if you nip along, dear, you can easily catch him up. And I *do* want that stuff out of the way.'

'Catch him up?' he asked, standing still in the doorway.

'Yes, dear, *catch him up*,' she answered rather sharply (the Efficient Young Mother knows when to be Firm). 'He can't possibly be more than a very short way down the road.'

Before she had finished Eric was outside the door and running. This was a technique he knew. It was the same as getting into icy cold water. If it was the end, if the Pig-man seized him by the hand and dragged him off to his hut, well, so much the worse. Swinging the paper carrier in his hand, he ran fast through the dusk.

The back view of the Pig-man was much as he had expected it to be. A slow, rather lurching gait, hunched shoulders, an old hat crushed down on his head (to hide his ears?) and the pail in his hand. Plod, plod, as if he were tired. Perhaps this was just a ruse, though, probably he could pounce quickly enough when his wicked little eyes saw a nice tasty little boy or something . . . did the Pig-man eat birds? Or cats?

Eric stopped. He opened his mouth to call to the Pig-man, but the first time he tried, nothing came out except a small rasping squeak. His heart was banging like fireworks going off. He could hardly hear anything.

'Mr. Pig-man!' he called, and this time the words came out clear and rather high.

The jogging old figure stopped, turned, and looked at him. Eric could not see properly from where he stood. But he *had* to see. Everything, even his fear, sank and drowned in the raging tide of his curiosity. He moved forward. With each step he saw more clearly. The Pig-man was just an ordinary old man.

'Hello, sonny. Got some stuff there for the old grunters?'

Eric nodded, mutely, and held out his offering. What old grunters? What did he mean?

The Pig-man put down his bucket. He had ordinary hands, ordinary arms. He took the lid off. Eric held out the paper carrier, and the Pig-man's hand actually touched his own for a second. A flood of gratitude rose up inside him. The Pig-man tipped the scraps into the bucket and handed the carrier back.

'Thanks, sonny,' he said.

'Who's it for?' Eric asked, with another rush of articulateness. His voice seemed to have a life of its own.

The Pig-man straightened up, puzzled. Then he laughed, in a gurgling sort of way, but not like a pig at all.

'Arh Aarh Harh Harh,' the Pig-man went. 'Not for me, if that's whatcher mean, arh harh.'

He put the lid back on the bucket. 'It's for the old grunters,' he said. 'The old porkers. Just what they likes. Only not fruit skins. I leaves a note, sometimes, about what not to put in. Never fruit skins. It gives 'em the belly-ache.'

He was called the Pig-man because he had some pigs that he looked after.

'Thank you,' said Eric. 'Good-night.' He ran back towards the house, hearing the Pig-man, the ordinary old man, the ordinary usual normal old man, say in his just ordinary old man's voice, 'Good-night, sonny.'

IESS

So that was how you did it. You just went straight ahead, not worrying about this or that. Like getting into cold water. You just *did* it.

He slowed down as he got to the gate. For instance, if there was a question that you wanted to know the answer to, and you had always just felt you couldn't ask, the thing to do was to ask it. Just straight out, like going up to the Pig-man. Difficult things, troubles, questions, you just treated them like the Pig-man.

So that was it!

The warm light shone through the crack of the door. He opened it and went in. His mother was standing at the table, her hands still working the cake mixture about. She would let him scrape out the basin, and the spoon—he would ask for the spoon, too. But not straight away. There was a more important thing first.

He put the paper carrier down and went up to her. 'Mum,' he said. 'Why can't Dad be with us even if Donald *is* here? I mean, why can't he live with us as well as Donald?'

His mother turned and went to the sink. She put the tap on and held her hands under it.

'Darling,' she called.

'Yes?' came Donald's voice.

'D'you know what he's just said?'

'What?'

'He's just asked . . .' She turned the tap off and dried her hands, not looking at Eric. 'He wants to know why we can't have Jack to live with us.'

There was a silence, then Donald said, quietly, so that his voice only just reached Eric's ears, 'That's a hard one.'

'You can scrape out the basin,' his mother said to Eric. She lifted him up and kissed him. Then she rubbed her cheek along his, leaving a wet smear. 'Poor little Ekky,' she said in a funny voice.

She put him down and he began to scrape out the pudding-basin, certain at least of one thing, that grown-ups were mad and silly and he hated them all, all, *all*.

L. E. JONES

The Bishop's Aunt

A PICTURE of peace and happiness. That is how most of us who are inclined to think in simple terms, would have described the appearance of the compact and ancient town of P. had we been gazing at it, on a May day in the year 1946, from the café terrace across the river. The warm brown roofs hung in folds, as if a massive rug had been thrown across the descending ridge; at the top of the town rose the castle and the thin flèche of the little cathedral (for P. was an old Catholic see), round which the swifts swooped and shrilled; between the river and the town a row of chestnut trees, still in full bloom, drew, with their continuous shadows, a bold, dark line. The May sunshine, bright and beneficent, lay over all.

But in the town itself was neither peace nor happiness. For P. was in Eastern Europe; the Red Army was occupying the country, and tragedy had come to this quiet little place.

Two days earlier a Russian soldier, sitting unarmed in a café on the small cobbled square, had been assassinated, stabbed in the back by an assailant who had escaped. Even today the edges of a thin, paper-like crust of dried blood and dust lifted and fell in the breeze below the iron chair in which the dead soldier had been sitting. The general of the Division occupying the district had immediately arrested twenty of the leading citizens, including the Catholic Bishop and the Mayor, and had issued a proclamation announcing that, unless the assassin surrendered, or was given up, within forty-eight hours, the twenty hostages would be shot. That period had expired at eleven o'clock on this lovely May morning. At half-past eleven the Bishop and the Mayor were brought, under guard, from the Castle to the small Gothic Town-hall. Here, in the Mayor's parlour, sat the General, with a list of the hostages upon the table before him. There was nothing typical of Russian generals—if photographs can be trusted—in his appearance.

His face could have been that of a thoughtful, energetic and
efficient senior officer in any Western army; it was strong, but
not hard; and he had the air, uncommon in generals, of being
capable of listening as well as of speaking. All the same, he
could shut his mouth tightly indeed. At the moment his
expression was stern, but his grey eyes were not happy.

The two prisoners who now stood before him, the Bishop
and the Mayor, had nothing, so far as appearances go, in
common. The Bishop, who was in cassock and skull-cap, was
a slight wisp of a man in his fifties, with a touch of the peasant
about him; his thin face was unremarkable except for the
candour, the trustfulness of his wide-open blue eyes. He stood
there very much at his ease; even if born a peasant, he moved,
stood and spoke like a bishop. The Mayor, on the contrary,
was a great bull of a man with angry eyes. His stiff black hair
was *en brosse* over a creased forehead; he had a habit of jerking
back his head and moving his heavy shoulders under his loose
alpaca jacket, that came from his habitual impatience with
stupid people—among whom he placed the Bishop. For the
Mayor was an aggressive infidel.

When the guards had finished with all those noisy stamp-
ings and time-markings, ending with the thump, as they
grounded arms, which punctuates military justice everywhere,
the General spoke:

'Well, gentlemen, I am sorry it has come to this. The time
is up: you have not given up your man: you know the consequences.'

'Naturally we have not given anybody up,' said the Bishop,
with a touch of indignation in his rather flat voice. 'Firstly because we do not betray one another, and secondly because we
don't know who he is.'

'I know who he is,' said the Mayor.

'Oh you do, do you?' said the General, but before he could
say more the Bishop had turned on the Mayor, red in the face.

'In that case, Mr. Mayor, you should have persuaded him
to give himself up.'

'I beg your pardon?' The Mayor swung round, genuinely
surprised.

'Murder,' said the Bishop, 'is always a sin, and a deadly one.' The Mayor turned to the General, putting, for the Bishop's benefit, a weary note into his voice.

'There he goes again, General.' He turned once more to the Bishop. 'As I have wasted far too much of the public's time on telling you and them, Bishop, you always get things mixed up. Murder is a sin: all right. But killing a lance-corporal in the General's army is not murder. It's an act of war. You yourself used to appoint days of prayer for Victory——'

'But the war is over,' interrupted the Bishop. 'We capitulated. And the man was unarmed—stabbed to death, while drinking coffee. It was a cowardly, as well as a wicked murder.'

'Cowardly!' The Mayor began to shout. 'My dear Bishop, I should like to know if *you* would have the guts to allow twenty of your fellow-citizens, including my worshipful self, to be executed, rather than let the General here get away with this futile game of hostages? The man's a hero!'

The Bishop smiled. 'I agree that I might never have had the nerve to let *you* be shot, my son. The thought of your almost certain fate in the next world would be too much for me. But when your man assassinated that poor fellow in the café——'

The General cut him short.

'You can save your sympathy for the "poor" fellow, Bishop. His C.O. tells me he was suspected of Trotskyism, and is better dead. And of course the Mayor is right. If you are going to have a Resistance movement, there can be no rules. But my business, gentlemen, is to suppress the Resistance movement——'

'Which remains unsuppressed,' said the Mayor. 'Our man has beaten you.'

'Don't be too sure, Mr. Mayor,' said the General. 'For one hero, as you call him, there will be fifty others who will think twice before sending a Bishop to Paradise and a Mayor to—where did you hint that the Mayor may be before six o'clock, Bishop?'

'I never claimed Paradise, General,' said the Bishop hastily.

'I shall be fortunate if, by Divine Grace, it proves to be Purgatory.'

'I'm in Purgatory now, General,' said the Mayor. 'It's this sentry of yours—I can't abide garlic—could he stand a little farther off?'

'But of course,' said the General, with a glance at the N.C.O. in charge of the guard. There was a bark; a rattle; some more stamping, and the sentry retreated two paces.

'Thank you,' said the Mayor.

'Don't mention it,' said the General. 'No, Mr. Mayor,' he continued, 'I cannot admit that my system of hostages has failed. At the same time I agree that in this particular case things might have gone better. Perhaps I arrested the wrong people. In a town like this there are bound to be individuals whom public opinion would like to see shot.'

'Our Mayor,' said the Bishop, 'is enormously—and from my point of view I must add deplorably—popular.'

'Our Bishop,' said the Mayor, 'muddle-headed though he is, is universally beloved.'

'Were some of the other hostages thought to be expendable, perhaps?' asked the General.

'They are all most highly respected,' said the Bishop.

'It may have been a mistake to include the Inspector of Taxes,' said the Mayor.

'I see,' said the General. 'Do you think that if I released the Inspector of Taxes your man would surrender to save the rest?'

'Not a hope,' said the Mayor. 'Actually he raised the point with me last night.'

The General, for a second or so, looked more startled than a general should.

'Are you telling me,' he replied, 'that you have been in touch with this man since your arrest?'

The Mayor spoke soothingly. 'Our Resistance is not an amateur movement, General. As I was saying, he did mention the Inspector of Taxes. It's one grain of comfort to him in his heroic unhappiness.'

'Aha. So he is unhappy?'

'Undoubtedly,' said the Mayor. 'But then he's a very sensitive type. For most of us these shootings of yours have become just a thing that happens. If I may say, you make them too common, General.'

'It is interesting that you should say that,' said the General, 'because it is exactly what I have been thinking myself. An announcement that so many notables have been executed at dawn in a prison-yard—it has become rather *vieux-jeu*. Our capacity for being horrified is strangely limited, don't you agree, Bishop?'

'Alas, it is only too true,' said the Bishop. 'Compassion, the most divine of virtues, is also by far the most fatiguing. It is perhaps the supreme horror of atrocities—that in the end they cease to excite horror.'

'Then it looks,' said the General, 'as if you may both feel at any rate an intellectual sympathy with my decision—a decision which I have come to since it appeared pretty certain that the murderer was not going to be given up. It seemed to me that I must do something more horrifying, more spectacular, better calculated to impress than a mere routine execution. So I am going to make you an offer, Bishop. I shall not insist upon it, if you refuse: but if you will volunteer to be publicly crucified in the market-place tomorrow, I will let the other nineteen go free, including your admirable Mayor.'

'Never!' shouted the Mayor, on whose great neck two veins were swelling.

'Silence, sir!' rapped out the General, 'I am speaking.' He turned to the Bishop. 'I think a crucifixion should make a decided impression. The mere announcement of it might cause your man to surrender at the eleventh hour. What do you say?'

'Never!' yelled the Mayor once more. 'It's an outrageous suggestion. It shall never be allowed. Never!'

'I am speaking to the Bishop, Mr. Mayor,' the General shouted back. 'He can allow it, or he can refuse it. Well, Bishop?'

'What time, tomorrow?' inquired the Bishop.

'The General looked a little puzzled. 'Whenever I order it, of course. But what has the time got to do with it?'

'It has a great deal to do with it,' said the Bishop. 'How could I possibly face the sublime honour of crucifixion without due preparation? I must make my Confession, I must get shaved and bathed. I must choose the proper vestments in which to approach the Cross; above all, I must have time for prayer and meditation. I cannot be rushed. This is not a small thing you offer me, General. And you must let me go home tonight—under guard, of course.'

'That will be quite in order, Bishop,' said the General. 'You may go home now, under guard, and the crucifixion will be at noon tomorrow.'

'Then I accept your offer,' said the Bishop.

The Mayor, who had been listening to the Bishop's words with his mouth as wide open as his eyes, again broke in.

'It can't be allowed! It's too utterly horrible!'

The Bishop looked shocked.

'Hush, my son. That is not the way to speak of a crucifixion.'

'Of course it's horrible,' said the General, 'but I thought we were agreed that, from my point of view, a little more horror is indicated. And *I* am the one who allows things in this town, Mr. Mayor.'

'There is just one question, General,' said the Bishop, 'that I should like to ask. Why don't you crucify the Mayor, instead of me?'

'A very good idea,' said the Mayor, turning eagerly towards the General. 'Why don't you?'

'Common sense, I suppose,' said the General. 'If one is compelled, unhappily, to destroy, one destroys the most dangerous man first.'

The Mayor actually laughed.

'Dangerous? Our good Bishop is the most harmless person alive. Why, he even wanted our brave Resistance fighter to give himself up to you.'

'That,' said the General, 'is the reason why he is so formidable compared to you, with your rather crude belief in violence. We can always beat you at that game—provided, that is, that the Bishop's fifth column is not permitted to corrupt us.'

The Bishop's face suddenly shone.

'Is it your meaning, General, that you chose me and not the Mayor for this great honour because of the Faith I hold?'

'It could be put like that, I suppose,' said the General.

'Then God be praised for His great goodness!' exclaimed the Bishop, radiant. 'I shall, after all, die for the Faith.' He held out a hand to the Mayor. 'Congratulate me, my son.'

The Mayor took his hand.

'You're a hero, Bishop.'

The Bishop laughed. 'Who's muddle-headed now?' he said. He turned to the General. 'What can we do, General, with a man so uninstructed that he confuses martyrs with heroes?'

The General looked puzzled.

'Is he so far wrong? I agree a hero need not be a martyr, but surely a martyr is a hero?'

'I see that I must pray for your brains too,' said the Bishop. 'If all goes well, I hope by tomorrow night to be in a position to do something substantial for both of you. Till then, good-bye, gentlemen, and once again my thanks, General.'

'Don't mention it,' said the General.

The General rose from his seat; the corporal of the guard barked out another order; there was stamping and banging and turning about, and the Bishop with his escort reached the door. The General called out to him:

'Won't you take my car, Bishop?'

'No, thank you,' said the Bishop, 'I shall enjoy the walk.' And he went out tranquilly, but with care to keep in step with his guards, up the narrow cobbled street to his home in the cathedral square.

The General turned to the Mayor. 'I expect you will wish to be the first to tell the good news to your friends, Mr. Mayor.'

'Send your own man,' said the Mayor. 'I haven't the courage to break it to them.'

It was past noon, an hour when the people went home to their dinners, and nobody noticed the Mayor as he walked, heavily and with his chin on his chest, to his house a few doors

away from the Town-hall. But in less than half an hour the
people were out in the streets again, for a military car equipped
with a loud-speaker was going at a foot's pace through the
town, blaring out the news that the hostages had been released,
all but the Bishop who, at his own free choice, would, unless
the assassin was delivered up, be crucified at noon tomorrow
in the market-square. Upon which there arose a murmuring
and a buzz of talk which kept the town pigeons restless and
uneasy for an hour or more.

At five o'clock that same afternoon a little old lady, all in
black and carrying a shopping-bag with no bulge in it, slipped
out of a postern door in the Cathedral and crossed the little
square to the Bishop's house. The square was almost deserted,
since the people still thought the Bishop to be a prisoner in the
Castle, and it was before the great doors of the inner keep
that they had gathered to cheer him. The old lady's eyes were
red, but her mouth was firm and her chin in the air. She
paused for a moment on the doorstep, and stared at the familiar, nail-studded door as if it had turned suddenly into
something strange and hostile; then, visibly pulling herself
together, she twisted the heavy iron stirrup-handle and
went into the house. Inside she paused again; again made an
effort, and opened the door of the Bishop's study. In it sat the
Bishop, reading, in his easy chair. On a hard chair by the
empty grate sat a Russian soldier. The little old lady appeared
thunderstruck.

'Joseph! What on earth are you doing here? I thought you
were dead.'

'I am reading the fifteenth chapter of the Gospel according
to St. Mark, Aunt.'

'But why haven't you been shot? Here I've been wasting
half the day in church, praying for your soul and weeping my
old eyes out, and all for nothing! Besides, I've only brought
home enough food for one supper. Have you seen to the
kitchen fire? And have you been reprieved? What's that man
doing here? Don't you stand up for a lady?'

The soldier, who understood nothing but Russian, remained
seated.

'He's a sentry,' said the Bishop. 'He's guarding me. But haven't they told you the news?'

'I tell you, I've been in the Cathedral since ten this morning. Are you really reprieved, dear Joseph?'

'Better than that, far better,' said the Bishop.

'Has he given himself up?'

The Bishop shook his head. 'No. But I—your nephew, dear Aunt—am to win a martyr's crown. I can still hardly believe it.'

'You a martyr? Don't be foolish, Joseph. You're a good man, but we don't have martyrs in our family. What have they been doing to you? Would you like a drop of cognac?'

'I know it sounds impossible,' said the Bishop, 'and nobody knows better than I do how unworthy I am. But God in His great goodness has willed it. Tomorrow I am to share the fate of my Blessed Lord. And only because of my Faith—the General made that perfectly clear.'

'Hush, Joseph—you musn't talk like that—what's come over you?' She moved quickly to his side, full of concern. 'Have they been hitting you over the head? If so, you must not on any account have cognac.'

The Bishop took her hand.

'Please listen, dear Aunt,' he said. 'It's the General's decision but God must have put it into his head. The other hostages are to be released, but I, because of my Faith—although unworthy—am to be publicly crucified in the market-place tomorrow at noon.'

'Crucified?' said his aunt, drawing away her hand. 'Don't be blasphemous, Joseph. How can *you* be crucified?' Suddenly her hands flew to her temples. 'Mother of God! You don't mean that those devils, these filthy heathen Communists, are going to dare to——'

'No, no,' said the Bishop, 'nothing of the sort. I freely chose it. There was no compulsion at all. The General could not have been fairer. Either we were all shot together, or I was to be crucified alone. He left it entirely to me.'

His aunt's face took on a look of blank incredulity.

'And you chose the—the *cross*, Joseph?'

'But of course,' said the Bishop.

'Then I'm ashamed of you,' said his aunt bitterly. 'I wouldn't have believed it of you? You were always a bit of a simpleton—but to walk into that trap! and you a Bishop! You'll go back to the General this minute, and tell him that you've changed your mind. Really, Joseph, there are times when one would take you for a small boy. Martyr indeed!'

It was the Bishop's turn to look blank.

'I don't understand. A trap? What do you mean by "walking into a trap"?'

'Oh, you noodle,' said his aunt. 'Can't you see their wicked thoughts? How could they better belittle and make a mock of our Blessed Saviour than by crucifying a little man like you, Joseph? What will your Master's Sacrifice and Passion mean to your people after they have watched *you* being tortured on a cross? Who do you suppose is going to have their prayers and adoration for the next hundred years—our Blessed Lord, or their own little St. Joseph, Bishop and Martyr? Aren't you always complaining that your flock seem to think more of our local saints than of the Christ? And who's going to be their favourite saint, do you imagine—when they've seen you, their own dear Bishop, martyred before their eyes?'

'Perhaps they won't come to the—er—market-place,' said the Bishop. 'They may not want to see me—it will be painful, of course.'

'Not come? Of course they'll come. It will be the day of their lives. No, my poor Joseph, you've been made a fool of, and the sooner you put things right the better.'

For thirty years the Bishop, although he did not know it, had been ruled by his aunt, and he had lost the capacity, through long disuse, of thinking her mistaken. He looked very downcast indeed.

'This is—this is rather a shock to me,' he said. 'I confess I had not looked at it from that point of view. It's all very difficult. I suppose, in a way, it does seem rather presumptuous——'

'It's downright blasphemy.'

'But since it was to save the lives of so many good men——'

His aunt snorted. 'The Inspector of Taxes, for instance?'

'Our Saviour died for him,' said the Bishop.

'All the less reason why you should. You've been altogether above yourself, Joseph.'

The Bishop sighed heartily. 'It's a terrible responsibility to go back now and ask for those men to be shot. Think of their families, Aunt.'

'I've been praying for their families for the last forty-eight hours—when I wasn't housekeeping. And it's not your responsibility, it's the General's. Besides, better a thousand men shot than let the Cross be mocked.'

The Bishop sighed again.

'You're a good woman, Aunt. And I'm afraid you are right. I didn't think, or worse, I was thinking of myself.'

'You were dazzled, Joseph. That's the plain truth of it.'

'Yes,' said the Bishop, 'I'm afraid I was dazzled. And now, oh dear, the thing must be undone. How shall I ever explain it to the Mayor?'

'Explain it?' said his aunt. 'Have you no sense, Joseph? Of course you can't explain it. Are you going to tell that atheist and his friends that the glory and holiness of our dear Lord's Crucifixion are not safe in the keeping of your own flock? That you can't trust Christians to know the difference between the Cross of Christ and the murder of a hostage? You know you are not.'

'No, I suppose not,' said the Bishop. 'No, I shall say nothing. They must just think me a coward.'

'Then they'll think wrong,' said his aunt. 'It won't be the first time. And now be off with you. You'd better go by the back lane, and avoid the crowds.'

'On the contrary, there is something I have got to say to the crowds. I'm afraid it will be bitter news to some of them.'

'Then I shall come with you,' said his aunt.

'Don't you trust me?'

'I don't trust crowds,' said his aunt.

'I am their Bishop. What are you afraid of?'

'Mightn't they,' said his aunt, '—oh, dear God, now it's my

turn to be blasphemous—mightn't they cry: Crucify him! Crucify him!'

'Nonsense,' said the Bishop. But she was not far wrong.

The Bishop, who knew a word or two of Russian, spoke to the sentry on the chair, and explained that he wished to be taken back to the Town-hall. The rest of the guard tramped in from the kitchen, but the Corporal made difficulties. The news had spread that the Bishop was now in his own house, and there was a big crowd gathering in the Cathedral Square, he said, in a highly excitable state. Women in tears, men crying: 'Long live our Bishop.' He had only six men; if a rescue were attempted, he would have to fire on the crowd.

The Bishop's aunt tried to explain to him that by 'Long live our Bishop' they did not mean that they wished their Bishop to live longer than noon tomorrow, and that an attempt at rescue was the last thing to be feared. She did not add that she herself was more afraid of an attempt on his life, but she did point out to the Corporal that the back lane, which avoided the Square altogether, would probably be deserted.

'I've only six men,' said the Corporal doubtfully.

'Only five,' said the Bishop. 'One of them must go to the General to tell him I wish to see him immediately in the Town-hall.'

'But I,' said his aunt, 'will be worth another six men at the least.'

'I must speak to the people first,' said the Bishop.

'Then you must speak from a window,' said the aunt. 'We will then slip out by the back door.'

The Bishop went to the formal parlour at the front of the house, a soldier on one side of him, his aunt on the other, and stood at an open window. A great roar went up from the crowd, and the town pigeons rose as one bird from the roofs. The Bishop put up his hand for silence. All sounds died away, for the Bishop's authority, always great, had become absolute by reason of his proclaimed martyrdom.

The Bishop's voice, when he spoke, was high and clear.

'My people,' he said, 'I have sad news for you. You have been told that, by my own free choice, I was to have been crucified tomorrow. Well, I have changed my mind. There will be no crucifixion. Together with my fellow-hostages, I shall be shot instead.'

He held up two fingers in sign of benediction and withdrew from the window.

For a few seconds the crowd was dumb. Then it began to murmur; the murmur turned to a growl; a man shouted something, and was answered by a roar; in no time the frightening 'rhubarb, rhubarb' noise of stage tradition filled the little square.

Inside the Bishop's house, the Corporal was hustling his captive out into the back lane which, as the aunt had guessed, was entirely deserted. Down it the little party marched briskly to the Town-hall. Only the Bishop's aunt failed to keep step; she trotted.

In the Mayor's parlour they had not long to wait. As the General strode in, spurs jingling, with a tight mouth, the noise of distant booing came through the open window.

'Shut that window, Corporal,' snapped the General. He turned to the Bishop as he took his seat.

'So a prisoner, Bishop, sends a peremptory summons to his captor? This is something new. Who is this lady?'

'Allow me to present to you my aunt, General,' said the Bishop.

The General made the slightest inclination of his head.

'I wish I could bid you welcome, madam. But this is highly irregular—may I ask to what I owe this honour?'

'Can't you hear them howling?' said the aunt. 'My nephew needed an escort.'

'He had my guards,' said the General.

'They would have eaten up your guards. But they still respect a woman—in this country,' said the aunt.

The General turned to the Bishop.

'What has happened to your people, Bishop? A little while ago they were cheering for you like——'

He was interrupted by a clatter of feet outside, the bursting open of the parlour door, and the bull-like rush of the Mayor, head down, angry, pushing a soldier out of his path. He ignored the General altogether.

'What the devil's the meaning of this, Bishop? The town's completely out of hand. There's a rumour going round that you've ratted—absurd, of course, but you'll have to come and speak to them yourself, at once.'

The General used his parade voice.

'Mr. Mayor, you forget yourself. *I* happen to be present.'

The Mayor took a pull at himself.

'I'm sorry, General. I apologise, but there's no time to be lost. You haven't a loud-speaker ready, have you?'

'I have already spoken to them,' said the Bishop.

'The devil you have! Then why the—what have you been telling them?'

'I told them that I had changed my mind. There will be no crucifixion tomorrow,' said the Bishop.

The Mayor stared at him. He had an air of never having seen the Bishop before. His eyes, for an instant, were full of curiosity. Then his great face flushed red.

'You—you bloody coward!' he cried.

'A lady present, Mr. Mayor,' said the General. 'This is news to me, Bishop.'

'Yes,' said the Bishop, 'I asked for this meeting in order to tell you.'

'You little rat,' said the Mayor.

'And you wish the previous arrangement to stand?' said the General. 'Mr. Mayor here and the other hostages are to be shot?'

'I'm afraid that follows,' said the Bishop. 'And me, of course.'

'Shooting hurts less, eh?' said the Mayor.

'Silence, sir,' said the General to the Mayor. 'You have no right yet to assume anything. Perhaps, Bishop, as you have put me to a good deal of trouble in arranging for your crucifixion, you will tell me your reasons for this sudden change of plan?'

'Careful, Joseph,' said the Bishop's aunt.

'I'm sorry, I have no reason to give,' said the Bishop.

'Aha!' said the Mayor.

'No explanation at all?' said the General. 'There's the people to be considered as well, you know, not to speak of your fellow-hostages and their families.'

'No explanation at all,' said the Bishop.

'So we draw our own conclusions,' said the Mayor.

The General looked grave. 'We draw our own conclusions,' he said.

The Mayor swung round to face the General.

'Then let me tell you, General, that there will be a crucifixion tomorrow. Your arrangements can stand.'

'I fail to understand,' said the General.

'You will crucify *me*,' said the Mayor. 'Better tell the people now, I think. It may quieten them.'

The Bishop, for the first time in the affair, lost his serenity. He all but shouted.

'No, no, no, General. You can't do that! It was to me you gave the chance, not to him.' He turned to the Mayor, speaking gently once more. 'You are a brave man, all the same.'

'Pray don't excite yourself, Bishop,' said the General. 'I have no intention of crucifying the Mayor. I don't believe in torture —if I did, I should have tortured him long ago. Doesn't he know all the names I am looking for? Not that he would have disclosed them.'

'Thank you, General. I wish I was as sure of that. But look here, you were quite ready to torture the Bishop. If him, why not me? It's so unfair on the other hostages. If you were ready to let them be ransomed by a crucifixion, what difference can it make whose crucifixion it is?'

'It makes the whole difference,' said the General. 'The Bishop represents a Faith which is one of the major obstacles, in this benighted country, to the spread of our own enlightened doctrines. I had hoped, by publicly crucifying him, to cheapen one of the central mysteries of the Faith. Your case is quite different. Like me, you are an atheist. To crucify instead of shooting you would be mere pointless savagery.'

The Mayor rubbed the back of his great head. 'You're an artful one, I must say, General. I should never have thought of it myself. So the failure of that wretched man's nerve has cheated you of your little game. It's almost funny in a way.'

'I don't think the Bishop's nerve failed him,' said the

General. 'I believe he saw through my little game, as you call it. Am I right, Bishop?'

The Bishop shook his head, mournfully.

'No, General, to my shame, I did not see through you. I have always been a bit simple. Fortunately my aunt here did see through you.'

The General turned to the aunt with an ironical inclination of the head.

'You did, madam? I congratulate you.'

'It was sticking out a mile,' said the aunt. 'I certainly can't congratulate *you*, General. And you, Mr. Mayor, will now kindly apologise for your disgraceful abuse of my nephew. He may be a simpleton—but he's certainly a hero.'

'I agree with you, madam,' said the General. 'It takes a brave man to choose crucifixion, but it takes a braver one still to send you, Mr. Mayor, and eighteen others to the firing squad, knowing that he will be branded for ever as a coward for doing so.'

The Mayor nodded.

'And perhaps you realise now,' continued the General, 'why I am so much opposed to the Bishop's Faith. It has qualities which, I am very much afraid, are almost invincible.'

The Mayor held out his hand to the Bishop.

'Bishop, I apologise. Forgive me.'

'You had every excuse, my son,' said the Bishop. 'There is nothing to forgive.'

'And you, Joseph,' said his aunt, 'must not let your head be turned. Brave as you have been, you are not in the same street for courage as the Mayor.'

'Right again, madam,' said the General.

'What nonsense is this?' said the Mayor.

'It's quite simple,' said the aunt. 'My nephew, crucified or not, dies with a sure and certain hope of his reward in Heaven. You, Mr. Mayor, are prepared to undergo the same sufferings with no hope at all. If there's to be a prize for sheer courage, you win hands down.'

'We must all agree there,' said the General.

'There can be no question,' said the Bishop.

'And it's a thousand pities, if you ask me,' said the aunt, still addressing the Mayor, 'that you should have to suffer eternal torment.'

'My dear aunt!' said the Bishop, 'God's mercy is infinite.'

'That may be, but He knows the Mayor,' said the aunt.

The General held up his hand.

'If I may interrupt these interesting conjectures, I would like to say that, if the Bishop—or perhaps I should say his lady aunt—has beaten me, you Mr. Mayor are also of an invincible type. What can I do against men who, without hope or faith, will face torture? Luckily such men are rare. If I get rid of you and the Bishop, I think I can afford to let the other hostages go free. I admit I did not realise at first what a valuable catch I had made. Would dawn tomorrow suit you, gentlemen?'

'Perfectly,' said the Bishop.

'Whenever you like,' said the Mayor.

'Don't be absurd, General,' said the Bishop's aunt. 'You have just admitted that the Mayor is invincible, and that such men are rare. But if you shoot him, you will be making them common. There's nothing like example to make men brave. For every one invincible you shoot, you will make fifty more invincibles. Heroism is catching. The dear God knows it's not for me to save you from weakening yourself, but I never could hold my tongue when I see stupidity, and to shoot the Mayor would be grossly stupid.'

The General looked hard at her. He blinked once or twice.

'Upon my word,' he said, 'you're a very intelligent person, madam. I wish I had you on my staff. I am greatly obliged to you. You have saved me from a blunder. Mr. Mayor, you are free.'

'I would rather you released the Bishop,' said the Mayor.

'I'm sorry,' said the General, 'but the Bishop's case is, as I told you, different. He is the product of a Faith. By shooting him I shall neither weaken nor strengthen this Faith. Besides, I must shoot somebody.'

'May I open the window, General?' said the aunt. Without waiting for his permission she crossed the room and opened it. Once more the sounds of booing were heard. She closed the window and resumed her position. 'Did you hear that?' she said. 'They are out for the Bishop's blood. Are you going to oblige them?'

'I shall of course explain to them that, so far from being the coward they think, the Bishop is a hero.'

'You can't make sense of that without giving away your own little plot, and how he beat you.'

'How *you* beat him, dear Aunt,' said the Bishop.

'Is that story going to be good for your prestige?' said the aunt. 'The attempt to crucify a Bishop which failed? Will Moscow think it funny?'

The General stroked his chin.

'They might not. You may be right. It would be difficult to explain to a mob, in any case. No, I'm sorry, Bishop, but I'm afraid it's not practical to explain. You must be content, as you were just now, with your own conscience being clear.'

The Bishop nodded.

'Then, General,' said his aunt, 'you will be shooting at dawn tomorrow the one man the people will be willing to see shot—the cowardly Bishop who ratted. As I said, I ought not to want to save you from yourself, but the pointlessness of it! It's so downright silly.'

For the first time the General looked savage.

'I know who I should *like* to shoot—madam!'

'Nobody but Joseph here would care a hoot if you did,' said the aunt.

'I imagine you are not popular,' said the General. 'People who are always in the right seldom are.' He made a gesture of annoyance. 'Very well, you can go, Bishop.'

'Into that howling mob?' said the aunt, 'with the stain of cowardice on him? You will stay here, Joseph, while I go and explain to the people.'

'Explain what?' said the Bishop.

'That the crucifixion was planned by the General as an insult to our Faith, and that you—that we saw through it. Goodbye, General. Good-night, Mr. Mayor.'

The General was a man of resource.

'Wait a moment, madam,' he said; 'I will save you any further trouble. I propose to send out my loud-speaker to

inform the crowd that the crucifixion had been already cancelled, not by the Bishop, but by myself, and that the hostages
have been released since it has come to light that the murdered
man was the aggressor in a brawl.'

'And our man killed him in self-defence?' said the Mayor.

'Exactly,' said the General.

'A dreadful lie, General,' said the Bishop. 'I have misjudged
you, I fear. I thought you were at least a man of truth.'

'And whose fault is it that I am not, I should like to know?
Who has driven me into a corner from which only a falsehood
can extricate me? There she stands, gentlemen—and she a
Bishop's aunt!'

'There's another thing,' said the Mayor. 'Your announcement does not clear the Bishop. Unfortunately he himself told
his people that he had changed his mind.'

'His aunt will clear him, you'll see,' said the General.

The Bishop shook his head.

'What I have said, I have said. My people may think me
a coward; they will never believe I could tell an untruth.'

'My dear Joseph,' said his aunt, 'I shall merely tell them
that you were acting under my orders. I shall take the full
responsibility.'

The Bishop smiled at her.

'You'll never convince them of that,' he said.

'I shan't have to convince anybody,' said his aunt. 'They've
known it for thirty years.'

Twenty minutes later the military car with the loud-speaker
was again patrolling the streets, blaring out the General's
announcement. And while the crowds were cheering for the
release of the hostages, a little old lady in black, with her chin
in the air, was passing from group to group, button-holing the
most talkative of the citizens. Within the hour a crowd was
in the Cathedral Square, cheering for the Bishop. The swifts
continued to swoop and shrill round the Cathedral spire, and
had you been seated on the café terrace across the river, you
would have thought the old town, now bathed in the yellow
evening light, the very picture of peace and happiness. And
this time you would have been right.

NADINE GORDIMER

Charmed Lives

THERE were two men in the town, a deaf man and a drunkard.

The one was a watchmaker and the other a doctor, and they never met except when the watchmaker consulted the doctor about his stomach ulcer, or the doctor's watch needed cleaning, but they belonged together in the mind of twenty-year-old Kate Shand. Extraordinary to think in what unimaginable partnerships one may exist in the minds of others, with what faces one's own may be bracketed for ever, through some categorical connection, of which one will never know, in the memory of a third person. The association between the watchmaker and the doctor in Kate Shand's mind began when she and her brothers were children. For the Shand children there were two kinds of people. There were people their mother had a lot of time for, and people she had no time for. The definitions were not only expressive, but literal; the people she had a lot of time for she would allow to delay her endlessly, talking to them on street corners when she met them out shopping, visiting them when they were ill, stretching telephone conversations far beyond her normal brusque limits; the people she had no time for took up no more than the duration of a curt nod, or a half-sentence of dismissal should their names come up in conversation.

Both the watchmaker and the doctor were in Mrs. Shand's favoured category. The deaf watchmaker, Simon Datnow, was employed by Kate's father in his jeweller's shop. I've got a lot of time for Simon, Mrs. Shand would say consideredly, with a 'mind you', a sage reservation in her voice. That was because, on the whole, she did not care for relatives, and this man was, in fact, one of the procession of Lithuanian and Russian relatives whom Marcus Shand had 'brought out' to South Africa, before Kate was born, in the early twenties, and whom, ever after, he regarded with a surly indifference quite out of character with his gentle nature—a churlishness created by the conflict in him between family feeling for them, and a resentment against them for being the kind of people he would not have expected his wife to like. For though he winced under his wife's scorn of his relatives, there was a perverse pride in him that he should have succeeded in marrying a wife who *would* scorn them. They were used to sleeping, these foreigners (Mrs. Shand said), on top of the stove. They did not bath more than once a week. They ate disgusting food, salted fish and soup made of beetroot. At that time the Shand kitchen still had a coal range; the children pictured these strange aunts and cousins huddled together on the sooty surface after the fire had been raked out in the evening, greasy-fingered, like Esquimaux. It would not have surprised Kate, William, and Dykie to hear that the aunts chewed their husbands' boots to soften them.

For most of the immigrant relatives, for the women, certainly, Mrs. Shand had no time at all. She would give them a moment or two if she met them in the town (and in no time they had established themselves there, the women getting busy and becoming the chief breadwinners almost at once, dressmaking—they all sewed most skilfully—or cooking in delicatessen shops, the men, slower to learn English and to unlearn the ways of the old country, picking up odd jobs in produce stores, or going from house to house, heavily dressed in dark suits in the African heat, employed as official collectors for charities connected with the synagogue or the Jewish Burial Society) but Mrs. Shand never visited them in their homes unless there was the ceremony of an occasion such as a wedding or funeral to demand her presence. Even then she sat stiffly, her plain clothes conspicuous among their elaborately festive or sorrowful garb, enquiring politely about the health and ages, to date, of their children, and refusing, with great courtesy and a careful aversion of her eyes from the proffered plate, their traditional refreshments. The only person with whom Mrs. Shand attempted conversation at these gatherings was the deaf watchmaker, Simon Datnow.

Simon Datnow was not actually a blood relation of Marcus
Shand, but merely the brother of one of Mr. Shand's sisters'
husbands. The husband was dead and Simon had 'come out'
with his sister-in-law as a kind of substitute protector. Perhaps
it was because there was no blood-tie to rein his resentment
with guilt that, if Mrs. Shand liked Simon most, Mr. Shand
liked him least of the immigrant relations. It seemed to annoy
Marcus Shand that, after the first year, the deaf watchmaker
really owed him nothing; had, unlike the others, nothing in
particular for which to be grateful to him. Simon Datnow had
paid back the passage money which Mr. Shand had advanced,
and he was a skilled watchmaker whose equal Mr. Shand
could not have hoped to find in South Africa. Kate always
remembered the watchmaker as she used to see him from the
door, whenever she entered her father's shop, sitting in his
little three-sided glass cage with the inscription, in gold leaf,
WATCH REPAIR DEPARTMENT, showing like a banner across his
bent head. As Kate grew up, the gold leaf began to peel, and
behind the faint loop of the first P, you could see his left ear
more and more clearly. In that ear, from time to time, a new
hearing-aid, flesh-coloured, black or pearly, would appear,
but usually, when he was working, he did not wear one. He
would put it on only when you approached to speak to him,
and in the moment before you did speak, the moment when the
device dropped into contact with his ear, you would see him
wince as the roar of the world, from which he had been sealed
off like a man dropped in a diving-bell to the floor of the ocean,
burst in upon him.

A curved bite had been sawn out of the work-table at which
he sat, and the edge of the wood had long since been worn
smooth by the rub of his body as he leaned forward over his
work, and it seemed to Kate that he fitted into the table as the
table fitted into its glass walls. Before him were tiny, shallow
receptacles and metal work-platforms a few inches square, on
which the delicate tweezers and probe-like instruments with
which he worked stalked like timid, long-legged insects among
specks of red jewel and minute wheels, and springs that looked
like a baby's hair you had run through thumb-and-fingernail.

Tiny glass bells protected the innards of watches on which he was not working. She felt she dared not breathe too near the exposed ones, lest they took off on the current and sailed into some crack in the scored and worn table-top. Yet the instruments that worried at them delicately, that picked them up and dipped them into a dewdrop of oil or spirit, and finally fitted them together, were controlled by a pair of blunt, curled hands with broken nails like plates of horn embedded in, rather than growing from, chapped fingers. The skin of these hands was permanently tarnished from contact with oil and metal, and in winter, was swollen and fissured with dreadful chilblains. The WATCH REPAIR DEPARTMENT was in the draughtiest corner of the shop, and it was then that the watchmaker, blue-nosed and pale above his grey muffler, reminded Kate of one of those zoo animals which, denied the lair of its natural habitat, shudders out the cold months in a corner of its cage.

In the summer the watchmaker worked in his shirt-sleeves, with shiny expanding armbands to pull the cuffs up out of the way, and a constant trickle of sweat making his short, greying hair spring out slowly into curl from its confinement of pomade. Summer and winter, most days he looked up only when Marcus Shand came stumping over to shove at him a watch for diagnosis, bellowing 'Loses twenty-five minutes in twenty-four hours' or 'Oiling and cleaning. See if it's in working order.' 'What?' the deaf man would say in his sibilant, half-audible voice, frowning vacantly and fumbling for his 'machine'—as he always called his hearing-aid—while he held back from the force of his employer in nervous distaste. Shand would shout in impatient repetition, so that half of what he said would not be heard by the watchmaker, and the other half would thunder in upon him as his aid was switched on. The force of this half-sentence would strike the watchmaker like a blow, so that for a moment he was bewildered and unable to understand anything. Then Shand would become more impatient than ever, and shout twice as loud. Because of this communication at cross purposes, Marcus Shand tended to phrase everything he had to say to his watchmaker as shortly as possible, and to dispense with all graces of politeness, and so

almost all that came to Simon Datnow of the outside world for
eight hours a day was an assault of surly questions and
demands.

Because his watchmaker and relation by marriage was
sensitive to the tick of a watch but not an undertone of the
human voice, Marcus Shand got into the habit of abusing
Simon Datnow in mumbled asides, before his very face. It
was a great comfort to Shand to be able to abuse someone
with impunity. Yet although it was true that he was able to
say abusive things without being heard, it was, of course, not
possible for these not to show on his face while he said them,
and so it was that Simon Datnow felt the revilement more
cuttingly than if it had come to him in words, and a wall of
thick, inarticulate hostility, far more impenetrable than that of
deafness, came to exist between the two men.

It infuriated Mrs. Shand that the only person whom her
husband should have the courage to abuse should be someone
only half of this world, and, as a result, too uncertain of his
ground to take a stand upon it. She herself had tried, and, in
fact, went on trying all her life, to get her husband to stand up
to *her*. But no; the only person before whom Marcus would
dare raise the timid flag of his spirit was a man who couldn't
trust himself to interpret the challenge clearly. Mrs. Shand
retaliated by championing Simon Datnow. Datnow, she gave
her children to understand, was a natural gentleman, a kind of
freak incidence among the immigrant relations. His drudgery
became an ideal of conscientious service; his enforced remote-
ness from the world, an ideal of contemplation. The bewildered, impotent rage that showed in his eyes—the repressed
daze of savagery in the eyes of the bull who cannot see where
the darts have lodged in the nerves of his shoulders—before
the rudeness of her husband which he could not hear, she
interpreted as the self-control of a superior being. The meek
aspect which his deafness imposed upon him as he went about
the town during his lunch hour, seemed to her the quality
that should inherit the earth. Even the stomach ulcer from
which he suffered as a result of the tension of his work and the
fragmentary intensity of his communication with the world,

came, through their mother, to be associated in the minds of the Shand children with a quality of exceptional sensitivity.

When Kate was small she would sometimes stand for a long time with her face close to the glass cage, smiling respectfully at the watchmaker when he smiled his low, saliva-gleaming smile back at her, and nodding her interest when he held up some part of a watch, a piece of metal confetti, for her to see. At the approach of her father she would go still; taking cover from the crude and puzzling aspect of him which showed when he spoke to Simon Datnow. This gruff man with the thick strings of vein rising against his collar had nothing to do with the father who would put his cheek to hers and ask, humbly, for a kiss.

One day, a week before Christmas in the year when Kate was nine years old, she was hanging about her father's shop. In the burning midsummer December of South Africa, the gold-mining town was seedily festive with borax snow in the shop windows, red and blue lights strung round the Town-hall, and the beery voices of miners in sports blazers slapping each other on the back outside the bars. The jeweller's shop was very busy. Kate ran errands for her father and the young Afrikaans sales-girl, and drank lukewarm lemon squash in the room behind the shop where cardboard boxes and straw and sheets of tissue-paper for packing were kept, and the mice were so impudent that anything edible disappeared while you turned your back.

At this time of year, the watchmaker was constantly interrupted at his work by requests to fit gleaming new watch-straps to customers' watches, or to make minor adjustments to necklaces that were too long, or to mend silver bracelets with faulty catches. In order to get his watch repairing done, he came to work early in the morning, before the shop was open, and stayed behind long after it was closed. And all day, while the bustle of customers and the rustle of parcels and the ring of the cash register filled the shop around him, he was bent over his table, trying to do several things at once, often under the harassing, impatient eye of Marcus Shand or the sales girl. His lunch sandwiches remained uneaten. Once, a

mouse from the back room ventured into the shop to gnaw at
them. His morning and afternoon tea turned pale and
scummy in the cup. On the crowded table before him, the
tiny viscera of his watches got mislaid beneath the metal straps,
the necklaces, the bracelets. He looked like a worried mouse
himself, grey-backed, rustling furtively over his jumble of work.

On this particular day, he was so busy that the face of the
little girl, who had wandered over to watch him through the
glass, did not penetrate his concentration. She watched him a
minute or two, nevertheless. He fitted a tiny spring into the
intricacy of a watch's belly; over it went a wheel; into some
pin-sized holes, three chips of ruby. Then he put out his long
tweezers to peck from its spirit-bath something that proved not
to be there; he felt about with the tweezers, looked in another
dish; at last, lifted his eyebrow so that the jeweller's loop in his
left eye-socket fell out into his hand. He stood up from his
stool and looked carefully and methodically under every glass
bell, in every dish. He rummaged systematically through the
cardboard box-lid where he kept the filings, little twirls of
yellow and silver metal like punctuation marks, from the
watchstraps, the necklaces, the bracelets. He paused a moment,
as if deliberating where he should look next. And then, the
light of a solution, a calm relief relaxed his face. Slowly, he
stood back, creaking his stool away behind him over the
cement floor. Then he grasped his work table firmly, palm
up under its top, and brought it over, crashing and slithering
all its conglomeration of contents on top of himself.

He stood there with his hands hanging at his sides, amid the
wreckage. His eyes glittered and his mouth clenched, so that
the skin, in which the growing beard showed like fine blue shot,
was white above and below his stiffened lips. He was breathing
so loudly that it could be heard right across the sudden silence
of the shop full of people.

Before the shock of that silence broke, Kate ran. Her running broke the silence; she heard, as she pulled the heavy back
door of the shop closed behind her, babble and movement spill
out. She went trembling across the dirty yard which the shop
shared with several others contiguous with it, and sat on a

rotting packing-case against the wall of the lavatory. It was dank there, with the solitude of dank places. She stayed a long time, playing with some old letterheads, puffy with rain.

When she went back into the shop again, there was a cheerful delegation from a mine, in the part of the shop known as the jewellery department, choosing a canteen of cutlery for presentation to a retiring official. Behind the WATCH REPAIR DEPARTMENT, the watchmaker was putting the last of his tiny containers back at the angle at which it had always stood; only the glass bells were missing, and they must have been swept away by Albert, the African cleaner. The face of the watchmaker, behind the gold-leaf letters, was pale and calm.

Presently, he looked up and beckoned to her across the shop, and, hesitantly, she went to him. He gave her one of the three-cornered buns filled with poppyseed which he had brought for his tea, and that he knew she loved. Holding it between finger and thumb, she took the bun to the back room and hid it in a corner, for the mice.

Mrs. Shand had even more time for the doctor than she had for the watchmaker. When Kate, or William, or Dykie were ill, and Mrs. Shand was expecting Dr. Connor on his morning round of calls, she would have a plate of fresh scones baked ready for tea from before ten o'clock. And if he happened to come earlier, while the Shand house was still in the uproar of cleaning which not even consideration for the patient was allowed to interrupt, Amos and Fat Katie, the servants, and their shining vacuum-cleaner and buzzing floor-polisher were banished at his approach, trailing the cords of their machines behind them. Mrs. Shand would stand smiling, with her hands on her hips, while the doctor did his examination of the patient. Even if she had been voicing the gravest misgivings about the nature of the child's malady to her sister or mother over the telephone ten minutes before, Mrs. Shand always seemed to be transformed into a mood of level-headed confidence the moment the doctor appeared. Her attitude became jocular and skittish: 'Show doctor the old tum-tum, darling—really, Dykie, must you wear these pyjamas? Why *do* they take

fancies to the most unsuitable things, sometimes? Children, oh
children . . .!'

Then, the moment the examination was completed, Mrs.
Shand and the doctor would disappear into the living-room,
talking in an intimate undertone, and the child, fevered with
self-importance and the desire to know if the pain really might
be appendicitis, would lie cross and rigid, straining to separate
the murmuring voices into words. If the other children were at
home, they would hang about the passage outside the living-
room, and now and then the door would open suddenly and
their mother's face would appear, requesting more hot water,
or another jug of milk. There would be a glimpse of the
living-room, blue with cigarette smoke, fragrant with tea, the
doctor sitting in the big armchair—and then the door would
shut firmly again. When Dr. Connor rose to leave, Mrs. Shand
would accompany him all the way down the garden path and
then stand talking over the gate, or at the window of his car.

She would come slowly back up the path to the house after
he had driven off, holding carefully in her hand the prescrip-
tion he had written. Slowly through the house and into the
bedroom where her child lay. The child seemed almost a surprise to her. . . . 'Well, there you are, darling,' she would
say, absently. 'No school for you for a few days. Now I must
go down to the chemist and get this made up. And you're to
stay in your bed and not jump about, do you hear? Dr.
Connor says——' Then she would go to the telephone and
speak to her mother and her sister again. 'Well, he's been.
That's what I like about him, when you need him, he's there at
once. And, of course, it's just as I thought, a real chill on the
stomach, that's all, and he recognised it at once. Good old
Robert Eldridge, I'd trust him with my life, any day, in spite of
his faults.'

Their mother always talked about Dr. Connor by the two
imposing Christian names which she had seen on his degree
diplomas at his consulting-rooms, Robert Eldridge. For years,
Kate thought of this form of address vaguely as some sort of
description; it was like speaking of The Major, or The General
Manager, or The Editor. The 'faults' in spite of which Mrs.

Shand, and, indeed, half the town, trusted Robert Eldridge were, of course, his drunkenness. He was not merely addicted to drink, he was dejectedly chained to it, as the great sheepish dog whom he resembled might be chained to a kennel. He did not drink at parties, or with friends, but in no company but his own, in solitary, irregular and frequent bouts; sometimes every week, sometimes at intervals of several months, sometimes every day for a month. Once he was sober for more than a year; once he was scarcely sober at all for a year. Unless he had had a particularly long bout and was in very bad shape indeed, he did not drink at home, but drove out into the veld with his African garden boy and a case of raw South African brandy—the cheapest brand; he did not care what he drank. There he would stay for two or three days. The brandy ensured oblivion, and the African, who asked no questions and offered neither protest nor sympathy nor arguments for reformation, ensured survival. For the odd thing was that this wretched man, who crept away to drink himself not into euphoria but into stupor and delirium, shamefully, like a sick animal following the instinct to hide its sickness from the sight of others of its kind, wanted to survive. The desire was so strong in him that it seemed to protect him from harm; he drove his car when he was drunk and did not kill himself, and he operated on his patients when he was drunk and did not kill them. So it was that he came to bear, for the people of the town, the legend of a charmed life, and they were not afraid to entrust themselves to him.

He lived alone with his old mother in a large, neglected house which had the stunned, withdrawn atmosphere of walls, furniture, possessions which have absorbed the unhappy stare of silent inmates. Here, in the living-room with the empty vases, he had sat in morose penitence with his unreproachful mother. Here, in the consulting-room where he examined his patients beneath a pale photograph of his first wife in a Suzanne Lenglen tennis outfit (his wives had come and gone without any sympathy from anyone), he had, in desperate times, concealed brandy in bottles bearing the labels of medicaments. And here, in the hall, where years of dust had turned the black shaggy curls of a mounted wildebeest head into a powdered wig, he had lain at the foot of the stairs whole nights, unable to get up to his room. The house was silent, yet spoke of all this. Kate, when she was thirteen, heard it. She was going to Dr. Connor's house every day at the time, to have a course of penicillin injections for an outbreak of adolescent boils. She was filled with a bewildering self-disgust because of the boils (her body was punishing her, or being punished; she was guilty, that she knew, though she did not know of what) and there was something in this house of Dr. Connor that recognised, instantly, found common cause with, self-disgust. The wildebeest head, the vases, the pale dead girl in the bandeau claimed kinship with her. You are not alone, they said; there is a whole side of life along with which your feelings belong. The claim filled her with dismay and a sense of struggle against some knowledge being forced upon her that she did not want. For the first time, the bony, prematurely white head of Dr. Connor, bent over his big, clean hands as they snapped the top off an ampoule and plunged into it the needle of a syringe, did not seem to her the image of succour and skill and reassurance that it had been all those other times, the times of measles, of tonsillectomy, of the broken arm. He was a mouth-breather, with a loose, wet, kindly lower lip; but today there was no comfort in that audible intake and out-let of breath. Today the uninhabited blue eyes—she had not noticed before that there was no one there—filled her with an indignant, frightened questioning. Where was he gone, and why did everyone go on pretending he was still there? Why, why, why? He had been someone to revere; someone for whom her mother had had a lot of time, 'in spite of'. Yet why must there always be excuses for grown-ups? Why couldn't they be strong, beautiful, happy? Lying down on the white-covered couch and baring her behind for the needle, she felt her young heart fill with cold cruelty toward the mild-voiced, broken man bending over her.

As Kate Shand grew up, she went less and less often into her father's shop. She was away from the town, of course; first at a boarding-school, then at a university. When she did come home, it was always with something of a shock that she saw the shop exactly as it had always been, the watchmaker still at his work in the booth behind the gold-leaf lettering. At seventeen, eighteen, she felt the world revolving with her; how could it be that *these* remained static, were found as you had left them, like the castle where the princess pricked her finger and put everything to sleep for a hundred years? She smiled at the watchmaker across the shop, but she did not cross to speak to him, as if to do so would be to fill with substance again the shadow of the little girl who used to stand there, on the other side of the lettering, watching. The little girl who had seen, one hot Christmas time, the work-table turn over shuddering to the ground, as if some beast that slept beneath industry and submissiveness stirred in impotent protest.

Once the childish ills were behind her (the Shand children had run through the whole alphabet of them, from croup to whooping cough, under Dr. Connor) Kate did not need a doctor again for many years, but her mother often did, and, home from the university one vacation, Kate was irritated to hear that Mrs. Shand had 'just been over to see Robert Eldridge'. 'Good God, mother, why can't you go to a *doctor*?' 'That's all right. I'd rather have him than any of these fancy young men.' Dr. Connor still drove in the car that people gave way to as if it were a sacred cow wandering about the streets, was still accepted, without comment, back under the photograph in the consulting-room in the old house after his periodical disappearances.

In books, worms turned, drunkards ended violently in the gutter, the world moved; in the small town, Kate felt, everything held back tolerantly to the pace of—well, for example, those two men for whom her mother had such a lot of time, two men who apprehended the world from a remove, the one looking through glass into an aquarium where silent, mouthing fish swam up to him incomprehensibly and swam away, the other through the glassiness of his own eyes, through which he saw even his own hands as if he had escaped from them, going on mechanically stitching flesh and feeling pulses.

Less

When Kate graduated and her mother, with her usual capability, announced that she had used her influence with the school board (there were people on it who had a lot of time for *her*) and that a post awaited Kate in a local school, all the reasons the girl gave why she would not, could not, ever live in the town again were the logical, rational ones which children have always used in the process of severing themselves from their parents. But, oddly, for Kate, even as she argued them, pleaded them, they were not true. She was not thinking about the greater academic opportunities, the wider social choice, the cultural stimulation of the city to which she would go; and even if she had dropped the clichés and bluntly substituted for them more money, more men, more pleasure, she would have been no nearer the real reason why she had to go. This reason—and it was a kind of panic in her—had taken shape for her, slowly, out of all her childhood, in the persons of those two men whom she had known, really, so slightly—the deaf man and the drunkard. Why them? Two harmless and handicapped people who, as her mother often said, had never done a scrap of harm; whom, as a child, Kate had automatically respected because they belonged to the people for whom her mother had a lot of time.

And yet, at twenty, it was because of *them* that Kate knew she could not come back to live in the town. They belonged together in her mind, and from them, from the shards of their images there, she must turn away, to live.

PETER USTINOV

The Man in the Moon

JOHN KERMIDGE walked down the street in Highgate to
the letter-box, a bulky package in his hand. He felt as
though he had been plunged backwards into another, more
ample century, when the legs of men were still in constant use
as a means of propulsion, not just as members groping for
brake and accelerator. He smiled at the sky as though greeting
a half forgotten friend. There was a trace of troubled conscience in his smile. He had kept the sky waiting for so long.
Usually, when he looked up, he saw nothing but the perpetual
night of his laboratory.

Since he was a scientist, it would have been inhuman if he
had not in some measure surrendered to tradition and been a
little absent-minded. Not in his work, but in relatively unimportant matters. When he wrote, he did so with vast applica-
tion, and the meaning of his words could only be fathomed by
a few dozen endowed creatures in various universities; but
often, as now, having filled pages with mysterious logic, he
forgot to stick any stamps to the envelope. The letter was
addressed to Switzerland, to a Doctor Nussli, in Zurich.
Considering that Dr. Nussli was perhaps John's best friend, it
was strange, if typical, that the name on the envelope was
spelled with a single *s*.

'Where did you go?' asked his wife anxiously when he
returned.

'I posted that letter to Hans.'

'Couldn't it have waited until the morning?'

Although the weather was cold, John mopped his brow with
his handkerchief. 'No,' he said.

'The last mail's gone anyway,' Veronica grumbled.

It was curious that John should feel irritated in his hour of
triumph, but he allowed himself a moment of harshness.

'No,' he repeated, unnecessarily loud.

There was a pause, with thunder in the air.

For quite a few months, Veronica and John had seen very little of each other. Veronica had permitted herself quite a few questions during this time; John had failed to gratify her with even a single answer.

'I thought you might like to see the children before they went to bed,' she said.

He grunted and asked, 'Where's Bill?'

'Bill? I don't know. Sir Humphrey called.'

'Sir Humphrey?' John started angrily. 'What the hell did he want?'

'He didn't say, but he was unusually nice to me.'

'That's a bad sign.'

'Seemed very elated.'

'Elated?' John kicked a chair.

'What's the matter with you?' Veronica almost shouted.

The doorbell rang.

'That'll be the champagne,' John said, going into the entrance hall.

'Champagne?'

It wasn't the champagne. It was Bill Hensey, John's assistant, a bearded fellow in an old sports jacket, with a dead pipe permanently in his mouth. He seized John by the arm, didn't even acknowledge Veronica, and started speaking agitatedly in a soft voice. Veronica wished she'd married a bank clerk, a man with simple problems and a little courtesy. She heard nothing of the conversation apart from an occasional reference to Sir Humphrey, but she saw Bill's baleful blue eyes darting hither and thither with excitement.

She was a pleasant girl without much temperament, the ideal wife for John, if there was such a thing. She didn't wish to attract attention to herself, since she knew that both men were engaged in important work and that they were under some strain which it was her unhappy duty to understand without being inquisitive. Just then, however, the children burst into the room, engaged in a running fight over the cactus-covered plains of the frontier badlands. Dick, dressed as a sheriff over his pyjamas, opened murderous fire with a cap pistol from behind an armchair, while Timothy plunged into cover behind the radiogram, his eyes shining evilly through the slits of his bandit's mask.

John exploded. 'Get out of here,' he yelled.

It was only natural for Veronica to leap to her children's defence. 'They're only playing,' she cried. 'God Almighty, what's the matter with you?'

'Can't you see we're working?' answered John, covering up his guilt in testiness.

But Veronica was roused, and launched into a big scene. While the children slunk out unhappily, she released all her resentment in a flood of tears and invective. She had been packing for this blasted trip to Washington. Did he think she wanted to go to Washington? She'd much rather stay home. Why didn't he go alone? And if he went, why didn't he stay? What thanks did she get? To her the unglamorous lot: the paying of bills, the checking of accounts, the necessary bedtime stories which taxed the imagination. Why didn't he marry Bill?

She was interrupted by the doorbell. The champagne, no doubt.

It wasn't the champagne. It was Sir Humphrey Utteridge, accompanied by an affected youth in a bowler hat.

'Kermidge, allow me to congratulate you,' Sir Humphrey said in a voice that was quivering with emotion.

John and Bill exchanged a quick, anxious look.

'Thank you, Sir Humphrey,' John answered, with some impatience.

'This event will mark the beginning of a new era, not only in the annals of recorded history, but in the indelible odyssey of the British Commonwealth of Nations.'

This was the fine, rolling language for launching a ship, but nobody wants a ship launched in his living-room.

'Old ass,' thought John, but said, 'It's very good of you to say so.'

'D'you remember me, Kermidge?' asked the affected youth, leaning heavily on his umbrella. 'Oliver de Vouvenay. We were at Charterhouse together.'

Good gracious. No wonder John didn't remember him, he
hadn't changed a bit. John's hair was turning white, but this
immaculate, pink creature looked exactly as he had at school.
If he was now successful it was a triumph of conformity. He
was successful.

After John had grudgingly shaken hands, Oliver de Vouvenay announced that he hadn't done badly, since he was now
the Principal Private Secretary of the Prime Minister, the
Right Honourable Arthur Backworth, and hoped to stand in
the next election.

'Not as a Socialist,' said John.

Oliver de Vouvenay laughed uproariously and expressed his
conviction that the joke was a good one.

Before there was time for more banter, the doorbell rang
again.

'That'll be——' Sir Humphrey began, but John interrupted
him.

'I ordered some champagne,' he said. 'I'll go.'

John opened the door and found himself face to face with a
detective. The man didn't say he was a detective, but it was
obvious. His disguise would only have deceived another
detective. 'This is it, sir,' called the detective to a waiting
Rolls-Royce.

The door of the limousine opened slowly, and an elderly man
of some distinction struggled cautiously on to the pavement.

John felt the colour draining from his face. He recognised
the man as the Right Honourable Arthur Backworth, Prime
Minister of Great Britain and Northern Ireland.

'May I come in?' said the Prime Minister, with a vote-
catching smile.

Here was a wonderful, perverse moment to say no, but John
said yes.

Veronica, amazed, and with an intense feeling of shame at
having even mentioned such trivialities as accounts and packing, watched her humble suburban boudoir gradually filling
with celebrities who had only graced it previously as guests on
the television screen.

'You will probably wonder why I am here,' crooned Mr. Backworth.

Once again John was seized with a desire to say no, but to the Prime Minister the question was a rhetorical one, and he continued in august and measured tones.

'When Sir Humphrey informed me early today of the success of your experiment, I immediately called a Cabinet meeting, which ended not half an hour ago. It goes without saying that what you have achieved is perhaps the most glorious, the most decisive step forward in the history of science—nay, of the human race. What recognition a mere government may accord you will be yours, rest assured.'

'It would have been impossible without Bill here——' John said.

'Yes, yes, both of you, both of you,' the Prime Minister went on with some impatience. He was used to the interruptions of politicians, but the interruptions of laymen were an impertinence. 'Now, it must be obvious to you,' he continued, 'that what you have accomplished is of such magnitude that it cannot fail to affect the policy of nations, and,' he added, with a trace of exalted mischief, 'of this nation in particular. After all, the Russians will, at any moment, be able to land a dog on the moon; the Americans have, I am told, a mouse in readiness; but we, without fanfares of magniloquence, have by-passed these intermediary stages and are ready to land a man, or men. You may not realise what this means.'

John smiled and said modestly, 'I am very fortunate, sir, that it should have fallen to me to head the team which managed, perhaps more by luck than by virtue, to achieve this success. I am, of course, looking forward immensely to my visit to Washington, and to the possibility of breaking this news to our American friends.' John was slightly annoyed with himself for adopting this formal tone, but in talking to Prime Ministers one apparently didn't talk, one made a speech.

Mr. Backworth looked at John curiously, and smiled. 'I want you to come to dinner on Thursday at Number 10,' he said.

'I can't, I'll be in Washington.'

'No, you won't.'

'What?'

The Prime Minister nodded at Sir Humphrey, who cleared his throat and spoke. 'It has been decided by the Cabinet— and I was present at the meeting—to send Gwatkin-Pollock to Washington in your place. We need you here.'

'But Gwatkin-Pollock knows not the first thing about inter- planetary travel!' John cried.

'Then he will give nothing away,' said the Prime Minister, pleasantly.

'This is outrageous. I want to go!'

'You can't,' replied the Prime Minister.

'Can't!' echoed John, and then fell back on the conven- tional reaction of the perplexed democrat. 'This is a free country.'

'Yes,' growled the Prime Minister, in his heroic style, 'and we must keep it free.'

His remark didn't mean much, but any student of politics will recognise the fact that it is more important to make the right noise than to talk sense.

The Prime Minister smiled, relaxing the unexpected tension. 'Do you really think that we have sunk so low as to reward you by curbing your liberties?' he asked.

John felt childish. 'I was looking forward to Washington,' he said.

'You scientists take such a long view of events that it needs simple souls like ourselves to open your eyes to the obvious on occasion. Of course you are flushed with pride of achievement. Of course you wish to announce your world-shattering dis- covery to your colleagues. That is only human. But alas! Your colleagues may be near to you in spirit, but they also carry passports, they also speak their various languages and boast their various prejudices. There can be no pure relationship between you and, say, a Russian scientist because you both have divergent responsibilities, however warm and cordial your contact in your laboratories or over a cup of coffee. Now, you harbour a tremendous, a dangerous secret. Have you the experience to keep it, all by yourself, without help from us? Will not the strain on you be utterly inhuman, however loyal your intentions? These are questions to which we must find answers within the next few weeks.'

'How do you intend to go about it?' asked John, too surprised to be really angry.

'By keeping your mind occupied,' said the Prime Minister, earnestly. 'Thursday is the day after tomorrow. I wish you to dine with me and with General Sir Godfrey Toplett, Chief of the General Staff.'

'We will have absolutely nothing in common,' said John.

'Before dinner, perhaps not. After dinner, I believe you will,' replied the Prime Minister coolly.

'I presume that I may go on seeing which friends I please?' asked John, his voice charged with irony.

The Prime Minister ignored the irony and said, 'Up to a point.'

John looked at Oliver de Vouvenay, who smiled fatuously.

Bill rose from his seat. He hadn't said anything, but was visibly dismayed. 'If you'll excuse me . . .' he began.

'Don't be alarmed if you should feel yourself followed,' said the Prime Minister. 'You will be.'

Gwatkin-Pollock was a man of science often selected by the British Government for official missions, since he had a quality of aloof and calculating majesty which those seated with him round a conference table never failed to find disturbing. He always seemed to be hiding something. He also had a habit of suddenly, unreasonably laughing at a comic situation of a day, a week, a year ago, usually while a serious statement was being read by someone else. His enigmatic quality was completed by his utter silence when it was his turn to make a statement.

It so happened that at the very moment Gwatkin-Pollock was seated with American scientists at a top-level conference in Washington, John was puffing one of the Prime Minister's better cigars and rather losing his critical sense in its lullaby of fumes. The dark plans of the British Government were working well for the time being on both fronts. A brilliant American scientist, who spoke for some reason with a thick German accent, was just expounding a remarkable plan for projecting a whole battalion of white mice into space, when Gwatkin-Pollock, remembering a humorous event from his youth, laughed loudly. The American delegation looked at each other with consternation and asked themselves whether the President had been wise to let the British into these top-secret conferences.

In London, meanwhile, General Toplett, a soldier with a face like a whiskered walnut, was busy producing some large photographs from his portfolio.

'You see,' he said to John and to the Prime Minister, 'it's quite clear that whatever nation is the first to land even light forces on Crater K here—I've marked it in red—will control all the lateral valleys on this side of the moon's face. My plan, therefore, is to land light air-borne forces as near the perimeter of the crater as possible, and to advance from there in four columns until we reach this green line here.'

This was too much for John, who leaped to his feet. 'It's revolting!' he cried. 'I didn't evolve a man-carrying moon rocket in order to see it subjected to the kind of thought which has made such a mess of our planet! I don't want dim soldiers and soiled politicians to pollute my moon!'

'Steady there, steady,' snarled the General, holding the photograph of the crater in the air as though it were a hand-grenade.

The Prime Minister laughed. 'Don't you think, Kermidge,' he said quietly, 'that there is a pleasant irony in this turn of events? Don't misunderstand me; the Americans are, and always will be, our allies. That goes without saying. But in a way, we do have a . . . a friendly score to settle, don't you think?'

'In the world of science there is always an element of quite innocuous rivalry——' John said, as reasonably as he could.

'I wasn't referring to the world of science,' the Prime Minister interrupted. 'I was referring to history. Kermidge, we are taxing our ingenuity to the limit to keep over fifty million people fully employed and well fed on this tiny island. Naturally our rules are stringent, our taxation inhuman, and naturally we tend to appear to other nations as somewhat avaricious in our methods and as almost ludicrously inflexible in our regulations. Can this give us pleasure? We, who gave the world so much?'

'We took quite a lot, too,' said John.

'I must ask you to listen to me without interruption,' replied the Prime Minister with a trace of irritation. He had to put up with this kind of thing from the opposition all the year round. There was no reason, he felt, why he should put up with contradiction in his own dining-room, in his own cigar smoke. 'The Americans are a most generous people,' he continued, 'but they can afford to be. A man with one hundred pounds in the bank giving a penny to a beggar is making the same financial sacrifice as a man with one million pounds in the bank giving four pounds, three shillings, and four pence to a beggar.' These statistics were so glib that they obviously formed a staple argument of the Prime Minister's.

'The widow's mite,' said John.

The Prime Minister gave him a withering look, which dissolved rapidly into a winning smile. Politics taught a man self-control as no other profession.

'Call it what you will, the facts are clear. We need space. We need to expand, not only in order to survive, but in order to conserve our national character, our even temper, our serenity.'

'Even Hitler thought of better reasons than that,' John heard himself saying.

The Prime Minister was unruffled.

'Would we ever attack our neighbours to achieve this end? Never. But'—and he leaned forward, searchingly—'once there is space, who knows? We've never shied at adventure. And think of it—rolling acres on the moon, or on other planets. Untold mineral wealth. Kermidge, we are in the shoes of Columbus, with the added proof of the unknown continent's existence. Look out of the window. You will see it. And we have the ship to get us there.'

'You want to paint the moon red,' murmured John. 'You want a moon worthy of Kipling, on which the sun never sets.'

'Rather well put,' said the General, now that the conversation had taken an understandable turn.

'Exactly—and why not?' cried the Prime Minister. 'Nothing in history is final. History is like the sea, constantly changing, a patchwork of phases, a mosaic of impermanent achievements. We were an occupied people once. The Saxons, the Danes, and the Romans had their will of us. Then we rose, with the determination of underdogs, and conquered the greatest empire the world has ever known. Times changed, and with them the conception of Empire. Whether we like it or not, we now live in an Era of Liberality, in which every tinpot republic has its own voice in the United Nations. We, in our great wisdom and experience, must sit silently by while Guatemala lays claim to British Honduras. This kind of thing taxes our dignity to the uttermost, but need it last? Must we accept the defeat of Burgoyne as final? We say we lose every battle but the last. Has the last battle been fought?' He dropped his voice from a rhetorical level into the intimacy of sincerity. 'Please understand me, I do not advocate war, least of all war with America. That would be unthinkable and stupid. In any event, we would lose it. However, I, for one, do not accept Burgoyne's defeat as the end of a story.'

'Burgoyne was a fool,' said the General gratuitously.

'Let us reach the moon first. This would not only give us the space we need, it would also give us the enormous moral ascendancy necessary to resume the leadership of the free world. There can be no doubt whatever that Russia is working rapidly towards the results you have so brilliantly attained. She is, as it were, breathing down our neck. Sharing our information with the Americans would only waste valuable weeks at this juncture, and by the time we had put our mutual scheme into operation the Americans would be taking all the credit. They are too flushed with their own technological efficiency to admit that anyone can achieve anything without stealing their plans. Kermidge, we have made our gesture. We have sent them Gwatkin-Pollock. Let us do the rest ourselves.'

There was a pause.

John began speaking slowly, trying hard to control his voice, which was quivering. 'I hold no brief for American scientists, or for Russian scientists, or for British scientists for that matter. I have friends and enemies in all camps, since to the true men of science there are no frontiers, only advances; there are no nations, only humanity. This may sound subversive to you, but it is true, and I will explain, as temperately as I can, why it is true, what has made it true. You, sir, talked of Columbus. In his day, men for all their culture, fine painting, architecture, humanism, the rest, were still relatively savage. Life was cheap. Death was the penalty for a slight misdemeanour, slavery the penalty for an accident of birth. And why? Because there was space to conquer, horizons full of promise. Conquest was the order of the day. The avid fingers of Britain, France, Spain, and Portugal stretched into the unknown. Then, abruptly, all was found, all was unravelled. Germany and Italy attempted to put the clock back, and behaved as everyone had once behaved, and were deemed criminal for no other reason than that they were out of date and that their internal persecutions were carried against men of culture, and white men at that, instead of against their colonial subjects. They were condemned by mankind, and rightly so, because they were hungry for glory at a time when other nations were licking their chops, sated by a meal which had lasted for centuries. And why did we all become civilised, so abruptly? Because, sir, there was nothing left to conquer, nothing left to seize without a threat of general war; there was no space left.' John mopped his brow briefly and continued. 'Now what has happened? We have become conscious of space again. Cheated of horizons down on earth, we have looked upwards, and found horizons there. What will that do to us? It will put us back to pre-Columbian days. It will be the signal for military conquest, for religious wars. There will be crusades for a Catholic moon, a Protestant moon, a Muslim moon, a Jewish moon. If there are inhabitants up there, we will persecute them mercilessly before we begin to realize their value. You can't feel any affection for a creature you have never seen before, especially if it seems ugly by our standards. The United

Nations will lose all control, because its enemy is the smell of space in the nostrils of the military. Life will become cheap again, and so will glory. We will put the clock back to the days of darkness, and our growing pains in the stratosphere will be at least as painful as those we suffered here on earth. I want no part of it.'

The Prime Minister looked at him with genuine affection and offered him another cigar, which he accepted automatically, with a shaking hand.

'You are looking at the world with the eyes of a historian,' said the Prime Minister, 'but the world is not run by historians. It is a luxury we cannot afford. We can't study events from such a comfortable distance, nor can we allow ourselves to be embittered so easily by the unfortunate parallels and repetitions of history. As a historian, you are no doubt right, since you look back so far in order to look forward, but as a politician you are wrong, you are wrong as a patriot.'

'I have no ambitions as a patriot,' John answered. 'I want to be a man the world is proud of.'

'You are young,' said the Prime Minister, lighting a match for John. 'Incidentally, the Archbishop of Canterbury has expressed an urgent desire to meet you.'

'I knew it,' cried John, 'a Church of England moon!'

When he returned home, John sat up all night writing a letter. Veronica, as she lay sleepless, heard the febrile stutter of the typewriter and an occasional angry outburst. The cabin trunks still stood half-filled in the bedroom, a measure of how disappointed John and Veronica were at not going to Washington and of their uncertainty about the future.

John didn't go to bed that night, but left the house at six-thirty to post his letter. He noticed a detective loitering on the opposite pavement, but ignored him.

There was practically no conversation between Veronica and John all day, and even the children modified their games. It was as though disaster had struck the family.

After lunch, they suffered the surprise visit of a grave Sir Humphrey, accompanied by Oliver de Vouvenay at his most

petulant, and a rosy-faced inspector from Scotland Yard called
Peddick.

'What may I offer you?' asked John, investing his question
with sarcasm. He seemed incapable of saying anything without sarcasm these days.

'Nothing. Nothing at all,' answered Sir Humphrey.

'Perhaps we could sit down?' said de Vouvenay.

'I see nothing to prevent you,' said John.

There was a brief, awkward silence.

'Well?'

In silence, Oliver de Vouvenay opened his briefcase and
produced the letter which John had posted that morning. It
was open.

'What are you doing with that?' John asked hotly.

'Perhaps I should take over, sir?' It was Inspector Peddick
speaking. 'Did you write this?'

'What business is it of yours?'

'It's addressed to Switzerland, sir.'

'I can explain that. It is addressed to Switzerland because I
intended it to arrive in Switzerland.'

'I gather, sir, that it contains information of a highly secret
nature.'

'It contains information which emanated from my brain and
which I do not consider secret. And in any case, for how long
has it been the practice, in this free country, for the police to
intercept private letters?'

'We have authority, sir, under the Official Secrets Act.'

'Could you tell me what you find particularly secret about
the information contained in this letter?'

The inspector smiled. 'That's hardly my province, sir. It
doesn't make much sense to me, but I've been told it's secret
from higher-up, and I acted accordingly.'

'But you've read it?'

'Oh, I skimmed through part of it, yes, sir, in the course of
duty.'

John broke a vase and shouted a profanity.

Sir Humphrey raised a restraining hand. 'You must realise,
John, that you must be in some measure subject to government

policy. You can't go on being a rebel all your grown life. What you have accomplished is far too important for us all for you to attempt to destroy it by what you imagine to be scientific integrity. John, I implore you to regard yourself as the care-taker of a secret, and not to do anything in your moment of imminent triumph which will bring you into disrepute.'

'I am not the caretaker of a secret,' thundered John, 'I am the inventor of a public utility!'

'You wrote a letter to Switzerland, to a Professor Nussli. Professor Nussli has been to Moscow recently,' said de Vouvenay, smoothly.

'So what?' snapped John. 'I've been to Trinidad, that doesn't mean I sing calypsos all day. What god-awful idiots you all are. Just because a man is inquisitive, just because he wants to find out, you think automatically that he's tarnished by whatever he went to investigate.'

'I didn't insinuate that at all.'

'Why did you mention it then? What do people mean when they say the word "Moscow" out of the blue? How naïve do you think I am? I've known Nussli for nearly forty years—in other words, all my life. I was brought up in Switzerland when I was young because I had asthma. I went to school with Hans. We were firm friends. He's a brilliant man now as he was a brilliant boy then, and he knows probably more about my particular field than any other man alive today. He's a thoroughly enlightened, liberal chap.'

'I'm very gratified to hear it,' said de Vouvenay.

'*You're* gratified to hear it?' shouted John, losing his temper. 'And who the hell d'you think you are? I very much regret leaving my Swiss school, where I worked and had fun, to come back here for the sole privilege of watching your nasty little career developing from the selfrighteous goody-goody with the only unbroken voice in school which could do justice to the soprano solos in the *Messiah* to the pompous prig who has the impertinence to ventilate opinions about which he knows noth-ing, nothing, nothing! Get out of here.'

De Vouvenay rose, flushed with anger, his yellow hair falling over one eye. 'Your letter will be confiscated for the time being,' he said, 'and perhaps, in time, you will learn to behave yourself sufficiently for us to be able to entrust you with Herr Nussli's answers.'

John was aghast. 'D'you mean——'

Sir Humphrey looked at him steadily and openly. 'I will apologise for Mr. de Vouvenay,' he said, 'since Mr. de Vouvenay evidently hasn't the resources to apologise himself.'

'Letters to me——'

'Yes, John. I deplore the practice of opening other people's mail. Especially do I deplore it when it is perpetrated by a government. But, as an Englishman, and as one who recognised your great talent early in your life, I must say that I realise the necessity for such an emergency measure at this time. We must not only protect our secret from any enemy, but we must protect you from yourself. I don't know what you have been writing to Professor Nussli during these past months, but the one answer in our possession suggests that he has a detailed and even a brilliant insight into our methods. What is especially disturbing is his apparent knowledge of our fuel——'

'Our fuel, fiddlesticks. It was his fuel as much as mine. How do you think two friends work when they are fired by the same ambition? They share their information, selflessly, for the common good.'

'In the mail? Neither of these letters was so much as registered.'

'Surely the mail is more discreet than the telephone, and it's certainly less expensive. I never for one moment believed that my letters would be opened. Had I known that, I would have found other methods of communication.'

'Such as?' asked de Vouvenay.

'Pigeons,' spat John.

When the visitors had left, John chided himself for not having hit de Vouvenay. He had actually been forced to defend himself from a position which was as strong as any position could be in a country with democratic traditions. His correspondence had been confiscated, and yet somehow he didn't feel that he had been able to bring it home to his tormentors how unethical their conduct had been. He had certainly become very angry, but his anger had somehow been dissipated by his sheer amazement that such things were possible in this day and age, in the twentieth century. The twentieth century? The threshold of the second fifteenth century more likely: the age of discovery, of casual death and roughshod life.

He made a quick decision. Lifting the telephone, he called British European Airways and booked a flight on the plane to Zurich. With two hours to kill, he paced the room reconstructing the scene with his three visitors and his dinner with the Prime Minister, his mood settling into one of cold and righteous indignation as he thought of all the choice phrases he would have used had he had the presence of mind.

Then, with forty minutes to go, he put his passport in his pocket, decided not to say goodbye to his wife, since explanations would only dilute his fury, and left the house, quietly closing the front door. The taxi arrived at London Airport with some minutes to spare, and John went into the departure hall. The young ladies were very polite and directed him into Immigration. Here, a colourless gentleman looked at his passport for a small eternity, seeming to read mysterious meanings into old visas. Eventually the colourless gentleman looked up, not at John, but past him.

A voice in John's ear said, 'I'm sorry, Mr. Kermidge.'

It was Inspector Peddick.

Veronica worried about John for the next three weeks. Although he was not ill, he showed no inclination to rise, and began to grow a beard out of sheer indolence. He never spoke except to say on one occasion, 'I'm a patriot, my dear. I'm staying in bed to make it easy for the police. In these hard days of intensive burglary and juvenile delinquency, it would be unfair to put too much pressure on the Yard by moving around.'

Sir Humphrey came to the house once or twice, but John just stared at the ceiling, refusing to say a word. Preparations were being made to launch John's rocket, and Sir Humphrey, a kind of devoted man at heart, sought to cheer up Veronica by telling her that a peerage was in the air. 'Even if John bridles at being Lord Kermidge, he'd surely wish to see you Lady Kermidge.'

'I don't care so long as he eats.'

One night, some twenty-five days after John's attempt to fly to Zurich, the Press the world over noticed mysterious and intensive diplomatic activity.

It was remarked by vigilant American journalists that the Secretary of State left a public dinner at Cincinnati in order to fly to Washington. A few minutes later, the President of the United States interrupted a fishing holiday and left for Washington by helicopter. The faces of these two dignitaries were exceptionally grave.

Newspapermen in Moscow observed that a meeting of the Supreme Soviet had been called at only an hour's notice and that grim-faced deputies were disrupting the traffic as they poured into the Kremlin. Areas were cordoned off, and the police were uncommunicative. In Paris, a crisis was stopped in midstream as a rumour spread, making the rising spiral of the cost of living seem frivolous indeed.

The Right Honourable Arthur Backworth left Chequers at four in the morning for Number 10 Downing Street. Observers caught a glimpse of his ashen face in the dark bowels of his Rolls-Royce.

The wires from America reported not only the unexpected presence of the President and the Secretary of State in the federal capital, but also of an unusual number of generals and admirals, all of them sullen and thunderous. Businessmen attempting transatlantic calls found that there were endless delays. Tempers were frayed the world over.

One of the last to know the reason why was John, who was fast asleep when Veronica and Bill burst into his room with all the morning papers. He glanced at the headline of the first paper and began to laugh, slowly at first, then hysterically, until the tears poured from his eyes in a stream, coursing through his young beard, staining his pyjama top. For a full quarter of an hour he laughed, weeping, moaning, gripping his sides, tearing the sheets with a delight which overlapped into anguish, panting like a dying man, and dragging Bill and Veronica with him in his lunatic joy. Suddenly the laughter stopped, and John, Bill, and Veronica looked at each other without energy, without emotion.

John, breathing deeply, took up the newspaper and read the headline again.

It said, in banner type, SWISS REACH THE MOON.

MAY C. JENKINS

I can play 'Schools'

I WAS writing to my mother, one sunny afternoon in the school holidays, while my daughter Marian sat on the grass, just outside the french window. She was playing 'Schools' with her dolls. Annoyed because they were 'not attending', she was scolding them, making expressive gestures with her hands, as her teacher might have done; it was interesting to watch her.

What would I write about Marian? It was never easy to find something new to say, and I did not want to use the same phrases as last week and—probably—the week before. Mother was in Canada, eager for news of home; she would scan the lines for news of Marian, for whom she had an anxious love.

Studying the child now, as if for inspiration, I thought for the thousandth time how lovely she was, with dark curls framing her small pointed face, dark serious eyes—too serious, perhaps, for a seven-year-old—and full, sensitive lips. Deep, loving pride in her stirred in me. She was such a dear, intelligent girl. But I felt disappointment too, for I had dreamed of a different child. I had seen a golden girl, golden voiced, moving with confidence through the world.

'Anne, you're being very stupid,' my husband had said, when, in the months before she was born, I drew this picture for him. 'You don't even know that you'll have a girl—and, supposing you do, you can't order one to a pattern like that. You're just heading for trouble.'

He was right, of course; the baby was a girl, but not as I had imagined her. I still thought wistfully, sometimes, of the child that might have been, and never would be, now. For my husband had been killed in a car crash, shortly before Marian was born. I did not have him now, to share my days, to comfort me.

Sometimes my friends spoke of re-marriage. But I had loved

Tom very much, so much that our days together, alight with love, were still too close to me. Then there was Marian. Step-parents—in fiction and fact—were apt to cause disharmony, that might have deep, far-reaching consequences. She had to come first.

This afternoon her game did not satisfy her. Without being told, I knew what was wrong; she wanted Christabel. This was her favourite doll, left that morning in the attic. The game was tasteless without her, Marian decided, and rose, shaking the grass off her blue cotton dress.

Turning, she saw the amusement in my eyes; her own lit up with rare and lovely laughter. 'I know it's silly, they seemed to say, 'but I can't help it, I must have her.' She went off; the garden seemed cold with her absence, the dolls forgotten. She is my love, my lamb, my darling, after all, I thought; we understand each other, words are unnecessary; how many parents can say that? and, my spirits lighter, I bent again over the desk.

'As you know, Marian is at home just now. It is wonderful to have her. I wish the holidays were longer——'

A shadow passed in front of the french window, dulling the sunny garden. For a moment, foolishly, I expected to see Marian. But it was a long way up to the attic; besides once there, she would probably become interested in something else. I looked up. It was the little girl from next door. She was tossing an orange into the air and catching it again. 'You'd think this was *her* garden!' I said inwardly. 'No shyness there!'

Her family had come only two short weeks before, but already it seemed a long time to me. I had not yet 'called on' the mother—in our small town it is still considered friendly to visit new neighbours—but I could not count the number of times that her daughter had appeared in the garden saying,

'Please may I play with your little girl today?'

She was perhaps a year or two older than Marian. Slim and fair-skinned, her hair was like ripe corn in sunlight, her eyes a sparkling, vivid blue. As if this were not enough, she had a voice as clear and careless as a mountain stream. I suppressed that ever-recurring envious ache.

'I've come again,' she announced.

'Is that so?' I was amused, in spite of annoyance.

(When would I get back to my letter? Mother would be looking for it, would worry if it did not come. That was the worst of agreeing to send mail at a certain time.)

'I saw your little girl in the garden. I can play "Schools" too, I love it.'

'How often have I told you——'

'But she plays all by herself, all the time. She'll be lonely.'

'Marian likes to play by herself.' It was true, I reflected sadly. She shrank from children in the neighbourhood, thinking she could not play their games properly; feared their laughter, thinking it was at her expense; did not understand their jolly, slangy conversations.

'Still, she must be lonely,' the other child said shrewdly. She was, but knew no way to avoid it; all the avenues which she had tried had led her further away, if anything from that carefree, shouting world. 'I am too. I haven't got brothers or sisters. And I don't know anyone here yet.'

Well, you won't be long before you do, I thought grimly, wishing that Marian had one quarter of the self-confidence which this child scattered so blithely to the four winds. In the face of her stubborn persistence I almost gave way. But what was the use? It had been tried so often before. The result was always the same. Marian would come home as soon as she could, her drooping shoulders expressing a despair that went to my heart.

With me, she was quite different. We played together contentedly, or went for walks. It was always a pleasure to go for a walk with Marian. She loved to see small, delightful things; a new bud, a wild rose, or thistledown floating like magic through the air, would bring a dreamy softness to her eyes, a lightness to her feet. Released, enchanted, she would run over springy grass, among kindly trees; it was her unassailable world. What was that poem, left by an unknown writer in an air-raid shelter, during the war? 'Beauty has ramparts nothing can destroy.' Marian had already discovered that.

I pulled myself together. 'It's no use, dear.' All the irritation had left me; I felt only gentleness. 'It's very good of you to say you'll play with Marian. It's good of all the children to come. But the thing is—you just don't know what it means. You get tired of her and then she thinks you don't like her—she doesn't understand. For a child like her you need so much patience.'

Evidently at a loss, she stared at me. 'Why? What's wrong with her?'

'Didn't you know?' Of course, she had been next door for a very short time. But I had assumed that she knew, that someone would have told her. I had thought, as we are apt to do, that my private tragedy was large and important to others, too.

'No. What is it?'

'She is deaf and dumb.'

After a minute she said, 'Does she speak on her fingers?'

'A bit . . . and in other ways as well . . . she goes away to a school.' Suddenly I was immensely tired. 'So you see why you can't play with her, child.'

'Don't call me Child, my name's Freda,' she said impudently. Then she moved from the window. 'Give this to Marian, I brought it for her.' She handed me the orange and was gone, walking with a lazy grace down the path, her yellow pigtails swinging.

I thought, it never does to open your heart to a child. Try it and she slaps your face. 'Give her the orange,' Freda had said, salving her conscience; she did not want to play with Marian, now. Well, what had I expected? I had tried to discourage her, hadn't I?

Turning, I saw Marian. How long had she been there? How much had she understood? Her eyes were following Freda—for a moment, surprised, I thought she was sorry to see the gate open and close. But I decided I had been mistaken. She never wanted to play with other children.

Then, speaking rapidly 'on her fingers' as Freda had put it, Marian said,

'Mother, would you rather have her than me?'

Deeply shocked, I put my arms round her. She had sensed my desire for a child without her handicap . . . she had been bitterly hurt. . . . Did that account, partly, for her great unhappiness, her sense of inadequacy, in the world of other children? Oh, my darling, my best-loved—and this time I did not add, after all. It came to me at last how much my love meant to her—so much more than it would have meant to Freda, who was so well-equipped to look after herself. I pressed my lips on the shining dark hair, and finally and forever my foolish longings died.

When I released her, she looked at me intently for a minute. Then, seemingly satisfied, she ran outside with Christabel. I finished my letter—cheerfully, in spite of the chaos of my thoughts—and went upstairs, to prepare for the afternoon shopping.

When I came down, half-an-hour later, Freda was in the garden with Marian. She had brought her own dolls over; the 'class' seemed larger and brighter, and had a comfortable air. Marian, the Headmistress, sat in her 'office'; Freda, as Assistant Teacher, pretended to consult her, and made notes in a little book. She looked up, carelessly, when she saw me.

'I said I could play "Schools",' she remarked.

MORLEY CALLAGHAN

Last Spring They Came Over

ALFRED BOWLES came to Canada from England and got
a job on a Toronto paper. He was a young fellow with
clear, blue eyes and heavy pimples on the lower part of his
face, the son of a Baptist minister whose family was too large
for his salary. He got thirty dollars a week on the paper and
said it was surprisingly good screw to start. For five a week he
got an attic room in a brick house painted brown on Mutual
Street. He ate his meals in a quick-lunch near the office. He
bought a cane and a light-gray fedora.

He wasn't a good reporter but was inoffensive and obliging.
After he had been working two weeks the fellows took it for
granted he would be fired in a little while and were nice to
him, liking the way the most trifling occurrences surprised
him. He was happy to carry his cane on his arm and wear the
fedora at a jaunty angle, quite the reporter. He liked to explain
that he was doing well. He wrote home about it.

When they put him doing night police he felt important,
phoning the fire department, hospitals, and police stations,
trying to be efficient. He was getting along all right. It was
disappointing when after a week the assistant city editor, Mr.
H. J. Brownson, warned him to phone his home if anything
important happened, and he would have another man cover it.
But Bowles got to like hearing the weary, irritable voice of the
assistant city editor called from his bed at three o'clock in the
morning. He liked to politely call Mr. Brownson as often and
as late as possible, thinking it a bit of good fun.

Alfred wrote long letters to his brother and to his father, the
Baptist minister, using a typewriter, carefully tapping the
keys, occasionally laughing to himself. In a month's time he
had written six letters describing the long city room, the fat
belly of the city editor, and the bad words the night editor
used when speaking of the Orangemen.

The night editor took a fancy to him because of the astounding puerility of his political opinions. Alfred was always willing to talk pompously of the British Empire policing the world and about all Catholics being aliens, and the future of Ireland and Canada resting with the Orangemen. He flung his arms wide and talked in the hoarse voice of a bad actor, but no one would have thought of taking him seriously. He was merely having a dandy time. The night editor liked him because he was such a nice boy.

Then Alfred's brother came out from the Old Country, and got a job on the same paper. Some of the men started talking about cheap cockney labourers crowding the good guys out of the jobs, but Harry Bowles was frankly glad to get the thirty a week. It never occurred to him that he had a funny idea of good money. With his first pay he bought a derby hat, a pair of spats, and a cane, but even though his face was clear and had a good colour he never looked as nice as his younger brother because his heavy nose curved up at the end. The landlady on Mutual Street moved a double bed into Alfred's room and Harry slept with his brother.

The days passed with many good times together. At first it was awkward that Alfred should be working at night and his brother in the day-time, but Harry was pleased to come down to the office every night at eleven and they went down the street to the hotel that didn't bother about Prohibition. They drank a few glasses of good beer. It became a kind of rite that had to be performed carefully. Harry would put his left foot and Alfred his right foot on the rail and leaning an elbow on the bar they would slowly survey the zigzag line of frothing glasses the length of the long bar. Men jostled them for a place at the foot-rail.

And Alfred said: 'Well, a bit of luck.'

Harry grinning and raising his glass said: 'Righto.'

'It's the stuff that heals.'

'Down she goes.'

'It helps the night along.'

'Fill them up again.'

'Toodleoo.'

Then they would walk out of the crowded bar-room, vaguely pleased with themselves. Walking slowly and erectly along the street they talked with assurance, a mutual respect for each other's opinion making it merely an exchange of information. They talked of the Englishman in Canada, comparing his lot with that of the Englishman in South Africa and India. They had never travelled but to ask what they knew of strange lands would have made one feel uncomfortable; it was better to take it for granted that the Bowles boys knew all about the ends of the earth and had judged them carefully, for in their eyes was the light of far-away places. Once in a while, after walking a block or two, one of the brothers would say he would damn well like to see India and the other would say it would be simply topping.

After work and on Sundays they took a look at the places they had heard about in the city. One Sunday they got up in good time and took the boat to Niagara. Their father had written asking if they had seen the Falls and would they send some souvenirs. That day they had as nice a time as a man would want to have. Standing near the pipe-rail a little way from the hotel that overlooks the Falls they watched the water-line just before the drop, smooth as a long strip of bevelled glass, and Harry compared it favourably with a cataract in the Himalayas and a giant waterfall in Africa, just above the Congo. They took a car along the gorge and getting off near the whirlpool, picked out a little hollow near a big rock at the top of the embankment where the grass was lush and green. They stretched themselves out with hats tilted over their eyes for sunshades. The river whirled below. They talked about the funny ways of Mr. Brownson and his short fat legs and about the crazy women who fainted at the lifted hand of the faith healer who was in the city for the week. They liked the distant rumble of the Falls. They agreed to try and save a lot of money and go west to the Pacific in a year's time. They never mentioned trying to get a raise in pay.

Afterwards they each wrote home about the trip, sending the souvenirs.

Neither one was doing well on the paper. Harry wasn't

much good because he hated writing the plain copy and it was
hard for him to be strictly accurate. He liked telling a good
tale but it never occurred to him that he was deliberately
lying. He imagined a thing and straightway felt it to be true.
But it never occurred to Alfred to depart from the truth. He
was accurate but lazy, never knowing when he was really
working. He was taken off night police and for two weeks
helped a man do courts at the City Hall. He got to know the
boys at the press gallery, who smiled at his naïve sincerity and
thought him a decent chap, without making up their minds
about him. Every noon-hour Harry came to the press gallery
and the brothers, sitting at typewriters, wrote long letters all
about the country and the people, anything interesting, and
after exchanging letters, tilted back in their swivel chairs,
laughing out loud. Heaven only knows who got the letters
in the long run. Neither one when in the press gallery seemed
to write anything for the paper.

Some of the men tried kidding Alfred, teasing him about
women, asking if he found the girls in this country to his
liking; but he seemed to enjoy it more than they did. Seriously
he explained that he had never met a girl in this country,
but they looked very nice. Once Alfred and Bun Brophy, a
red-headed fellow with a sharp tongue who did City Hall for
the paper, were alone in the gallery. Brophy had in his hands
a big picture of five girls in masquerade costumes. Without
explaining that he loved one of the girls Brophy asked Bowles
which of the lot was the prettiest.

'You want me to settle that,' said Alfred, grinning and
waving his pipe. He very deliberately selected a demure little
girl with a shy smile.

Brophy was disappointed. 'Don't you think this one is
pretty?'—a colourful, bold-looking girl.

'Well, she's all right in her way, but she's too vivacious. I'll
take this one. I like them kittenish,' Alfred said.

Brophy wanted to start an argument but Alfred said it was
neither here nor there. He really didn't like women.

'You mean to say you never step out?' Brophy said.

'I've never seemed to mix with them,' he said, adding that

the whole business didn't matter because he liked boys much better.

The men in the press room heard about it and some suggested nasty things to Alfred. It was hard to tease him when he wouldn't be serious. Sometimes they asked if he took Harry out walking in the evenings. Brophy called them the heavy lovers. The brothers didn't mind because they thought the fellows were having a little fun.

In the fall Harry was fired. The editor in a nice note said that he was satisfied Mr. H. W. Bowles could not adapt himself to their methods. But everybody wondered why he hadn't been fired sooner. He was no good on the paper.

The brothers smiled, shrugged their shoulders and went on living together. Alfred still had his job. Every noon-hour in the City Hall press room they were together, writing letters.

Time passed and the weather got cold. Alfred's heavy coat came from the Old Country and he gave his vest and a thin sweater to Harry, who had only a light spring coat. As the weather got colder Harry buttoned his coat higher up on his throat and even though he looked cold he was neat as a pin with his derby and cane.

Then Alfred lost his job. The editor, disgusted, called him a fool. For the first time since coming over last spring he felt hurt, something inside him was hurt and he told his brother about it, wanting to know why people acted in such a way. He said he had been doing night police. On the way over to No. 1 station very late Thursday night he had met two men from other papers. They told him about a big fire earlier in the evening just about the time when Alfred was accustomed to going to the hotel to have a drink with his brother. They were willing to give all the details and Alfred thankfully shook hands with them and hurried back to the office to write the story. Next morning the assistant city editor phoned Alfred and asked how it was the morning papers missed the story. Alfred tried to explain but Mr. Brownson said he was a damn fool for not phoning the police and making sure instead of trying to make the paper look like a pack of fools printing a fake story. The fellows who had kidded him said that too.

Alfred kept asking his brother why the fellows had to do it. He seemed to be losing a good feeling for people.

Still the brothers appeared at noontime in the press room. They didn't write so many letters. They were agreeable, cheerful, on good terms with everybody. Bun Brophy every day asked how they were doing and they felt at home there. Harry would stand for a while watching the checker game always in progress, knowing that if he stood staring intently at the black and red squares, watching every deliberate move, he would be asked to sit in when it was necessary that one of the players make the rounds in the hall. Once Brophy gave Harry his place and walked over to the window where Alfred stood watching the fleet of automobiles arranged in a square in the courtyard. The police wagon with a load of drunks was backing toward the cells.

'Say, Alfie, I often wonder how you guys manage,' he said.

'Oh, first rate.'

'Well, you ought to be in a bad way by now.'

'Oh no, we have solved the problem,' said Alfred in a grand way, grinning, as if talking about the British Empire.

He was eager to tell how they did it. There was a store in their block where a package of tobacco could be got for five cents; they did their own cooking and were able to live on five dollars a week.

'What about coming over and having tea with us sometimes?' Alfred said. He was decidedly on his uppers but he asked Brophy to visit them and have tea.

Brophy, abashed, suggested the three of them go over to the café and have a little toast. Harry talked volubly on the way over and while having coffee. He was really a better talker than his brother. They sat in an arm-chair lunch, gripped the handles of their thick mugs, and talked about religion. The brothers were sons of a Baptist minister but never thought of going to church. It seemed that Brophy had travelled a lot during war-time and afterwards in Asia Minor and India. He was telling about a great golden temple of the Sikhs at Amritsar and Harry listened carefully, asking many questions. Then they talked about newspapers until Harry started talking about the East, slowly feeling his way. All of a sudden he told about standing on a height of land near Amritsar, looking down at a temple. It couldn't have been so but he would have it that Brophy and he had seen the same temple and he described the country in the words Brophy had used. When he talked that way you actually believed that he had seen the temple.

Alfred liked listening to his brother but he said finally: 'Religion is a funny business. I tell you it's a funny business.' And for the time being no one would have thought of talking seriously about religion. Alfred had a casual way of making a cherished belief or opinion seem unimportant, a way of dismissing even the bright yarns of his brother.

After that afternoon in the café Brophy never saw Harry. Alfred came often to the City Hall but never mentioned his brother. Someone said maybe Harry had a job but Alfred laughed and said no such luck in this country, explaining casually that Harry had a bit of a cold and was resting up. In the passing days Alfred came only once in a while to the City Hall, writing his letter without enthusiasm.

The press men would have tried to help the brothers if they had heard Harry was sick. They were entirely ignorant of the matter. On a Friday afternoon at three-thirty Alfred came into the gallery and, smiling apologetically, told Brophy that his brother was dead; the funeral was to be in three-quarters of an hour; would he mind coming? It was pneumonia, he added. Brophy, looking hard at Alfred, put on his hat and coat and they went out.

It was a poor funeral. The hearse went on before along the way to the Anglican cemetery that overlooks the ravine. One old cab followed behind. There had been a heavy fall of snow in the morning, and the slush on the pavement was thick. Alfred and Brophy sat in the old cab, silent. Alfred was leaning forward, his chin resting on his hands, the cane acting as a support, and the heavy pimples stood out on the lower part of his white face. Brophy was uncomfortable and chilly but he mopped his shining forehead with a big handkerchief. The window was open and the air was cold and damp.

Alfred politely asked how Mrs. Brophy was doing. Then he asked about Mr. Brownson.

'Oh, he's fine,' Brophy said. He wanted to close the window but it would have been necessary to move Alfred so he sat huddled in the corner, shivering.

Alfred asked suddenly if funerals didn't leave a bad taste in the mouth and Brophy, surprised, started talking absently about that golden temple of the Sikhs in India. Alfred appeared interested until they got to the cemetery. He said suddenly he would have to take a look at the temple one fine day.

They buried Harry Bowles in a grave in the paupers' section on a slippery slope of the hill. The earth was hard and chunky and it thumped down on the coffin case. It snowed a little near the end.

On the way along the narrow, slippery foot-path up the hill Alfred thanked Brophy for being thoughtful enough to come to the funeral. There was little to say. They shook hands and went different ways.

After a day or two Alfred again appeared in the press room. He watched the checker game, congratulated the winner and then wrote home. The men were sympathetic and said it was too bad about his brother. And he smiled cheerfully and said they were good fellows. In a little while he seemed to have convinced them that nothing important had really happened.

His last cent must have gone to the undertaker, for he was particular about paying bills, but he seemed to get along all right. Occasionally he did a little work for the paper, a story from a night assignment when the editor thought the staff was being overworked.

One afternoon at two-thirty in the press gallery Brophy saw the last of Alfred, who was sucking his pipe, his feet up on a desk, wanting to be amused. Brophy asked if anything had turned up. In a playful, resigned tone, his eye on the big clock, Alfred said he had until three to join the Air Force. They wouldn't take him, he said, unless he let them know by three.

Brophy said, 'How will you like that?'

'I don't fancy it.'

NESS

'But you're going through.'

'Well, I'm not sure. Something else may come along.' It was a quarter to three and he was sitting there waiting for a job to turn up before three.

No one saw him after that, but he didn't join the Air Force. Someone in the gallery said that wherever he went he probably wrote home as soon as he got there.

NORAH LOFTS
Forty Years On

J OHN BULLYER and I met for the first time in 1956 when
we were both in our early sixties, but it is true to say
that he did more to shape my life than any other person,
and is largely responsible for the diffidence which has, I
know, been a handicap to me, though I am told that I conceal
it very well.

John Bullyer came into my life when my Uncle George,
who lived close by us, married, rather late in life, a most
delightful woman who thus became my Aunt Carrie and
quite my favourite relative. In those days wholesale in-
dulgence of the young had not yet come into full fashion,
and a pretty aunt always free with caresses, sweets, words of
praise and excuses for misdoings was something of a rarity
and greatly to be treasured. For me she had but one draw-
back; she was also aunt to John Bullyer, the son of her sister
who lived in Gloucestershire. She invariably referred to him
as 'Little-John-my-other-nephew' all in one word, and she
referred to him far too often.

Later in my life I could see her motive; she came to us as
a stranger; my mother was a relative by marriage, a near
neighbour and a potential friend; we children were common
ground, a safe topic for those early, difficult conversations
over the teacups.

From Aunt Carrie's point of view it was fortunate, from
mine, disastrous, that John Bullyer and I were of comparable
age, practically twins, in fact, having been born within four
days of one another. Probably hundreds of comparisons were
made before I became aware of them. The first that I remember
with any clarity was made soon after I began school where I
had lain on the floor and wailed that I wanted to go home.
Shortly after that my mother reported in a voice that was to
become all too familiar, that Little-John-Aunt-Carrie's-other-

nephew had started school on the same day and taken to it like a duck to water.

And so it went on. Incredible boy, he knew his nine-times table while I was still hopelessly bogged in the fours; he was dealing expertly with fractions what time I wrestled unsuccessfully with tens and units. I began to dread Aunt Carrie's erstwhile most welcome visits. She was still just as pretty and gay, still as sweet-smelling, still ready to take part in any childish game, to be enthusiastic about any pursuit, certain to produce chocolate or sixpence from her reticule; but, as soon as she had gone, Mother was sure to say the dread words:

'Aunt Carrie was telling me that John Bullyer . . .'

The comparisons were, without exception, to my detriment. The wretched boy never set foot upon a football field without scoring a goal; never took bat in hand without making some notable number of runs. I was hopeless at games; at football I fell in the mud, and caught a cold which became bronchial; at cricket I made ducks, dropped easy catches and was afflicted with nose-bleeding. I became so conscious of my inferiority that even when I overheard my parents speak of John Bullyer as 'The Child Wonder' I never even suspected the irony; I took it literally and believed that they regarded him with the same awe and envy as I did.

To me it seemed sinister that Mother always passed on, with pitiable pride, any small achievement of mine. Once, at my prep. school, I had a story in the magazine and Mother was momentarily jubilant.

'I must have another copy of that,' she said, 'so that Aunt Carrie can send it for John Bullyer's mother to see.' What a boomerang that proved! By return of post came the news that John had won a scholarship.

To anyone now on the bright side of forty it will seem strange that we boys never met, but in those days Gloucestershire was as far removed, in travelling time, from Suffolk, as New York is today, and my father was a man who preferred his own bed to any other. Aunt Carrie kept saying, 'Really, you boys should know one another, I'm sure you'd be such friends,' and once or twice she tried to arrange that John should stay with her in the holidays. Mercifully for me something always prevented him from doing so.

I did have, however, one horribly narrow escape. An elderly couple, distant relatives of my father's, were celebrating their Golden Wedding. They lived in London, reasonably accessible, and they issued such a pressing, sentimentally-worded·invitation that even Father was bound to accept. As soon as he had done so Aunt Carrie came over in a state of high excitement. Wasn't the world a small place, the Bullyer family and Father's old relatives had once been near neighbours and all three Bullyers had been bidden to the feast.

I saw my mother look at me, not, I admit, with any lessening of affection, but with a strange, anxious appraisement. When Aunt Carrie had gone Mother said to me:

'You sit there huddled over a book until your back is bent like a bow. Go out and get some air.' I stood up, obediently, and she added, 'Oh, I wish the sun would shine; you look so much better with a little tan.' I realised from that that she and I visualised John Bullyer in the same way, tall, big for his age, straight as a ram-rod, with a handsome brown face and hair like the man pictured on Father's bottle of hair tonic.

Walking made no perceptible difference to my posture and the sun remained disobliging, so Mother, like the practical believer in self-help that she was, tried another tack:

'You'll need a new suit at Easter anyway, you might as well have it now. *And* I'm going to find a different barber. I *cannot* believe that that piece of hair would stick up like that if it were properly cut.'

It was plain to me that I was repulsive to look at as well as being a clown at games and a booby at arithmetic.

On the evening before we were to make our early morning start for London, Mother came into my room and made me try on the new suit. I could see, by the expression on her face, that it worked no miracle. Nor, alas, had the new barber. But Mother did not take defeat easily; looks weren't everything, my manners, at least, should pass muster! So while I glumly divested myself of the wasted suit, she gave me a few final instructions. I kept saying, 'Yes, Mother' and 'No, Mother', and 'I'll remember, Mother', and gritted my teeth together until my jaws ached.

'Have you anything in your mouth *now*?' she demanded.

'No, Mother.'

'Well, hurry into bed and get a good night's sleep.' (Everything looks better in the morning!) She kissed me, fondly, but at the same time she stroked down the obstinate tuft of hair. I felt exactly like a very ugly dog of low pedigree which some doting owner has entered for a show!

I did not sleep well; I had, in fact, the worst night I had ever known. Although I had ceased gritting my teeth my jaws still ached. The pain spread up into my head, back into my ears, down into my throat. With the covers over me I broke into a hot sweat, when I pushed them off deadly chills shook me. In addition to my physical woes I had mental agonies, including that first sad loss of simple faith; I had prayed, as never before, that something might occur to prevent this meeting. The smallest excuse would have served; Father was already regretting his acceptance, he would have seized gladly at any chance to retract it.

I saw the dawn that morning, watched my window grow grey, heard the first bird chorus. After several centuries had dragged by I heard the strident alarm go off in my parents' room and thankfully rose from my bed of torment. I felt little, if any, better when I was on my feet. I washed more thoroughly than usual, hopefully plunging the whole of my stuffy-feeling head into the cold water; then I dressed and, in honour of the occasion, went to the looking glass to arrange my tie. For a moment, I swear, I thought that nervousness had affected my eyesight; the face that looked back at me was a dreadful caricature of my own, only just recognisable. My ears, ordinarily so prominent, were hidden by the bulge of my jaws and I seemed to have no neck.

Horrified I reeled into my parents' room; Mother was settling a beribboned corset-cover over her bosom and Father was gloomily stropping his razor.

'Do *you* think I look funny this morning?' I blurted.

They both turned. Mother screamed. Father said:
'I wouldn't say *funny*. You look damned peculiar.'
It was mumps. It left me very open-minded about prayer.

Aunt Carrie thought it a great pity that John and I could
not go to the same public school; I was spared that by the
intransigence of our respective fathers. Harrow, in its charity,
accepted my unpromising self; John took his talents to
Winchester.

Time went on; so did the comparisons. By word of mouth
during the holidays, by phrases that leaped out of letters
during term time, I was kept up to date with John's prowess
and progress. Thus goaded I began at last to look round for
something that I *could* do, something at which I could excel.
When I found it I worked with a savage intensity, minding
nothing else; let this be mine, John Bullyer could have all the
rest.

I was, however, still a Grub Street hack, counting it a
good week in which I made five pounds, when John attained
some glittering appointment in India. That ability to master
the nine-times table had proved no flash-in-the-pan; he had
developed into some kind of financial wizard and was now
being 'lent' to the Maharajah of a native state whose ex-
chequer was in a deplorable tangle. There was a paragraph
in the daily papers about it.

Aunt Carrie took the cutting to show to my mother. I was
glad later that she had that pleasure, for that was her last
visit, her last report. She was dead before her other nephew
reached his destination. The line which had for so many
years vibrated between Gloucestershire and Suffolk was life-
less and dumb.

Three or-four times during the next forty years I saw
mention of John Bullyer in the press. His was not the kind of
career to attract much publicity but those rare paragraphs
charted a steady success which culminated in a knighthood
when he retired in 1956. On that occasion there was a half
column about him; it said that his last job, the handling of
some currency crisis in a young South American Republic,

had forestalled a revolution. When asked, in an interview, what he intended to do with his leisure, Sir John replied, 'I hope to take up golf; I have never had time to take it seriously.' I pictured him again, lean and tanned, with a head of well kept grey hair, getting his handicap down in record time. I was sorry that Aunt Carrie could not cut out that half column, sorry too that there was no photograph; I could have looked at it almost unflinching, I thought. I was, by that time, not unsuccessful in my own line.

Late that year, in November, I was in my club, sipping a glass of sherry before dinner. A rather deprecating cough at my elbow made me look round. I saw a short stout man, a round dumpling of a man, glitteringly bald, with a little snub nose that looked too small to support the framework of his heavy glasses. They were of that peculiarly thick kind which reduce the eyes to pin-points. Diffidently, with more than a suggestion of a stammer, he spoke my name and I somewhat grudgingly admitted my identity. Since I attained some measure of fame I have on occasion been accosted by strangers and no matter how flatteringly they speak I am always horribly embarrassed.

'You d-don't know m-me,' said the little man. 'My name's John B-Bullyer. We once sh-shared an aunt, C-Caroline Lacey.'

I leaped up and shook hands, expressing my pleasure at meeting him at last, and then we settled down to drink sherry together. His stammer, like my shyness, soon wore off.

'I used to hear so *much* about you,' he said with a grin. 'Then I learned that you were a member here and I could not resist asking someone to point you out to me. Though, if you'd looked the least bit as I always imagined I don't think I'd have d-dared to approach you. You see . . . I grew up with the idea that you were at least eight feet tall, tremendously handsome and more talented than da Vinci.' His grin broadened—and I knew why! 'Really,' he said, 'the letters Aunt Carrie used to write about you and the way my mother used to read them out. You were the b-bug-bear of my life.'

'They were nothing,' I said, 'to the letters *your* mother used to write about *you*. I was told every time you got a sum right. I always thought of you as nine feet high, better looking than Robert Taylor and more versatile than Churchill. So they played the game both ways, did they?'

We laughed.

'But it was worse for me,' he said. 'I've always been under-sized, and I always had these.' He touched his glasses. 'And there were you, tall and handsome, with *such* nice manners. And so clever too. I had to do something; and all I could ever do was sums, and jolly well kill myself at games in an effort to be popular. I might almost say,' he said, with something like resentment, 'that because of you I've been doing sums all my life!'

'Substitute spinning yarns for doing sums and you have exactly my story,' I said.

We looked at one another. Then it probably dawned on us both that the place in which we sat is not the haunt of men who have been failures in life, and that, boys being what they are, an occasional prod in the rear is no such bad thing. Together we lifted our glasses, and though neither of us spoke, I know that we drank to the memory of Aunt Carrie.

DAVID OWOYELE

The Will of Allah

THERE had been a clear moon. Now the night was dark. Dogo glanced up at the night sky. He saw that scudding black clouds had obscured the moon. He cleared his throat. 'Rain tonight,' he observed to his companion. Sule, his companion, did not reply immediately. He was a tall powerfully-built man. His face, as well as his companion's, was a stupid mask of ignorance. He lived by thieving as did Dogo, and just now he walked with an unaccustomed limp. 'It is wrong to say that,' Sule said after a while, fingering the long, curved sheath-knife he always wore on his upper left arm when, in his own words, he was 'on duty'. A similar cruel-looking object adorned the arm of his comrade. 'How can you be sure?' 'Sure?' said Dogo, annoyance and impatience in his voice. Dogo is the local word for tall. This man was thick-set, short and squat, anything but tall. He pointed one hand up at the scurrying clouds. 'You only want to look up there. A lot of rain has fallen in my life: those up there are rain clouds.'

They walked on in silence for a while. The dull red lights of the big town glowed in crooked lines behind them. Few people were abroad, for it was already past midnight. About half a mile ahead of them the native town, their destination, sprawled in the night. Not a single electric light bulb glowed on its crooked streets. This regrettable fact suited the books of the two men perfectly. 'You are not Allah,' said Sule at last. 'You may not assert.'

Sule was a hardened criminal. Crime was his livelihood, he had told the judge this during his last trial that had earned him a short stretch in jail. 'Society must be protected from characters like you,' he could still hear the stern judge intoning in the hushed court-room. Sule had stood in the dock, erect, unashamed, unimpressed; he'd heard it all before. 'You and your type constitute a threat to life and property and this court will always see to it that you get your just deserts, according to the law.' The judge had then fixed him with a stern gaze, which Sule coolly returned: he had stared into too many so-called stern judges' eyes to be easily intimidated. Besides, he feared nothing and no one except Allah. The judge thrust his legal chin forward. 'Do you never pause to consider that the road of crime leads only to frustration, punishment, and suffering? You look fit enough for anything. Why don't you try your hand at·earning an honest living for a change?' Sule had shrugged his broad shoulders. 'I earn my living the only way I know,' he said. 'The only way I've chosen.' The judge had sat back, dismayed. Then he leaned forward to try again. 'Is it beyond you to see anything wrong in thieving, burglary, crime?' Again Sule had shrugged. 'The way I earn my living I find quite satisfactory.' 'Satisfactory!' exclaimed the judge, and a wave of whispering swept over the court. The judge stopped this with a rap of his gavel. 'Do you find it satisfactory to break the law?' 'I've no choice,' said Sule. 'The law is a nuisance. It keeps getting in one's way.' 'Constant arrest and imprisonment—do you find it satisfactory to be a jail-bird?' queried the judge, frowning most severely. 'Every calling has its hazards,' replied Sule philosophically. The judge mopped his face. 'Well, my man, you cannot break the law. You can only attempt to break it. And you will only end up by getting broken.' Sule nodded. 'We have a saying like that,' he remarked conversationally. 'He who attempts to shake a stump only shakes himself.' He glanced up at the frowning judge. 'Something like a thick stump—the law, eh?' The judge had given him three months. Sule had shrugged. 'The will of Allah be done. . . .'

A darting tongue of lightning lit up the overcast night sky for a second. Sule glanced up. 'Sure, it looks like rain. But you do not say: It will rain. You are only a mortal. You only say: If it is the will of Allah, it will rain.' Sule was a deeply religious man, according to his lights. His religion forbade being dogmatic or prophetic about the future, about anything. His fear of Allah was quite genuine. It was his firm conviction that Allah left the question of a means of livelihood for each man to

decide for himself. Allah, he was sure, gives some people more
than they need so that others with too little could help themselves to some of it. It could certainly not be the intention of
Allah that some stomachs remain empty while others are
overstuffed.

Dogo snorted. He had served prison sentences in all the
major towns in the country. Prison had become for him a home
from home. Like his companion in crime, he feared no man;
but unlike him, he had no religion other than self-preserva-
tion. 'You and your religion,' he said in derision. 'A lot of
good it has done you.' Sule did not reply. Dogo knew from
experience that Sule was touchy about his religion, and the
first intimation he would get that Sule had lost his temper
would be a blow on the head. The two men never pretended
that their partnership had anything to do with love or friend-
ship or any other luxurious idea; they operated together when
their prison sentences allowed because they found it convenient. In a partnership that each believed was for his own
special benefit, there could be no fancy code of conduct.

'Did you see the woman tonight?' Dogo asked, changing the
subject, not because he was afraid of Sule's displeasure, but
because his grasshopper mind had switched to something else.
'Uh-huh,' grunted Sule. 'Well?' said Dogo, when he did not
go on. 'Bastard!' said Sule without any passion. 'Who? Me?'
said Dogo thinly. 'We were talking about the woman,' replied
Sule.

They got to a small stream. Sule stopped, washed his arms
and legs, his clean-shaven head. Dogo squatted on the bank,
sharpening his sheath-knife on a stone. 'Where do you think
you are going?' 'To yonder village,' said Sule, rinsing out his
mouth. 'Didn't know you had a sweetheart there,' said Dogo.
'I'm not going to any woman,' said Sule.

'I am going to collect stray odds and ends—if it is the will of
Allah.' 'To steal, you mean?' suggested Dogo. 'Yes,' conceded
Sule. He straightened himself, pointed a brawny arm at
Dogo: 'You are a burglar too . . . and a bastard besides.'

Dogo, calmly testing the edge of the knife on his arm,
nodded. 'Is that part of your religion, washing in midnight

streams?' Sule didn't reply until he had climbed on to the further bank, 'Wash when you find a stream; for when you cross another is entirely in the hands of Allah.' He limped off, Dogo following him. 'Why did you call her a bastard?' Dogo asked. 'Because she is one.' 'Why?' 'She told me she sold the coat and the black bag for only fifteen shillings.' He glanced down and sideways at his companion. 'I suppose you got on to her before I did and told her what to say?' 'I've not laid eyes on her for a week,' protested Dogo. 'The coat is fairly old. Fifteen shillings sounds all right to me. I think she has done very well indeed.' 'No doubt,' said Sule. He didn't believe Dogo. 'I'd think the same way if I'd already shared part of the proceeds with her. . . .'

Dogo said nothing. Sule was always suspicious of him, and he returned the compliment willingly. Sometimes their suspicion of each other was groundless, other times not. Dogo shrugged. 'I don't know what you are talking about.' 'No. I don't suppose you would,' said Sule drily. 'All I'm interested in is my share,' went on Dogo. 'Your second share, you mean,' said Sule. 'You'll both get your share—you cheating son without a father, as well as that howling devil of a woman.' He paused before he added, 'She stabbed me in the thigh—the bitch.' Dogo chuckled softly to himself. 'I've been wondering about that limp of yours. Put a knife in your thigh, did she? Odd, isn't it?' Sule glanced at him sharply. 'What's odd about it?' 'You getting stabbed just for asking her to hand over the money.' 'Ask her? I didn't ask her. No earthly use asking anything of characters like that.' 'Oh?' said Dogo. 'I'd always thought all you had to do was ask. True, the coat wasn't yours. But you asked her to sell it. She's an old "fence" and ought to know that you are entitled to the money.' 'Only a fool would be content with fifteen shillings for a coat and a bag,' said Sule. 'And you are not a fool, eh?' chuckled Dogo. 'What did you do about it?' 'Beat the living daylight out of her,' rasped Sule. 'And quite right too,' commented Dogo. 'Only snag is you seem to have got more than you gave her.' He chuckled again. 'A throbbing wound is no joke,' said Sule testily. 'And who's joking? I've been stabbed in my time, too.

You can't go around at night wearing a knife and not expect to get stabbed once in a while. We should regard such things as an occupational hazard.' 'Sure,' grunted Sule. 'But that can't cure a wound.' 'No, but the hospital can,' said Dogo. 'I know. But in the hospital they ask questions before they cure you.'

They were entering the village. In front of them the broad path diverged into a series of tracks that twined away between the houses. Sule paused, briefly, took one of the paths. They walked along on silent feet, just having a look around. Not a light showed in any of the crowded mud houses. Every little hole of a window was shut or plugged, presumably against the threatening storm. A peal of languid thunder rumbled over from the east. Except for a group of goats and sheep, which rose startled at their approach, the two had the village paths to themselves. Every once in a while Sule would stop by a likely house; the two would take a careful look around; he'd look inquiringly down at his companion, who would shake his head, and they would move on.

They had been walking around for about a quarter of an hour when a brilliant flash of lightning almost burned out their eyeballs. That decided them. 'We'd better hurry,' whispered Dogo. 'The storm's almost here.' Sule said nothing. A dilapidated-looking house stood a few yards away. They walked up to it. They were not put off by its appearance. Experience had taught them that what a house looked like was no indication of what it contained. Some stinking hovels had yielded rich hauls. Dogo nodded at Sule. 'You stay outside and try to keep awake,' said Sule. He nodded at a closed window. 'You might stand near that.'

Dogo moved off to his post. Sule got busy on the crude wooden door. Even Dogo's practised ear did not detect any untoward sound, and from where he stood he couldn't tell when Sule gained entry into the house. He remained at his post for what seemed ages—it was actually a matter of minutes. Presently he saw the window at his side open slowly. He froze against the wall. But it was Sule's muscular hands that came through the window, holding out to him a biggish gourd. Dogo took the gourd and was surprised at its weight. His pulse quickened. People around here trusted gourds like this more than banks. 'The stream,' whispered Sule through the open window. Dogo understood. Hoisting the gourd on to his head, he made off at a fast trot for the stream. Sule would find his way out of the house and follow him.

He set the gourd down carefully by the stream, took off its carved lid. If this contained anything of value, he thought, he and Sule did not have to share it equally. Besides how did he know Sule had not helped himself to a little of its contents before passing it out through the window? He thrust his right hand into the gourd and the next instant he felt a vicious stab on his wrist. A sharp exclamation escaped from him as he jerked his arm out. He peered at his wrist closely then slowly and steadily he began to curse. He damned to hell and glory everything under the sun in the two languages he knew. He sat on the ground, holding his wrist, cursing softly. He heard Sule approaching and stopped. He put the lid back on the gourd and waited. 'Any trouble?' he asked when the other got to him. 'No trouble,' said Sule. Together they stooped over the gourd. Dogo had to hold his right wrist in his left hand, but he did it so Sule wouldn't notice. 'Have you opened it?' Sule asked. 'Who? Me? Oh, no!' said Dogo. Sule did not believe him and he knew it. 'What can be so heavy?' Dogo asked curiously. 'We'll see,' said Sule.

He took off the lid, thrust his hand into the gaping mouth of the gourd, and felt a sharp stab on his wrist. He whipped his hand out of the gourd. He stood up. Dogo too stood up, and for the first time Sule noticed Dogo's wrist held in the other hand. They were silent for a long time, glaring at each other. 'As you always insisted, we should go fifty-fifty in everything,' said Dogo casually. Quietly, almost inaudibly, Sule started speaking. He called Dogo every name known to obscenity. Dogo for his part was holding up his end quite well. They stopped when they had run out of names. 'I am going home,' Dogo announced. 'Wait!' said Sule. With his uninjured hand, he rummaged in his pocket, brought out a box of matches. With difficulty he struck one, held the flame over the gourd, peered in. He threw the match away. 'It is not necessary,' he said. 'Why not?' Dogo demanded. 'That in there is an angry cobra,' said Sule. The leaden feeling was creeping up his arm fast. The pain was tremendous. He sat down. 'I still don't see why I can't go home,' said Dogo. 'Have you never heard the saying that what the cobra bites dies at the foot of the cobra? The poison is that good: just perfect for sons of swine like you. You'll never make it home. Better sit down and die here.' Dogo didn't agree, but the throbbing pain forced him to sit down.

They were silent for several minutes while the lightning played around them. Finally Dogo said, 'Funny that your last haul should be a snake-charmer's gourd.' 'I think it's funnier still that it should contain a cobra, don't you?' said Sule. . . . He groaned. 'I reckon funnier things will happen before the night is done,' said Dogo. 'Uh!' he winced with pain. 'A couple of harmless deaths, for instance,' suggested Sule. 'Might as well kill the bloody snake,' said Dogo. He attempted to rise and pick up a stone from the stream; he couldn't. 'Ah, well,' he said, lying on his back. 'It doesn't matter anyway.'

The rain came pattering down. 'But why die in the rain?' he demanded angrily. 'Might help to die soaking wet if you are going straight to hell from here,' said Sule. Teeth clenched, he dragged himself to the gourd, his knife in his good hand. Closing his eyes, he thrust knife and hand into the gourd, drove vicious thrusts into the reptile's writhing body, breathing heavily all the while. When he crawled back to lie down a few minutes later the breath came whistling out of his nostrils; his arm was riddled with fang-marks; but the reptile was dead. 'That's one snake that has been charmed for the last time,' said Sule. Dogo said nothing.

Several minutes passed in silence. The poison had them securely in its fatal grip, especially Sule, who couldn't suppress a few groans. It was only a matter of seconds now. 'Pity you have to end up this way,' mumbled Dogo, his senses dulling. 'By and large, it hasn't been too bad—you thieving scoundrel!' 'I'm soaked in tears on account of you,' drawled Sule, un-utterably weary. 'This seems the end of the good old road.

But you ought to have known it had to end sometime, you rotten bastard!' He heaved a deep sigh. 'I shan't have to go up to the hospital in the morning after all,' he mumbled, touching the wound in his thigh with a trembling hand. 'Ah,' he breathed in resignation, 'the will of Allah be done.' The rain came pattering down.

ANGUS WILSON

Ten Minutes to Twelve

PALE shafts of winter sunshine lit up Lord Peacehaven's great walnut desk as he began to write; before he had ended, the gentle melancholy of twilight had driven the more acute sadness of the sunshine from the room. On the desk stood an old-fashioned brass lamp with a smoke-grimy, dark green silk shade. He snapped on the lamp switch irritably. He was a vast, heavy man—too heavy it seemed even for the substantial leather chair in which he sat. His head was square and his neck bulged thickly over his stiff collar. His cheeks, which should surely have been an apoplectic purple, were pale from a life confined indoors. Across their flabby pallor, however, ran little purple and blue veins that recalled his former unhealthy flush. His grey moustache was neatly clipped, but the thick white hair that fringed his shining bald head was perhaps a shade too long. Hairs, too, projected from the nostrils of his fleshy, pitted nose. His green-brown eyes had a melancholy, anxious look, but as he wrote they gleamed both with anger and with bitter amusement. He muttered continuously the words he was writing. The emotions his face expressed seemed unsuitable to such an old and compact looking man. Yet his pepper and salt rough tweed suit was neat and cared for, his brown brogue shoes were brightly polished. Now and again water collected at the corners of his eyelids and he wiped it away with a large Paisley silk handkerchief.

MEMORANDUM TO THE BOARD OF DIRECTORS OF HENRY BIGGS AND SON, he wrote at the top of his folio sheet of paper. And then after a pause, when he chuckled slightly—FROM THEIR CHAIRMAN. Then at the side of the paper he wrote in even larger letters TEN MINUTES TO TWELVE.

The following, he wrote on, are the *only* conditions on which I am prepared to continue to serve as Chairman. N.B.

When I say the *only* conditions, the merest simpleton (supposing there to be any such on the Board and there most certainly are) may understand what I mean and will not, I trust, waste my time by sending me *alternative* conditions or any damn fool nonsense which I will not under any conditions entertain. (This means that they will go into the waste-paper basket with all the other bumph that idiotic fools continue to bother me with.)

1. I am to have *sole* direction of Henry Biggs—the organisation which I *built up from nothing* in days before it was thought necessary for a pack of self-styled experts and interlopers to poke their noses into all sorts of business that does not concern them.

2. The direction of Henry Biggs is here intended to include any and every 'associated' or subsidiary firm whatsoever and wheresoever. (Subsidiary it should be clear to any fool means subordinate and the 'associated' firms only associated themselves because they were incapable of running their own businesses and knew that they would make greater profits if they *were* subordinated to *me*.)

3. The organisation will revert to its original name of Henry Biggs and cease to be called Henry Biggs and Son. The incorporation of 'and Son' has only led to the interference of a lot of petty officials and jacks in office who have their own interest in mind and not that of the firm. Indeed it is probable that the whole 're-organisation' of the last years was engineered solely for that purpose and *not* as was stated in the interests of my son Walter. In any case the Son has being in and through the Father. This is an IMMUTABLE MORAL LAW and nothing to do with re-organisation for efficiency, being in line with the contemporary market, the wishes of foreign customers, satisfactory labour relations or any other canting claptrap.

4. Those who do not like the conditions *must quit*. I cannot undertake to run an organisation where burkers, shirkers and the rest of it are undermining confidence behind my back. I haven't time for such pettiness and if I had I shouldn't choose to use it that way.

5. *In any case* the following gentlemen will leave the organisation forthwith—Messrs Powlett, Rutherford, Greenacre, Barton (T. C.) and (R. L.), Timperley and Garstang. They are well aware that I have done everything possible to work with them and that only their own obstinacy has prevented it.

6. THERE MUST BE UNITY.

7. The Annual dividend will be declared on my sole responsibility. I will, of course, consult the accounting branch, but it must be clearly understood that they are *an advisory body not an executive power*.

8. The wage structure of the organisation will be decided by me and by me alone. I should like to place it on record that I have the highest opinion of Trade Unions and have worked excellently with them *when they have remembered that they are a British Institution*. I do not propose to deal with foreigners or with those who ape their ways. (No names, no pack-drill.)

9. Henry Biggs always dealt in perfect harmony with customers abroad within and without the Empire while I was in sole charge. Our customers respected us because we dealt with them in good faith and *stood no nonsense*. This practice *must be reverted to*. (They were perfectly satisfied with the tune we played until we started all this business of asking them whether they wanted to hear something else. From now on we shall play 'Rule Britannia' and they will like it.) If anybody doesn't understand what this means, it can be quite simply stated in a few words: Foreign branches and the Foreign Orders branch will stem as they should from the parent tree—that is to say MYSELF.

10. The watchword of the firm will henceforth be ACTION and plenty of it. The Orders for the day will be ACTION STATIONS. Henry Biggs is a living organism and organisms must be active (Keep your bowels open is an old and true saying). Shilly shallying, red tape, passing the buck and other practices of that sort will cease.

Staff Managers will concern themselves with what concerns them, i.e. canteen arrangements, sanitary conditions and the like. Sales Managers will concern themselves with *getting sales orders. The Board will meet for action.* Everything else must be left to THE MAN AT THE TOP.

These are the *only* conditions on which I will continue to act as Chairman. *An immediate Affirmative is absolutely necessary.* Look at the top of this memorandum and you will see TEN MINUTES TO TWELVE. That means the SANDS OF TIME ARE RUNNING OUT. (Any fool knows what 'wait and see' led to with that dangerous old woman Asquith.)

The old man read the memorandum through slowly, smiled to himself and signed neatly but with a concluding flourish: Peacehaven. He then shook a small Benares ware handbell. The door opened and a sadly smiling woman of thirty-five or so appeared. 'I want you to see that this letter goes immediately, Miss Amherst,' Lord Peacehaven said. He folded it, placed it in a long envelope, addressed the envelope 'The Board of Directors. Henry Biggs' and handed it to the woman. 'Certainly, Lord Peacehaven,' she said. The old man looked suddenly tired and a little puzzled. 'And, and,' he hesitated in his speech, 'I think I should like my breakfast.'

Nurse Carver's high heels clicked along the parquet flooring of the upstairs landing. The panelling of the walls, the broad light oak staircase and the wooden railing always reminded her of a man-of-war in olden times. When she reached the large panelled lounge hall the whole family were assembled there, cocktail glasses in their hands, awaiting the summons to dinner.

Walter Biggs was standing, legs apart, warming his bottom before the red brick open log fire. His wife Diana was crouched on the long low tapestried fireside seat. They both looked up at the sound of Nurse Carver's high heels.

Walter's lined red face showed petulance at the interruption. He knocked his pipe noisily against the fireside wall and said sharply, 'Yes, nurse?'

Diana turned her swan neck towards him and frowned at his tone. She got up from the low seat, letting her lemon scarf drape around her waist and the crooks of her arms.

Old Lady Peacehaven, too, was stirred by the note in her son's voice. She sat forward on the sofa, hurriedly, slopping a little of her drink on her dove grey evening dress. Mopping it up with a little handkerchief, she said, 'How is he this evening, Carvie?' Her voice was cracked and flat; the vowels more faintly common than Cockney.

'Ready for bed, I think, Lady Peacehaven,' Nurse Carver answered, 'when he's had his supper. He seemed a little agitated earlier this afternoon, but he's done his bit of writing and that's worked it off. I shall give him a sedative though at bedtime.'

'Then I won't come up to say good-night,' the old lady decided, 'it will only unsettle him.'

Her younger son Roland's thin face twitched for a moment. He was seldom at home and he found so much there that made him want to snigger. He ran his hand over his face and through his greying fair hair, hoping that his mother had not noticed his flickering smile.

'This is the paper Lord Peacehaven wrote,' Nurse Carver announced, holding out the long envelope.

'Yes, yes,' Walter said irritably, 'I imagine you can dispose of it though.'

Nurse Carver's sad, sweet, somewhat genteel smile threatened for a moment to freeze, but she was accomplished at thawing. 'Dr. Murdoch has asked for all Lord Peacehaven's writings to be kept, Mr. Biggs,' she said, 'he wants to show them to the new specialist he's bringing down next month.'

'Oh, yes, Walter, I forgot to tell you. We're keeping all Henry's writings now.' Lady Peacehaven announced it as though it were a new school rule about exercise books. Her plump body and heavy, old grey face looked more than ever 'comfortable' as she spoke and she stroked the grey silk of her dress complacently, but she looked for a second anxiously to Nurse Carver for support.

'Good Heavens,' Walter said, 'what on earth for?' He raised his eyebrows and his red forehead wrinkled up into the scurfy patches where his ginger hair was straggly and thinning. 'Murdoch's had father's case for years. He knows everything about him. There's no possible point in fussing now unless he's trying to use the old man as a guinea pig.'

Diana fussed again with her lemon scarf. Their daughter Patience looked up for a moment from *Anna Karenina* and stared at her father as though he had sneezed over her. Their son Geoff went on reading the evening paper, but he scowled over its pages.

'I'm sure Dr. Murdoch would only do what's best for your father, wouldn't he, Carvie?' Lady Peacehaven said.

Before Nurse Carver could answer, Roland Biggs had turned towards his brother and said contemptuously, 'You love to throw around words like "guinea pig", Walter, don't you? You've no knowledge of any branch of medicine any more than of any other science. At bottom you're as frightened as any primitive savage, but a bit of bluster helps to warm the cockles of your heart.'

Walter laughed to reduce the level of his brother's words to schoolboy ragging. 'A bio-chemist naturally understands every aspect of mental disease, I suppose,' he said, and when his brother gave no answer, his laughter ceased and he added aggressively, 'Well, isn't that what you're trying to claim?' Roland hesitated for a moment whether to accept the challenge, then he said wearily, 'No, no, Walter, only that a competent, modern business man knows nothing about anything.'

'Now, Roland,' his sister-in-law said, 'you're being absurd. Lots of business men are very intelligent even if Walter isn't.'

'Oh dear,' Lady Peacehaven cried, 'if I'd spoken to Henry like that . . .' She turned to Nurse Carver, 'You'll join us to see the New Year in, won't you, Carvie?'

Now Nurse Carver allowed herself the pleasure of a genuine smile, 'Unless you think I should be with the Finns and Sicilians. What do *you* think, Mr. Biggs?' she asked Walter. He hesitated at her remark for a second before he smiled in return, but the teasing relation between them was an old one and therefore acceptable to him.

'You're reprieved from the kitchen New Year, Miss Carver,' Roland said. He hoped to emphasise the fact that Walter appeared to take charge in their mother's house—or could one still say, their father's?

Diana gave her famous little mocking chuckle. 'You're frightfully good for Walter, Carvie,' she cried. 'That was enchanting.'

Her son Geoff turned his growl on her now rather than on the newspaper. 'Why is it enchanting to attack Daddy?' he asked. A lock of black hair fell over his glasses, but the recession at the temples pointed to his father's balding pate. 'Well,' he continued quickly to prevent a remonstrance from his sister, 'if I shouldn't say that, why is it enchanting to avoid a kitchen celebration? I should have thought it was just as clever . . .'

'I don't understand,' Patience finally pulled herself out of Levin's harvesting and announced it, 'I don't understand why there has to be a kitchen New Year. Couldn't they join us?'

'Oh, my dear,' her grandmother said quickly, 'they have their own ways—all sorts of foreign customs.'

'I shouldn't have thought Finnish ways could be much like Sicilian ones,' the girl insisted.

'You heard what your grandmother said, Patience,' Walter was stern, 'she knows best about it.'

'I can't imagine anybody could know more about foreign servants than we do at Four Mile Farm.'

'How true, how sadly true,' Diana smiled across at her daughter. 'You've only had Finns and Sicilians, dear mother-in-law'—Lady Peacehaven laughed dutifully as she always did when Diana addressed her so—'we have had Portuguese, Germans, Norwegians, Swiss, Belgians and—shall we ever forget her?—a Lapp as well.'

'The Lapp,' said Walter, 'was jolly pretty.'

Girolamo came to announce dinner and the company rose. Diana and Lady Peacehaven led the way in intimate laughter about the comic vagaries of foreign domestics.

Nurse Carver stood for a moment, looking at the great Tudory lounge hall with her sad-sweet smile. Then she sniffed, laid Lord Peacehaven's memorandum on the refectory table and made her clicketing way up the broad oak staircase.

After dinner they watched television for a short while. Patience read on in *Anna Karenina*.

'She gets such a lot of television at home,' Diana said in apology to her mother-in-law.

'You speak as though I was ten, Mother, instead of nearly seventeen,' Patience said.

'I'm afraid my set isn't as good as yours.' Lady Peacehaven had strange notions of appeasement.

'I don't think its a question of sets, Mother,' Walter declared, 'its more the programmes. They're designed for a mass audience and you naturally tend to get the lowest common multiple. On the whole, that is,' he added judicially. He was essentially balanced in his outlook.

'Ah,' Roland cried delightedly, 'I see we have a new class now. There used to be those who had the tele and those who were above it. Now we have those who have the tele and are still above it. Good, Walter, good.' Patience looked up at him from her corner for a moment with interest. 'I suppose,' he went on and his tone was now as judicial as his brother's, 'that like anything else it must be used discriminatingly.' She returned to her book.

'Fisher the new history man organised some discussion groups last term,' Geoff told them. 'I said I thought television was one of the chief reasons why everything was so dead to-day. I mean it puts everybody on a level and nobody does anything about anything because they're all so used to just sitting and watching.'

'They have such a lot of discussions at school nowadays, Mother,' Diana said. Patience looked up once more in the hope that her mother might have spoken sarcastically, but she returned to her book disappointed.

Lady Peacehaven, however, was suddenly more than disappointed. Her fat, fallen cheeks flushed pink. She got up and turned off the television.

There was an astonished silence for a moment, then Roland said, 'So you think everything's dead to-day, do you Geoff?' Have you any conception of the progress that's being made in the world?' He turned on Walter. 'It ought to be made a capital crime,' he cried, 'to give people a non-scientific education these days.'

Geoff blushed red, but he glowered at his uncle and answered, 'I don't think scientific progress . . .'

But Walter had had enough. 'Why don't we play contract, Mother?' he asked. 'Geoff's even better at that than he is on the soapbox.'

The card game left Roland to pace about the room. Finally he stopped before his niece. 'Can you be persuaded for a moment to come out of your wallow in romantic adulteries and use your brain for a bit?' he asked. She looked up in surprise. 'Come on. Play a game of chess.' He sounded so like a disgruntled small boy that she burst into laughter and accepted his offer.

After some time Lady Peacehaven began to lose interest in the game of bridge. Despite Walter's pursed lips and Geoff's frown, she made desultory conversation. Diana tried to answer politely without increasing the men's annoyance.

'Nineteen fifty-five has been a very good year on the whole, hasn't it, Walter?' the old lady said, 'considering, that is, how years can be these days.' After a pause, she added, 'Of course, we've got a sensible government and that makes a difference.' Then to their horror, she said, 'I wish so much I could tell Henry that we've got a proper Conservative majority now. But then he never knew that we had those dreadful Socialists, thank God.' She sighed.

Walter seemed to feel that a comment was preferable to the charged silence. 'I can't think what on earth need Murdoch has fussing about father's papers like that,' he said testily.

Lady Peacehaven was quite sharp. 'Henry's been very restless lately,' she said; 'sometimes Carvie's found him as much as she could manage. I'm only glad Dr. Murdoch is keeping an eye on things. You don't want your father to have to go away again, Walter, I suppose.'

Walter mumbled in reply, but once or twice again he returned to the charge during the game. 'I wish Murdoch wouldn't interfere in the old man's affairs,' he said. He seemed to feel that the doctor's interest was impertinent and indecent rather than medical.

'Things seem better in Russia from what I can read,' Lady Peacehaven said. 'Of course, they're up one day and down the next.'

'I've ceased to read the papers,' Diana seemed gently to rebuke her mother-in-law, 'they're so sensational.' Lady Peacehaven smiled a little patronisingly at her daughter-in-law. 'Oh, I think one ought always to keep abreast of the times, but then I suppose when you've been at the centre of things as I was in Henry's day. . . . The Geddeses made things hum,' she added, but no one seemed to care. 'Of course these wage claims are a bit disturbing,' she told them, 'but on the whole everyone seems very happy.'

Their lack of response to public affairs came home to her at last. 'When do you go to Switzerland, Diana?' she asked.

'At the end of next week,' Diana replied. 'We shall just get a fortnight before Geoff's term begins. This mild weather isn't very promising though.'

'Saint Moritz used to be so much the place,' Lady Peacehaven said, 'but I never took you children. Henry was very much against people going abroad in winter, although, of course, he was very good when I had that attack of pneumonia in 1928. He took me all the way to Monte Carlo himself and travelled back the next day. The Blue Train it used to be.'

'No Switzerland next year,' Diana announced, glancing at Patience, 'unless Geoff goes with some party. Patience and I will stay at the flat. It's high time she had a winter of London social life.'

'Next winter,' Patience's voice came from the corner of the room, 'I shall be busy working for Oxford entrance.'

'This is a game which demands concentration,' her uncle said, 'a thing that no humanist ever has.' He frowned at his niece in mock sternness.

'Oh heavens,' Diana cried, 'don't give her any more high sounding names. She's blue stocking enough as it is. Neither of the children have *any* sense of humour.'

Geoff said, 'If Granny can attend to the game, I should think you could, Mummy.'

Walter said, 'Now Geoff!'

While he was dummy, Walter got up and fussed around the room. Finally, he picked up Lord Peacehaven's memorandum. 'You've no objection to my opening this, have you, Mother?' he asked, and before she could answer he had done so. Soon he began mumbling the words of the Memorandum to himself and now nobody's attention was really on the games.

Roland, on occasions, of course saw Lord Peacehaven, but the old man seldom recognised his son for who he was and, when he did, more often than not he remained obstinately silent. Only in his memoranda, Roland was given to understand, did he retain a kind of lucidity. Diana never saw her father-in-law, on a plea, purely evasive and generally accepted as such, that it would only upset him. In fact, she disliked the idea of someone closely related who did not know of her existence. To the young people their grandfather was an alluring mystery. Only Lady Peacehaven remained detached. In her daily contact with her husband she lived as really in the past as he did and this existence was not wholly pleasure. But for all of them the memorandum was secretly an intriguing affair.

'The old man seems to have slipped back,' Walter said crossly. 'The last time he knew me properly, I'm pretty sure I got it over to him that the firm had been part of the Development Trust for years.' He prided himself on his capacity to reach his father's comprehending powers where no one else could.

'Poor old Timperley died last month,' he said, 'he was invaluable to the firm in his day.'

'Of course, the incredible thing is,' he said, 'that, allowing for the extravagance of a lot of this, the old man *did* run the firm almost as autocratically as he writes here. He could, of course, in those days, but even before I joined him, things were getting into a ghastly mess. People just wouldn't stand for it. I well remember how we lost three or four very big

South American customers in the crisis of '31 just because of the old man's attitudes.'

'Labour relations!' he exclaimed. 'I'd like to see some of the men's faces to-day if they read this.' And he began suddenly to read the memorandum aloud from the beginning.

'Really, darling, I don't think this is quite the place . . .' Diana began. But Roland turned on her angrily, 'I think I have as much right as Walter to hear what my father has to say. Jacob had the blessing, you know, not Esau.'

'I didn't mean you,' Diana cried, but Lady Peacehaven's voice put an end to the discussion.

'I'm sure,' she said quietly, 'that there is no reason for any-one not to hear what Henry has written. The children are old enough,' she looked in turn to Patience and Geoff, 'to appre-ciate that what their grandfather writes doesn't come from his real self. He's sick in mind. But we're not ashamed of his ill-ness. It's a misfortune not a disgrace.' She smiled at Diana to show her that no one attributed her attitude to ill intention, only to ignorance.

Both Lady Peacehaven's sons seemed a little discomforted by her words; it almost appeared that Walter would not con-tinue his reading. However their mother said, 'Go on, Walter, we're waiting,' and he felt obliged to continue. As he read Lady Peacehaven sat very quietly with her hands folded as she did when anyone insisted on hearing a 'talk' on the wireless.

When he had finished, Walter said, 'I don't know. Nobody seems to realise the scope and the complication of business to-day. In father's day they could bludgeon their way through things. Nowadays it's like a sensitive precision instrument—the least faulty handling in one department and the effects may be felt right through the whole Trust. And the nation depends on it for survival,' he added, in what should surely have been a proud manner, but came out in the same grumb-ling, whining voice as the rest.

Roland smiled; he could not believe in anything depending upon his brother. 'What I find so distressing,' he said, and his tone was genuinely sad, 'is the awful note of anxiety and fear that runs right through that document. And I don't believe it's just because father's not in his right mind. I think that's what he must have always felt, with all his courage and individualism and high handedness. Of course,' he went on, 'their certainty was so limited. In fact it wasn't there. There was only a bottomless pit beneath their strength of will. I wonder how he would have managed in a world like ours where we pretty well know the answers—technical and scientific. It probably wouldn't have been any good, he would never have had the patience to wait for results, and that's the essential.'

Diana handed her glass to her husband for a refill and began to rearrange her shawl preparatory to changing the subject, but she was too late, for Geoff burst out in a loud, excited voice:

'I think it's frightfully good what grandfather says. It's perfectly true we *do* want action. I mean a lot of us at school think that. And that about making things alive instead of flat and dull and having good reasons for doing nothing. I hate all those good reasons. I don't believe he's mad at all.'

Patience sprang up from her chair. 'Don't you? I do. I think it's appalling to write like that—ordering people about and demanding power for oneself and never stopping to think properly. I hope I should always fight bullying like that whenever I met it. It's no better than Russia.'

'Why shouldn't people be ordered about?' Geoff shouted, 'if they get in the way and don't pull their weight. What's the good of being in charge if you don't give orders? Anyway it's not like Russia. You didn't listen properly. The whole point is that the firm's *English*. Grandfather said so.'

'I know,' Patience said. Her eyes were large with anger. 'That's what's so shameful. Oh, I'm sorry, Granny, but it's made me feel so ashamed.'

'I should hope so,' Walter said sternly, 'what an exhibition from both of you. You should *both* apologise to your grandmother.'

'At least,' said Roland, 'it's brought the younger generation to life.'

Diana looked horrified. 'If it takes the words of someone who isn't . . .' She stopped and put her hand on her mother-in-law's arm. 'I'm sorry,' she said.

'That's all right,' Lady Peacehaven declared, 'perhaps it wasn't a very good thing to read poor Henry's letter really. But I don't know. He always liked to raise an argument.' She took up the pack of cards and began shuffling them. 'Your grandfather had great drive, you know,' she said to the young people, 'and he worked so hard. He liked to do it all himself. He was very good to people when they fitted in with his ways. But I think Roland's right. He *was* always very anxious. He seemed to want to reassure himself that things were as he wanted them—no matter how well everything went. And he never relaxed or took a holiday. I used to go with you children,' she spoke now to Walter and Roland, 'to Angmering or Budleigh Salterton, but if he came down for a day that was as much as he could manage. One year, it must have been when you were still at St. Stephens, Roland, some parents of a boy there, I think it must have been those Capels, suggested that we should go to Thorpeness, but we never did.' She paused, realising her digression. 'Your father used to ring up though, every evening. I don't think he felt convinced that I knew how to look after you. He *couldn't* let people do things their way. It was just the same when you grew up, it wasn't that he wasn't fond of you both, but he was shy and he couldn't believe you could manage on your own. Of course, it got worse, as time went on. I ought to have seen it really. I *did* make him go for a holiday. We went to Le Touquet and stayed at the Westminster. It was very comfortable although some people said we should have stayed at the Hermitage. But Henry only stayed three days. He started so many law suits then. He *knew* that right was on his side. And so it often was, but not always. He got so angry sometimes that I could hardly recognise him, and moody too. His face seemed different. Like someone changing in a dream. One minute it's them and the next minute it's someone else. I think the first time I really realised how ill he was came about through that. It was New Year's Eve 1935.' She stopped and then said, 'Perhaps I shouldn't tell it now, but there's no sense in superstition. Henry was sent out into the garden before midnight. You know—the darkest man must come in with something green. Although Henry was already turning very grey. But when he came in again, I didn't recognise him for the moment. It seemed as though someone else had been substituted for him when he was outside. And soon after that he had that terrible scene at the "office".' She put down the cards. 'Well, this isn't at all a cheerful sort of talk for a party evening,' she said.

'No, indeed,' Roland cried. He disliked personal revelations. 'Anyhow, now it is *really* ten minutes to twelve. Where's Miss Carver?'

A moment later Nurse Carver came down the stairs. 'He's fast asleep,' she said, 'so I thought I might join the merry-makers before I go off to bed myself.' She gazed at rather sombre faces. 'Well now, Geoff,' she cried, 'I don't know whether I ought still to call you that. You're so much the man. The darkest man present too. You'll have to go outside to bring the New Year luck in.'

Geoff jumped to his feet. 'All right,' he said, 'I'll bring in 1956. You'll see. I'll make it a year of adventure and action.'

Walter was about to stop him, but Lady Peacehaven said, 'Don't be silly, Walter. Of course he can go.'

There was silence when Geoff had left them. 'He's the spit image of Lord Peacehaven, isn't he?' Nurse Carver cried, 'perhaps *he'll* grow up to be quite a great man.'

Diana shuddered. Patience came behind her mother and put her arms round her neck. She kissed her cheek.

Nurse Carver looked at the downcast features of the family with consternation. 'Only a taste of champagne for me,' she said to Walter in the brightest voice she could muster.

RHYS DAVIES

Afternoon of a Faun

No one took any notice of the ordinary, strong-legged mountain boy as he stood in truant-looking calculation on a street corner that golden October afternoon. The day-shift miners were clattering their way home; a few women scuttled, concentratedly as crabs, in and out of the shops; in the gothic-arched porch of Lloyds Bank the minister of the prosperous Baptist chapel stood brandishing an unnecessary umbrella in debate under the long, doubtful nose of the Congregational minister, whose sermons were much bleaker than his rival's. Even the constable stepping out from the police station, which had eight cells for violent men, did not rest his pink-lidded eyes on the meditating boy. The afternoon remained entirely the property of grown-ups.

A few minutes earlier, Mr. Vaughan, the headmaster, had walked into his classroom in the grey school up behind the main street. After beckoning to him from behind the big globe atlas, which had just been wheeled in for a geography lesson, Mr. Vaughan had whispered, 'You have to go home at once, Aled; your mother has sent for you. . . .' The old duffer, in that unreliable way of his, had smiled, hesitated, attempted to pat the pupil's ducking-away head; then, giving the globe —skittishly it seemed—a spin in its sickle, he had stalked off to his own quarters. Had he come with good news which, in his punishing way, he decided finally to withhold? A back-row boy had made a whinnying neigh, and Aled's own departure was accompanied by a chorused groan from the others of Standard 4: they thought he was summoned out for the usual. In those days, corporal punishment was rife in the schools, and Mr. Vaughan's only authority lay in a resined willow cane, though his incessant use of this had about as much real body as a garrulous woman's tongue. All the boys of Standard 4 despised him, unerringly divining his lack of true moral stature, unforgiving him for not being masterful as a bloody oath.

Humming like a bee with a ripe peach in its vicinity, Aled had swooped down the hill from the stone jail and come to a bouncing halt in the main street. It was a full hour before the school would close for the day, and the liberation made time prodigal. A yellow sun wallowed high above the mountains. He half guessed why he had been called from school. His father, who lately had become more bad-tempered, was due to go to Plas Mawr, the hospital and rest home for sick miners, away in another valley, and the horse-drawn ambulance van must have arrived that afternoon; no doubt his mother had gone in it too, to see his father installed. He was only needed to look after the house until she returned by train. It wasn't necessary, he decided, to hurry home just for that. Willie Dowlais' mother, who lived next door, would be keeping an eye on the house meanwhile.

But what was there to do? He gazed dreamily at the Baptist preacher, and, in the style of a pigeon-fronted old gentleman of well-behaved disposition, he took an imitative strut down the main street, hands clasped behind him, a leisurely eye cocking into shop windows. Suddenly, he halted again and, neck stretched out, advanced closer to a window of Morgan's General Emporium, stared into it intently, and loped a rapid step backwards. The afternoon lost all its festival tints.

Morgan's hotch-potch window display included a bulky black perambulator, and in this sat, among silken cushions, a most successful-looking wax baby. Cosy as a cauliflower among leaves, its face bulged out from a price-ticketed bonnet of green ribbons. A snowy diaper, also priced, dangled from a triumphantly lifted hand. Other articles relevant to worship of this enthroned pest lay scattered below its carriage—garish toys, shoes of knitted blue wool, a little pot painted with garlands of roses, and embroidered bibs to catch dribbles from that smirking and overfed mouth.

Nose puckered, he continued to stare at the omen in mesmerized suspicion. *That* was why Mr. Vaughan had twitched into a smile and attempted to pat his head! About a month ago, while she was ladling baked custard on to his plate, his mother had confided in him that he might expect either a sister or a brother soon. Although withholding comment at the time, he had not been favourable at all. The sovereignty of his reign, now in its eleventh year, had never been disputed before.

'I'm sure it's a sister you'd prefer,' his mother had added, in that deciding-for-you manner of grown-ups, and looking at him as if it was only for his comfort that this act was being done. 'She'll be company for you. . . . But, of course, they *might* send you a brother instead. They handle so many that often they get careless and stupid.'

They, they—who were these mysterious, two-faced *theys*? He didn't believe in them, they were invented by treacherous grown-ups who wanted to hide their own mistakes. He had stared angrily at the photo of his grandfather above the chiffonier, and asked, 'Why don't *they* go on strike for shorter hours or more money, like the miners do?' It was his sole pronouncement at the time.

'That's enough, Aled!' his mother had said, escaping into another of the despotisms of grown-ups. 'You're a spoilt boy. Eat your custard.'

Since then, the news had been too outlandish to preoccupy him. He turned from the grinning wax horror at last, hesitated, and stood frowning on the gutter kerb. Further brooding weighed him down. The thought of Ossie Ellis had arrived logically, and, also logically, his stomach sank lower.

Ossie, often seen obediently pushing a battered old pram— usually it contained two babies—through the streets, was the derision of his fellow pupils of Standard 4. He was seldom in the position to enjoy a cowboy Saturday in the mountains because he was obliged to stay at home to look after his brothers and sister, all unjustly younger than himself. One Saturday, when called for at his home to go on a pre-arranged spree, he had put his head round the door and said, depressingly, 'Can't come, Aled. I'm the old nanny goat again today; four to mind and feed, and one of them's going to get measles, I think.' Shirt sleeves rolled up, Ossie wore a girl's stained pinafore, and a smelly noise came out of the ramshackle house. His mother was a befeathered tartar, his father a drunkard, but Ossie, always solemn behind steel-rimmed spectacles, never took umbrage when taunted by Standard 4 with his kowtowing to domestic tyranny.

'Do a bunk from home some day,' Aled advised, on another thwarted occasion. 'Run away and get lost all night—that will teach them.'

Ossie had blinked owlishly, and said, 'No, it won't. But I'll never get married, Al.'

'Nor me,' Aled had said, without just cause then.

He looked up. The pink-lidded eyes of the policeman, who was patrolling the main street in the usual suspicious manner of his kind, rested assessingly on him now. Without further delay, Aled turned on his heel, walked with laborious meekness up the street, and vanished into a quiet turning. But he hurried down the rough-stoned, deserted alleyway which lay in a homewards direction, leading to the bridge that he crossed twice a day, to and from school. He looked back over his shoulder furtively. It was as though the golden day had darkened into night and avenging footsteps plodded behind him, like the feet of pursuit in a nasty dream.

Forebodings of drastically curtailed pleasures, of assaults to dignity, bereft his sandalled hooves of their usual nimble leap as he climbed the gritty steps which led to the old iron foot-bridge. On the top step he paused to gaze up at the bluish green mountains encircling the valley. It was a look of fare-well. He was a great lover, even in winter, of the coarse high-ways and byways in the mountains; he knew their secrecies as shrewdly as the rams and ewes inhabiting those antique places. A baby's perambulator could never reach them.

Ahead, on the shivering middle span of the old bridge, tramped a last day-shift miner. The rickety Victorian structure linked, with three long, nervously zigzagged spans, two hillside communities. It was a short cut for pedestrians, and it crossed the big, sprawling colliery yard. In winter storms uneasy people avoided it. Two pit shafts, aerial wheels whirling, towered a quarter mile up the narrowing valley.

Downwards, lay a long view of swirls of mountain flank retreating from the valley in flowing waves ungrimed as a sea.

He began to increase his step, after a last backwards glance. The miner ahead had stopped to peer over the bridge railing —the colliery yard ended just there with a steep 'tip', down which rubble, slag and useless coal-dust from the pits was thrown every day—and Aled, when he reached him, stopped to peer down too, looking through an opening in the trellised ironwork.

What he saw below made him grip the railings. The afternoon flowered.

'His back got broken,' the old miner said, noticing the boy standing beside him. 'There's been a fall of roof down in Number 2 pit today. They had to stun him to put him out of his misery.' His voice was casual, and his hands hung from the dirtily ragged sleeves of his pit jacket like crumpled shapes of old black paper. For a miner, he looked frail and ghostly.

Aled drew away for a moment and, astounded, asked, 'They are going to throw him on the tip?'

'No. The wagon will be shunted back after they've emptied the stuff from the others. He was called Victor in Number 2.' The miner, his face anonymous in its mask of negroid dust, looked at the boy again. The whites of his eyes shone glossy as candlewax. 'Dan Owen's boy, aren't you?' he asked. 'How's your dad getting on?'

'He's going to Plas Mawr,' Aled replied, inattentive, a foot jerking in excited impatience. Why didn't the man go?

'Oh, aye. A good place for them.'

The miner tramped off unconcerned. The middle span quaked under his studded boots. Expert as a squirrel, Aled scrambled up the railing and sat on the shaky ledge. Now he could view unimpeded the train of four small-size wagons below. It had run on a narrow gauge track from the pit shafts and stood drawn up to the tip's edge. But no labourer was in attendance. A horse lay in the end wagon. The boy sat rigid. All the wealth of the Indies might have been below in the monotonous yard.

If only because of its size, a collapsed horse is an arresting

spectacle, and this one—he was of the cob breed suited to the
pits—had been dumped into a wagon much too mean for his
awkward proportions. From the chained body a foreleg was
thrust up stiffly into the air. The long neck, a sorrel gush under
the dishevelled, grit-dulled mane, hung inert over the wagon's
end. But the staid profile of the head could be seen, its eye
open in a dull, purposeless fixity. Gaunt teeth showed yellow
under lips drawn back as if in a snarl, and from the mouth
dripped—yes!—an icicle of purplish fluid. Victor looked an
old horse. Had he been stunned on that bone inset so strongly
down the long, desolate face?

No one crossed the bridge now, no one was visible in the
whole yard. All the smashed horse was his. He stared down
calculatingly, wanting to retain the exclusiveness of this treat,
jealously store this gala exhibit. An item from an elementary
school lesson of the past returned to him; *The horse is a quad-
ruped, a beast of burden, and a friend to man,* and he felt a brief
compassion. Everybody spoke well of horses. He remembered
seeing a couple of young ones trotting in fastidious energy,
tossing their bright manes, as they were led up the valley for
their life down in the pits. Horses dragged the small wagons of
coal from the facings to the bottom of the pit shafts, and he had
heard that when they were brought up for retirement, or to be
sent to the knackers, they could no longer see clearly in daylight: they would stand bewildered at the pit-head, neighing in
chagrin, lost from their warm, dim-lit stables deep under the
earth. . . .

He jerked up his head, glanced swiftly at the sky, swivelled
round on the ledge, made a clean jump, and galloped over the
bridge. Willie Dowlais' camera! The light would be good for a
long time yet, but the horse might be removed at any moment.
With snapshots of this treasure in his possession he would be a
prince among the other boys.

Anxiety began as he leapt the far steps and it occurred to
him that Mrs. Dowlais the Parrot might not be at home or,
alternatively, would be unwilling to lend Willie's camera.

Springing up the path on the slope, above which the piled

streets and terraces began, he heard Angharad Watkins singing as she pegged washing on a rope in the tilted, flower-cushioned garden of her old cottage, which stood isolated on the slope. She called to him when he stampeded past her gate, but he only waved an impatient hand; they were old friends and he owed money in her amateur shop. Above, the length of Noddfa Terrace was abolished in a flash.

On the corner of Salem Street, swarthy old Barney Window Panes shouted his customary, 'Hey, boy, know anyone with a broken window?' Barney was also called The Wandering Jew, because, with a load of glass pieces strapped to his bowed, homeless-looking back, he tramped over the mountains, never using trains even after sunset, and no one knew where he lived. He gave pennies to boys for information of people's broken windows. Although Aled knew of a couple, he dashed past heedlessly, rounding the corner into the empty roadway of Salem Street in champion galloping style.

His shouted name brought him to an abrupt halt. The call home! He had forgotten about it. He stood poised in the road, glaring sidewise towards the open door of his home, a leg still lifted. 'There you are at last!' Aunt Sarah's voice cried, further. 'Come here, Aled. You've taken a long time!'

Why was *she* there? She stood just inside the doorway with Willie Dowlais' mother. He lowered his leg and, cautiously, approached them. 'What do you want?' he demanded, his voice rising to a shout—'I've got to go back to school. . . . For the geography!'

Mrs. Dowlais the Parrot—as, usually, she was called—gave Aunt Sarah a bunch of the chrysanthemums which grew in her back garden and waddled past him silently to her own door: he watched her go in despair. Aunt Sarah never failed in reducing him to a surly feeling of guilt. She lived across the bridge, in the fashionable part, and always looked as though she had been awarded medals all her life. The owner of five terrace houses, and an influential member of the Baptist chapel, she sang solo in the chapel's famous annual performance of Handel's *Messiah*, heaving herself out of her seat on the specially erected platform, when her items came, and growing twice her size as she gave vent. Even now, statuesque, she stood as if expecting applause that she was there.

His kingdom came toppling down. He had forgotten about her, too, and anguish became more acute as he realized she would have been called across the valley for such a ceremonious event as the arrival of a baby. The usurper *had* arrived!

'Come in, Aled,' Aunt Sarah said, her voice different. He edged a step or two inside the doorway, avoiding her hand and throwing a glance of extreme anxiety in the tip's direction. 'Your father asked for you,' she said. 'He has left us.'

'Gone to Plas Mawr?' He still breathed heavily, but half in relief now. He did not proceed further into the house. A peculiar silence, such as comes after an important departure of a person, lurked about the interior.

'No.' Aunt Sarah's pince-nez glimmered down on him. 'He died this afternoon, Aled.' She added, in comforting afterthought, 'You wouldn't have arrived here in time, in any case.'

'Died?' The word dropped down his throat like a swallowed sweet. He stared at her. 'Why?'

'Why?' The familiar, other tone returned. 'He had a relapse. . . . A haemorrhage.' She used the word importantly and, noticing his uncomprehending stare, added, 'His lungs, my boy. The silicosis.'

Silicosis. It was a word he knew well. The blight word of the valley. Some men of the pits stayed at home with the disease for years, living on the compensation money paid by the colliery owners; others went to Plas Mawr for cure or not. Men got it from breathing the gritty dust of the pits. Now and again, in streets or shops, he had heard gossiping women relate, 'The test says he's got it hundred per cent.' Or it would be the gamble of eighty per cent; or a more cheerful fifty. Even men who were cured never went down the pits again, and always there were others, younger, coming up the valley to take their places.

'Your mother is upstairs with him,' Aunt Sarah said, returning to her grown-up oblivion. She bunched the neighbour's chrysanthemums and began to mount the staircase. Her voluminous grey skirt swished majestically.

'Shall I come up?' he mumbled, stretching his neck as he advanced. He wanted a cup of water.

'No; wait,' she replied, not turning. 'I'll call you when we're ready.'

He stood baulked before the staircase, gazing up. The sense of frustration became more desperate. That unfamiliar silence came down the stairs like an exhalation; it made his scalp contract. Yet he could hear the gentle press of feet shifting across the floor above. Then he heard his mother's voice—it sounded both swollen and hollow—saying, 'Give me the sponge, Sarah.' He made a headlong plunge to the open front door.

A new agony, as he banged on the neighbour's door, was the sudden thought that there would be no roll of negatives in the camera, though he knew Willie had bought one on Saturday. Mrs. Dowlais the Parrot was ages in answering the bang. 'Yes, Aled?' she said, bending a puce ear closer, as if she hadn't heard his immediate babbling request. 'Your mother wants something?'

'Willie's camera——' he panted.

'Willie's camera!' Her eyes widened in astonishment. Within the house, her aged parrot gave a squawk that sounded mocking.

His feet strutted on the doorstep like a dancer's. But he sensed that she was willing to grant any request because of what had happened next door. 'I've got to take photos of a horse on the tip, before it's taken away!' he shouted. 'For school! We're having lessons about horses. Willie said I could borrow his camera. . . . The CAMERA!'

His crescendo yell did not upset her. A comfortable woman, very esteemed in the valley, she waddled and sighed her way into her sympathetically darkened house, its blinds down. She rummaged there for an unbearably long time. A whine came from him when he snatched the camera from her hand. Running, he examined the indicator of the black, ten-shilling box, saw that only three negatives had been used, and streaked round Salem Street corner. The Wandering Jew was still there, sunk in reverie, waiting for informing boys to come from

school. In the sky the delicate mountain-blue of early October
had darkened a shade.

He had scrambled down to the yard by a workmen's path
on the slope and, chest bursting in foreboding of this last
frustration, arrived at the exact place below the bridge.
But the horse was gone. The three wagons of waste stuff
remained. But, again, no labourer was visible. He could have
gone in pursuit of the shunted wagon; the man in charge
would have understood this special flouting of the *Trespassers
will be Prosecuted* notices posted at the yard's main entrances.
He did not move. All desire to photograph the horse left him.

A fanfare of approaching yells made him start into attention, and, immediately, he dashed to the shadows under the
bridge. The boys were out of school. They stampeded over
the spans in whooping droves. Leaning against a trembling
stanchion, he listened to their cries as though hearing them
for the first time, and with no wish for their confederacy now.
The last feet pattered away into the distance. Still, passive
and exhausted, he lingered in the hiding place, looking at a
heap of mildew-green tree trunks maturing for use down in the
pits. He knew, now, that he would never brag to the boys
about the horse, never even mention it. He could hear them—
'Hark at Al! . . . You saw a dead horse, eh? Shoved into a little
wagon on top of the tip! Purple stuff dropping from his mouth,
eh? Sure he didn't have billiard balls for teeth, too?'

The yard stretched unfamiliarly silent and deserted. Had
he really seen a horse? Had a man with an unknown, dustily
black face spoken to him on the bridge, and asked a question
about his father? It seemed a long time ago, though yellow
sunlight still splashed on the tenacious clumps of seeded thistles
and thorn bushes growing from this grit-thick waste ground.
He looked about him vaguely. It no longer seemed unusual
that he had not seen a labourer. This closed territory, where he
trespassed, was not the same yard which he viewed daily from
the footbridge. It was his first visit to below.

When he came from the hiding place he stood irresolutely
on the tip's crest. The sun, veering towards a mountain, had

become a deeper gold; a seagull visitant winged through a shaft of thickening light, returning down the quiet valley to its coastal haunts. People were gathering into their houses. He took a few slow steps homewards, stopped, and moodily kicked a piece of slag down the tip.

Forgetful of prosecution, he stood looking everywhere but in the direction of his home. A rope of lazily flapping coloured garments caught his eye—Angharad's washing, hung above a spread of dahlias, chrysanthemums and Michaelmas daisies. He hesitated, remembering his debt, then slowly crossed the yard and scrambled up a slope to the path beside which her old, silverstone cottage stood alone, the only one remaining from the valley's remote rural days.

Angharad's grandmother had left the house as a legacy to her, together with its litter of pigs and a cow. After the funeral, about a year ago, she instantly got rid of the pigs and cow and almost as instantly married Emlyn Watkins, a sailor conveniently home on leave from the Royal Navy. But Aled could never think of her as a woman shut-up properly by a wedding: she didn't have that style.

A chewing woman customer, chronically married-looking and with a ponderous goitre, came out of the cottage. To companion herself during Emlyn's long absences—she had no children to bother her, so far—Angharad had opened a shop in her front parlour, the stock consisting mainly of confectionery, cheap remedies for sicknesses, household oddments, and cigarettes for workmen dashing in off the colliery yard. Credit was allowed some children, who were selected emotionally and not according to social prestige. He owed her for three lots of stopjaw toffee, a bag of marbles, and two cartons of chalk crayons.

A dramatic soprano shriek greeted him as he walked into the odorous parlour. 'Aled!' Anghared cried, 'I've only just heard about it from Mrs. Price the Goitre!' And, full-based, down she collapsed to a chair behind the big table, which was heaped with open boxes of sweets, satchels and bottles of stuff for toothache, bellyache and headache, culinary herbs, pencils and cotton reels, cards of hairpins, illustrated packets of flower seeds, and the kitchen scales of burnished brass on which she usually gave very good measure to favoured children. 'Another good man gone!' she wailed. 'It's wicked.' She might have been bewailing loss at sea of her own husband.

A chair, for gossiping, stood on the customer's side of her well-spread table. Aled sat on its edge, eyeing a newly-opened box of Turkish Delight. The rose and yellow chunks, elegantly perfumed and pearl-dusted, were always beyond his means. He felt he was there under false pretences. Why had he come?

'They're upstairs with him,' he mumbled, waiting for her outburst to subside, but also relieved by it.

'I'd close all the damned pits!' she went on, shrilly. 'Or make people dig for their own dirty coal!' Momentarily the origin of all sorrow, she yet managed to remain lavish as a lot of lambs gambolling on a hillock. A tight heliotrope frock, stamped with a design of pineapples and pale shells, held her body in precarious bondage.

He dreaded that she would ask him what he wanted—the room, after all, was a shop. Simmering down in her abuse of the pits, she peeped at him out of the corner of her blue eyes. At random, he said, 'My mother made a lemon jelly this morning—she said it would set in time for his tea. Dad liked lemon jelly. . . .' He lapsed into pondering. Because of all that was going on upstairs, he thought, no one would prepare a meal now, and the jelly would remain forgotten in the cool place under the kitchen sink.

Angharad's woe entirely ceased. She dabbed at her fresh-coloured face with a man's large handkerchief, and invited, 'Take a piece of Turkish Delight.' When, slowly, he shook his head, she urged, 'Aled, I'll let you off your account. You don't owe me anything!' She jabbed a tiny gift fork into a yellow chunk and, smiling, held it out.

'My Aunt Sarah is there,' he said, taking the honey-soft chunk. He heard the hiss of the goose-grey bombazine skirt going upstairs.

'*She's* got a good voice in the *Messiah*.' Angharad wagged her head. 'Too loud and showy for my taste, though.' She pushed a piece of Turkish Delight into her own mouth, which, shaped like a clover-leaf, was surprisingly small.

He sat back. The scented luxuriance melted in his mouth. 'She's always criticising me,' he remarked.

'A rose one this time?' Angharad held out another chunk, dismissing Aunt Sarah. A drop of juice, like a golden ooze from fruit, came from the corner of her mouth, and for a moment, staring, he remembered the horse. 'It's what they eat in harems in the East,' she said, and she, too, eating a rose piece, seemed to purr in understanding of women reclining lazy in satin bloomers on a marble floor. 'But these are made in Bristol,' she said.

'Have you been in a harem?' he asked, exact.

'No, certainly not! And neither has Emlyn, though his ship's been to the East.' Angharad remained amiably regal as her ancient name.

No one came in to buy: everybody, by that time, was gathered about the routine teapot and a plate of bread and butter. Angharad, after giving him another peeping glance, placed the lacefrilled box of Turkish Delight in a position convenient to both of them, and took a letter from a fat cookery book lying on the table. 'From Emlyn!' she whispered, confidentially. 'I'll read it to you. . . . Help yourself,' she said, pointing.

It was a long letter, and she read it in leisurely gratification, a hand reaching occasionally for Turkish Delight. Emlyn seemed to be exceedingly fond of her and interrupted anecdotes of life in ship and port to reiterate, like the last line in a ballad's verses, *'Angharad, girl—roll on, Christmas leave! You'll have to shut shop then!'* Once or twice, she paused to omit something, shaking her head and peeping at her guest.

Interest in Emlyn's ramblings dwindled from him. He watched her hand playing with beads distributed about her freckled throat, where it went into her sleepy-looking chest. Vaguely he thought of something tucked-in and warm, and, for some reason, he remembered the speckled thrush's egg which he and Willie Dowlais had taken from a nest last spring: the startling private warmth of the nest, as he put his hand in it, returned to him.

She folded the letter at last and gave a heave, murmuring, 'Home by Christmas! My big Santa Claus. . . .' She started, looked at Aled guiltily, craned her neck, and squealed, 'My God, we've eaten the whole boxful! Seven shillings' worth, at cost price! No wonder Emlyn always asks me what I've done with my profits.'

Aled said, rapidly. 'I've got a loan of this camera. I thought I'd take photos of you, to . . . to send to Emlyn.' He glanced at the window. 'We'll have to be quick.'

She jumped up with alacrity, crying, 'Oh yes, yes! But let me get my new hat and fur.'

Willie Dowlais would need appeasing for this unsanctioned use—far less understandable than for the eccentric treasure of a dead horse—of his roll of negatives. They hurried into the garden. He took nine shots of her, among the explosive dahlias, lolling chrysanthemums and dried washing; for some he, the expert in charge, commanded her to remove the cygnet-winged hat of Edwardian dimensions which was balanced on a head which always he had trusted. She posed with proud docility. The cherry-red sun leaned on a mountain top. He guessed the prints would be dim.

'Sailor though he is, Emlyn will break down and cry, when he sees me among my dahlias and washing!' Angharad, after stretching a hand to feel if a pale blue nightdress had thoroughly dried, began to pluck the freshest dahlias and chrysanthemums. 'But serve him right for joining the Navy!' She turned, quickly. 'All the same, Aled, don't go down the pits when you grow up! Join the Navy. It's healthier.'

He wound the completed rolls, and said, 'There was a dead horse on the tip this afternoon. I was going to take photos of it. But it had disappeared. . . .' His voice loitered and his eyes wandered in the tip's direction.

Angharad paused, turned to look at him again, then only remarked, 'Well, better a live woman inside that box than a dead horse, don't you think?'

Her face was serious, but, within the clear eyes, smiled.

She began to walk towards him, flowers—milky purple, golden, sorrel-red, russet, deep claret—in the crook of her arm. As, vaguely, he stood watching her approach, the apparition came again. But, now, the defeated neck, the dead eye, the snarling yellow teeth, the mouth from which thick liquid dropped, were like glimpses recalled from a long-ago dream . . . Angharad had come close to him; he did not look up to her face. Her right hand pressed his head into her, under the breast. He seemed to smell a mingle of earthily prosperous flowers, sweets and herbs, and warm flesh. She had to pull his head away by the hair.

'Aled,' she said. 'I've kept you too long. You must go home now. You'll be needed.'

'Yes,' he agreed, waking.

'Take these flowers with you?' she suggested.

He shook his head, definitely. 'No; I can't carry flowers through the streets.'

'What!' But she smiled at once, and, walking down the garden with him, only said, 'Men!'

'Bring them up to the house tonight?' he invited, adding, without dubiousness, 'My mother is going to have a baby.'

'Aren't you lucky!' Angharad said, unsurprised. 'When my time comes, you'll be able to advise me how to bring them up.' At the garden gate, she promised, 'I'll come up tonight with the flowers.'

'You can have the prints on Saturday,' he shouted from the slope, waving the camera.

The sun was slipping out of sight. Grey dusk already smudged the valley's far reaches. Soon, the air would stir under the crescent moon's rise, with the evening star sparkling in clear attendance. He hurried, without anxiety.

GEORGE LAMMING

A Wedding in Spring

LONDON was their first lesson in cities. The solitude and hugeness of the place had joined their lives more closely than ever; but it was the force of similar childhoods which now threatened to separate them: three men and a woman, island people from the Caribbean, who waited in separate rooms of the same basement, sharing the nervousness of the night.

The wedding was only a day away.

Snooker thought he could hear the sweat spilling out of his pores. Talking to himself, old-woman-like in trouble, he started: 'Is downright, absolute stupid to make me harness myself in dis mornin' costume. . . . I ain't no Prince Philip or ever want to be. . . .'

A pause drew his attention to the morning suit he had rented. The top hat sat on its crown, almost imitating itself. It provoked Snooker. He watched it, swore at it, then stooped as though he was going to sit on it.

'Now what you think you doin'?'

Snooker was alerted. He heard the closing creak of the door and the blurred chuckle of Knickerbocker's voice redeeming the status of the top hat.

Snooker was silent. He watched Knickerbocker hold the top hat out like some extraordinary fruit in his hand.

'Is what Beresford think it is at all?' he said, turning his back on the suit to face Knickerbocker. 'My body, not to mention my face, ain't shape for dis kind o' get-up.'

'Even de beggar can be king,' said Knickerbocker, 'an' dis is de kind o' headpiece kings does wear.' He cuddled the top hat to his chest. 'An' tomorrow,' he added, lifting his head towards Snooker, 'I goin' to play king.'

'You goin' to play jackass,' Snooker said sharply.

'So what?' Knickerbocker smiled. 'Christ did ride on one.'

'Is ride these clothes goin' ride you tomorrow,' said Snooker,
' 'cause you ain't got no practice in wearin' them.'

'You goin' see who ride what,' said Knickerbocker,' I sittin'
in de back o' dat limousine jus' so, watch me, Snooker.' He
was determined to prove his passion for formal dress. He had
lowered his body on to the chair, fitting the top hat on his head
at precisely the angle his imagination had shaped. He crossed
his legs, and plucked at the imaginary seams of his morning
trousers. The chair leaned with him while he felt the air for the
leather rest which would hold his hand.

Snooker refused to look. But Knickerbocker had already
entered the fantasy which the wedding would make real. His
head was loud with bells and his eyes turned wild round the
crowd, hilarious with praise, as they acknowledged his white
gloved welcome. Even the police had removed their helmets
in homage to the splendour which he had brought to a drab
and enfeebled London. He was teaching the English their own
tune. So he didn't hear Snooker's warning until the leather
rest refused his hand and the crowd vanished into the shadows
which filled the room. The chair had collapsed like a pack of
cards under Knickerbocker's body. He looked like a cripple
on his back.

Now he was afraid, and he really frightened Snooker too, the
way he probed his hands with fearful certainty under and
across his thighs. His guess was right. There was a split the
size of a sword running down the leg and through the crutch
of the only pair of trousers he owned.

'You break up my bes' chair,' Snooker said sadly, carrying
the top hat like wet crockery across the room. It had fallen into
the sink.

The crisis had begun. Knickerbocker crouched on all fours,
his buttocks cocked at the mirror, to measure the damage he
had done. The basement was still: Knickerbocker considering
his black exposure while Snooker collected the wreckage in
both hands, wondering how he could fit his chair together
again. They didn't speak, but they could hear, behind the door,
a quiet tumble of furniture, and after an interval of silence, the
sullen ticking of the clock in Flo's room.

QESS

She was alone, twisting her hair into knotty plaits that rose
like spikes out of her skull. She did not only disapprove of her
brother's wedding but she also thought it a conspiracy against
all they had learnt. Preoccupied and disdainful, she saw the
Vaseline melt and slip like frying lard over her hands. The last
plait done, she stuck the comb like a plough into the low shrub
of hair at the back of her neck. She scrubbed her ears with her
thumb; stretched the under lid of each eye to tell her health;
and finally gave her bottom a belligerent slap with both hands.
She was in a fighting mood.

'As if he ain't done born poor,' she said, caught in that
whispering self-talk which filled the basement night. 'Borrow-
in' an' hockin' every piece o' possession to make a fool o'
himself, an' worse still dat he should go sell Snooker his bicycle
to rent mornin' suit an' limousine. Gran Gran. . . . Gawd res'
her in de grave, would go wild if she know what Beresford
doin' . . . an' for what . . . for who he bringin' his own down-
fall.'

It was probably too late to make Beresford change his mind:
what with all those West Indians he had asked to drop in after
the ceremony for a drink: the Jamaican with the macaw face
who arrived by chance every Sunday at supper time, and
Caruso, the calypsonian, who made his living by turning every
rumour into a song that could scandalise your name for life.
She was afraid of Caruso, with his malicious tongue, and his
sly, secretive, slanderous manner. Moreover, Caruso never
travelled without his gang: Slip Disk, Toodles and Square
Dick; then there were Lice-Preserver, Gunner, Crim, Clarke
Gable Number Two, and the young Sir Winston. They were all
from 'back home', idle, godless, and greedy. Then she reflected
that they were not really idle. They worked with Beresford in
the same tyre factory.

'But idle or no idle,' she frowned, 'I ain't want Beresford
marry no white woman. If there goin' be any disgrace, let me
disgrace him first.'

She was plotting against the wedding. She wanted to bribe
Snooker and Knickerbocker into a sudden disagreement with
her brother. Knickerbocker's disapproval would have been

particularly damaging since it was he who had introduced the English girl to Beresford. And there was something else about Knickerbocker that Flo knew.

The door opened on Snooker who was waiting in the passage for Knickerbocker. Flo watched him in the dark and counted three before leaning her hand on his head. Her anger had given way to a superb display of weakness: a woman outraged, defenceless, and innocent of words which could tell her feeling.

'Snooker.'

'What happen now?'

'I want all you two speak to Beresford,' she said. Her voice was a whimper appropriate with grief.

'Let the man make his own bed,' said Snooker, 'is he got to lie down in it.'

'But is this Englan' turn his head an' make him lose his senses.' Flo crouched lower, tightening her hand against Snooker's neck.

'He keep his head all right,' said Snooker, 'but is the way he hearken what his mother say, like he walkin' in infancy all life long.'

'Ma wasn't ever goin' encourage him in trouble like this,' Flo said.

'Is too late to change anything,' said Snooker, 'except these kiss-me-tail mornin' clothes. Is like playin' ju-ju warrior with all that silk cravat an' fish-shape' frock they call a coat. I ain't wearin' it.'

'Forget 'bout that,' said Flo, 'is the whole thing we got to stop complete.'

Knickerbocker was slipping through the shadows, silent and massive as a wall which now rose behind Flo. The light made a white mask over his face. Flo seemed to feel her failure, sudden and complete. Knickerbocker had brought a different kind of trouble. He was fingering the safety-pins which closed the gap in his trousers. He trusted Flo's opinion in these details. He stooped forward and turned to let her judge whether he had done a good job.

'Move your tail out of my face,' she shouted, 'what the hell you take me for?'

Knickerbocker looked hurt. He raised his body to full height, bringing his hands shamefully over the safety-pins. He couldn't understand Flo's fury: the angry and unwarranted rebuke, the petulant slam of the door in his face. And Snooker wouldn't talk. They stood in the dark like dogs shut out.

Beresford was waiting in the end room. He looked tipsy and a little vacant under the light; but he had heard Flo's voice echoing down the passage, and he knew the others were near. It was his wish that they should join him for a drink. He watched the bottle making splinters with the light, sugar brown and green, over the three glasses and a cup. The label had lost its lettering; so he turned to the broken envelope on his stomach and went on talking to himself.

All night that voice had made dialogue with itself about his bride. His mood was reflective, nostalgic. He needed comfort, and he turned to read his mother's letter again.

. . . concernin the lady in question you must choose like i would have you in respect to caracter an so forth. i excuse and forgive your long silence since courtship i know takes time. pay my wellmeanin and prayerful respects to the lady in question. give flo my love and my remembrance to snooker and knick. . . .

The light was swimming under his eyes; the words seemed to harden and slip off the page. He thought of Flo and wished she would try to share his mother's approval.

. . . if the weddin come to pass, see that you dress proper, i mean real proper, like the folks in that land would have you. hope you keepin the bike in good condition. . . .

The page had fallen from his hand in a moment of distraction. He was beginning to regret that he had sold the bicycle to Snooker. But his mood didn't last. He heard a knock on the door and saw Knickerbocker's head emerge through the light.

'Help yuhself, Knick.'

Beresford squeezed the letter into his pocket while he watched Knickerbocker close in on the table.

'I go take one,' Knickerbocker said, 'just one.'

'Get a next glass if the cup don't suit you.'

'Any vessel will do,' Knickerbocker said.

Knickerbocker poured rum like water as though his arm could not understand the size of a drink. They touched cup and glass, making twisted faces when the rum started its course down their throats.

'Where Snooker?'

'Puttin' up the bike,' Knickerbocker said. 'But Flo in a rage.'

'She'll come round all right,' said Beresford. 'Is just that she in two minds, one for me an' one 'gainst the wedding.'

'You fix up for the limousine?'

'Flo self do it this mornin',' said Beresford, 'they comin' for half pas' four.'

'Who goin' partner me if Flo don't come to the church?'

'Flo goin' go all right,' said Beresford.

'But you never can know with Flo.'

Beresford looked doubtful, but he had to postpone his misgivings.

Knickerbocker poured more rum to avoid further talk, and Beresford held out his glass. They understood the pause. Now they were quiet, rehearsing the day that was so near. The room in half light and liquor was preparing them for melancholy: two men of similar tastes temporarily spared the intrusion of female company. They were a club whose rules were part of their instinct.

'Snooker ask me to swap places wid him,' Knickerbocker said.

'He don't want to be my best man?' Beresford asked.

'He ain't feel friendly with the morning suit,' Knickerbocker said.

'But what is proper is proper.'

'Is what I say too,' Knickerbocker agreed. 'If you doin' a thing, you mus' do it as the done thing is doed.'

Beresford considered this change. He was open to any suggestion.

'Snooker or you, it ain't make no difference,' he said.

'Then I goin' course wid you to de altar,' Knickerbocker said.

Was it the rum or the intimacy of their talk which had dulled their senses? They hadn't heard the door open and they couldn't guess how long Flo had been standing there, rigid as wire, with hands akimbo, and her head, bull shaped, feeding on some scheme that would undo their plans.

'Get yuhself a glass, Flo,' Beresford offered.

'Not me, Berry, thanks all the same.'

'What you put your face in mournin' like that for?' Knickerbocker said. He was trying to relieve the tension with his banter. 'Those whom God join together . . .'

'What you callin' God in this for?' Flo charged. 'It ain't God join my brother wid any hawk-nose English woman. Is his stupid excitement.'

'There ain't nothin' wrong wid the chick,' Knickerbocker parried.

'Chick, my eye!' Flo was advancing towards them. 'He let a little piece o' left-over white tail put him in heat.'

'Flo!'

Beresford's glass had fallen to the floor. He was standing, erect, wilful, his hands nervous and eager for action. Knickerbocker thought he would hit her.

'Don't you threaten me wid any look you lookin',' Flo challenged him. 'Knickerbocker, here, know what I sayin' is true. Look him good in his face an' ask him why he ain't marry her.'

'Take it easy, Flo, take it easy,' Knickerbocker cautioned. 'Beresford marryin' 'cause he don't want to roam wild like a bush beast in this London jungle.'

'An' she, you know where she been roamin' all this time?' Flo answered. Knickerbocker fumbled for the cup.

'Is jus' what Seven Foot Walker tell you back in Port-o'-Spain,' Beresford threw in.

Whatever the English girl's past, Beresford felt he had to defend his woman's honour. His hands were now steady as stone watching Flo wince as she waited to hear him through.

'That man take you for a long ride, Flo, an' then he drop you like a latch key that won't fit no more. You been in mournin' ever since that mornin' he turn tail an' lef' you waitin'.

An' is why you set yuh scorpion tongue on my English woman.'

'Me an' Seven Foot Walker . . .'

'Yes, you an' Seven Foot Walker!'

'Take it easy,' Knickerbocker begged them. 'Take it easy . . .'

'I goin' to tell you, Berry, I goin' to tell you . . .'

'Take it easy,' Knickerbocker pleaded, 'take it easy . . .'

Flo was equipped for this kind of war. Her eyes were points of flame and her tongue was tight and her memory like an ally demanding vengeance was ready with malice. She was going to murder them with her knowledge of what had happened between Knickerbocker and the English girl. Time, place, and circumstance: they were weapons which now loitered in her memory waiting for release. She was bursting with passion and spite. Knickerbocker felt his loyalty waver. He was worried. But Flo's words never came. The door opened and Snooker walked in casual as a bird, making music on his old guitar. He was humming: 'Nobody knows the trouble I've seen'. And his indifference was like a reprieve.

'The limousine man outside to see you,' he said. 'Somebody got to make some kind o' down payment.'

The crisis had been postponed.

London had never seen anything like it before. The spring was decisive, a hard, clear sky and the huge sun naked as a skull eating through the shadows of the afternoon. High up on the balcony of a fifth-floor flat an elderly man with a distressful paunch was feeding birdseed to a flock of pigeons. He hated foreigners and noise, but the day had done something to his temper. He was feeling fine. The pigeons soon flew away, cruising in circles above the enormous crowd which kept watch outside the church; then closed their ranks and settled one by one over the familiar steeple.

The weather was right; but the crowd, irreverent and forgetful in their fun, had misjudged the meaning of the day. The legend of English reticence was stone-cold dead. An old-age pensioner with no teeth at all couldn't stop laughing to the chorus, a thousand times chuckled: 'Cor bli'me, look at my

lads.' He would say, ' 'Ere comes a next in 'is tails, smashers the
lot o' them,' and then: 'Cor bli'me, look at my lads.' A con-
tingent of Cypriots on their way to the Colonial Office had
folded their banners to pause for a moment that turned to
hours outside the church. The Irish were irrepressible with
welcome. Someone burst a balloon, and two small boys, swift
and effortless as a breeze, opened their fists and watched the
firecrackers join in the gradual hysteria of the day.

Snooker wished the crowd away; yet he was beyond anger.
Sullen and reluctant as he seemed he had remained loyal to
Beresford's wish. His mind alternated between worrying and
wondering why the order of events had changed. It was half
an hour since he had arrived with the bride. Her parents had
refused at the last moment to have anything to do with the
wedding, and Snooker accepted to take her father's place. He
saw himself transferred from one role to another; but the
second seemed more urgent. It was the intimacy of their childhood, his and Beresford's, which had coaxed him into wearing
the morning suit. He had to make sure that the bride would
keep her promise. But Beresford had not arrived; nor Knickerbocker, nor Flo.

Snooker remembered fragments of the argument in the basement room the night before; and he tried to avoid any thought
of Flo. He looked round the church and the boys from 'back
home' looked at him and he knew they, too, were puzzled.
They were all there: Caruso, Slip Disk, Lice-Preserver, and an
incredibly fat woman whom they called Tiny. Behind him,
two rows away, he could hear Toodles and Square Dick
rehearsing in whispers what they had witnessed outside. There
had been some altercation at the door when the verger asked
Caruso to surrender his guitar. Tiny and Slip Disk had gone
ahead, and the verger was about to show his firmness when he
noticed Lice-Preserver who was wearing full evening dress
and a sword. The verger suddenly changed his mind and
indicated a pew, staring in terror at the sword that hung like a
frozen tail down Lice-Preserver's side. Snooker closed his eyes
and tried to pray.

But trouble was brewing outside. The West Indians had

refused to share in this impromptu picnic. They had journeyed from Brixton and Camden Town, the whole borough of Paddington and the Holloway Road, to keep faith with the boys from 'back home'. One of the Irishmen had a momentary lapse into prejudice and said something shocking about the missing bridegroom. The West Indians bristled and waited for an argument. But a dog intervened, an energetic, white poodle which kicked its hind legs up and shook its ears in frenzy at them. The poodle frisked and howled as though the air and the organ music had turned its head. Another firecracker went off, and the Irishman tried to sing his way out of a fight. But the West Indians were showing signs of a different agitation. They had become curious, attentive. They narrowed the circle to whisper their secret.

'Ain't it his sister standin' over yonder?'

They were slow to believe their own recognition.

'Is Flo, all right,' a voice answered, 'but she not dress for the wedding.'

'Seems she not goin',' a man said as though he wanted to disbelieve his suspicion.

'An' they wus so close,' the other added, 'close, close, she an' that brother.'

Flo was nervous. She stood away from the crowd, half hearing the rumour of her brother's delay. She tried to avoid the faces she knew, wondering what Beresford had decided to do. Half an hour before she left the house she had cancelled the limousine and hidden his morning suit. Now she regretted her action. She didn't want the wedding to take place, but she couldn't bear the thought of humiliating her brother before this crowd. The spectacle of the crowd was like a rebuke to her own stubbornness.

She was retreating further away. Would Beresford find the morning suit? And the limousine? He had set his heart on arriving with Knickerbocker in the limousine. She knew how fixed he was in his convictions, like his grandfather whose wedding could not proceed; had, indeed, to be postponed because he would not repeat the words: *All my worldly goods I thee endow.* He had sworn never to part with his cow. He had a thing about his cow, like Beresford and the morning suit. Puzzled, indecisive, Flo looked round at the faces, eager as they for some sign of an arrival; but it seemed she had lost her memory of the London streets.

The basement rooms were nearly half a mile from the nearest tube station; and the bus strike was on. Beresford looked defeated. He had found the morning suit, but there was no way of arranging for another limousine. Each second followed like a whole season of waiting. The two men stood in front of the house, hailing cabs, pleading for lifts.

'Is to get there,' Beresford said, 'is to get there 'fore my girl leave the church.'

'I goin' deal wid Flo,' Knickerbocker swore. 'Tomorrow or a year from tomorrow I goin' deal wid Flo.'

'How long you think they will wait?'

Beresford had dashed forward again, hailing an empty cab. The driver saw them, slowed down, and suddenly changed his mind. Knickerbocker swore again. Then: a moment of revelation.

'Tell you what,' Knickerbocker said. He looked as though he had surprised himself.

'What, what!' Beresford insisted.

'Wait here,' Knickerbocker said, rushing back to the basement room. 'I don't give a goddam. We goin' make it.'

The crowd waited outside the church, but they looked a little bored. A clock struck the half-hour. The vicar came out to the steps and looked up at the sky. The man in the fifth-floor flat was eating pork sausages and drinking tea. The pigeons were dozing. The sun leaned away and the trees sprang shadows through the early evening.

Someone said: 'It's getting on.'

It seemed that the entire crowd had agreed on an interval of silence. It was then the woman with the frisky white poodle held her breast and gasped. She had seen them: Beresford and Knickerbocker. They were arriving. It was an odd and unpredictable appearance. Head down, his shoulders arched and harnessed in the morning coat, Knickerbocker was frantically pedalling Snooker's bicycle towards the crowd. Beresford sat on the bar, clutching both top hats to his stomach. The silk cravats sailed like flags round their necks. The crowd tried to find their reaction. At first: astonishment. Later: a state of utter incomprehension.

They made a gap through which the bicycle free-wheeled towards the church. And suddenly there was applause, loud and spontaneous as thunder. The Irishman burst into song. The whole rhythm of the day had changed. A firecracker dripped flames over the church steeple and the pigeons dispersed. But crisis was always near. Knickerbocker was trying to dismount when one tail of the coat got stuck between the spokes. The other tail dangled like a bone on a string, and the impatient white poodle charged upon them. She was barking and snapping at Knickerbocker's coat tails. Beresford fell from the bar on to his knees, and the poodle caught the end of his silk cravat. It turned to threads between her teeth.

The crowd could not determine their response. They were hysterical, sympathetic. One tail of Knickerbocker's coat had been taken. He was aiming a kick at the poodle; and immediately the crowd took sides. They didn't want harm to come to the animal. The poodle stiffened her tail and stood still. She was enjoying this exercise until she saw the woman moving in behind her. There was murder in the woman's eyes. The poodle lost heart. But the top hats were her last temptation. Stiff with fright, she leapt to one side seizing them between her teeth like loaves. And she was off. The small boys shouted: 'Come back, Satire, come back!' But the poodle hadn't got very far. Her stub of tail had been safely caught between Flo's hand. The poodle was howling for release. Flo lifted the animal by the collar and shook its head like a box of bones.

Knickerbocker was clawing his rump for the missing tail of the morning coat. Beresford hung his head, swinging the silk cravat like a kitchen rag down his side. Neither could move. Flo's rage had paralysed their speech. She had captured the top hats, and it was clear that the wedding had now lost its importance for her. It was a trifle compared with her brother's disgrace.

The vicar had come out to the steps, and all the boys from 'back home' stood round him: Toodles, Caruso, and Square Dick, Slip Disk, Clarke Gable Number Two, and the young Sir Winston. Lice-Preserver was carrying the sword in his right hand. But the poodle had disappeared.

Flo stood behind her brother, dripping with tears as she fixed the top hat on his head. Neither spoke. They were too weak to resist her. She was leading them up the steps into the church. The vicar went scarlet.

'Which is the man?' he shouted. But Flo was indifferent to his fury.

'It don't matter,' she said. 'You ju' go marry my brother.'

And she walked between Knickerbocker and her brother with the vicar and the congregation of boys from 'back home' following like a funeral procession to the altar.

Outside, the crowd were quiet. In a far corner of sunlight and leaves, the poodle sat under a tree licking her paws, while the fat man from the fifth-floor flat kept repeating like an idiot to himself: 'But how, how, how extraordinary!'

BIOGRAPHICAL NOTES

BATES, HERBERT ERNEST (1905). Educated the Grammar School, Kettering. Worked as a provincial journalist and clerk before publishing first novel at the age of twenty; subsequently established an international reputation as a novelist and short-story writer. His stories are widely anthologized; his novels have been translated into sixteen languages. He has also written plays and many essays on country life. His publications include nearly twenty collections of short stories. *The Watercress Girl*, from which the selected story is taken, appeared in 1959.

CALLAGHAN, MORLEY (1903). Born in Toronto, and graduated from the University of Toronto. Is the author of six novels, an autobiographical work, and two volumes of short stories. The story by which he is represented here comes from *Stories I* (1962).

DAVIES, RHYS (1903). Educated Porth County School. Has published some two dozen books, including several volumes of short stories. The selected story comes from *The Darling of Her Heart and Other Stories* (1958).

GORDIMER, NADINE (1923). Born in South Africa, educated at Witwatersrand. Won the W. H. Smith Literary Award, 1961. Has published two novels and three volumes of short stories. The selected story is taken from *Six Feet of the Country* (1956).

HARTLEY, LESLIE POLES, C.B.E. (1895). Educated Harrow and Balliol College, Oxford. Has written literary criticism for a number of weekly reviews since 1923, but is renowned chiefly as one of the leading novelists of our day. He has also published five collections of short stories, including *Two for the River* (1961), from which the selected story is taken.

JENKINS, MAY C. Born in Morayshire, educated High School for Girls, Aberdeen, and Aberdeen University. Until recently taught English and Speech-Training; now a full-time free-lance writer. Has had poems, short stories, and articles published, and short stories and talks broadcast.

JHABVALA, R. PRAWER (1927). Born of Polish parents in Germany; came to England in 1939, and was educated here; has a University of London M.A. in English. Married an Indian architect, and now lives in Delhi. She has published five novels and a volume of short stories, *Like Birds, Like Fishes* (1962), from which the selected story is taken.

JONES, SIR LAWRENCE EVELYN, Bt., M.C., T.D., F.R.S.L. (1885–1969). Educated Eton and Balliol College, Oxford. Barrister, Inner Temple. Has published many works, including three auto-biographical volumes. The short story by which he is represented here is taken from *The Bishop's Aunt* (1961).

LAMMING, GEORGE (1927). Born in Barbados, where he was educated at Harrison College. Taught in Trinidad. Emigrated to England in 1950; worked as a free-lance broadcaster in the B.B.C. Caribbean Service for about six years. Has published four novels and a volume of travel essays. 'A Wedding in Spring' is taken from *West Indian Stories*, edited by Andrew Salkey (1960).

LAVIN, MARY (Mrs. William Walsh) (1912). Born in East Walpole, Mass., U.S.A., and educated National University of Ireland, Dublin (Graduate, M.A.). Member of Irish Academy of Letters. Guggenheim Fellow, 1959, 1961, 1962. Her published work include several volumes of short stories, among them *Tales from Bective Bridge* (1942) for which she received the James Tait Black Memorial Prize, and *The Great Wave* (1961), from which the selected story is taken.

LOFTS, NORAH (Mrs. Robert Jorisch) (1904). Educated West Suffolk County School. As Norah Lofts and as Peter Curtis she has published more than twenty books, including *Heaven in Your Hand* (1959), from which the selected story is taken.

MEYNELL, VIOLA (Mrs. John Dallyn) (died 1956). Author of many novels, of biographical works, and of poems and short stories. The story by which she is represented here is taken from her *Collected Stories* (1957).

NAUGHTON, BILL (1910). Born in County Mayo, and brought up in Bolton. Left school at fourteen to become a weaver and then a dyer. Married at nineteen, became unemployed, and got casual work as labourer, barman, salesman, and coal-heaver. For some years was a heavy-lorry driver. Has been a full-time writer since 1945; has published three books and more than a hundred stories, and has written radio and television plays. The selected story is taken from *Late Night on Watling Street* (1959).

OWOYELE, DAVID OLABODE (1934). Born in Nigeria. 'Trained to be a teacher but didn't do much of teaching. Did about two years in the drawing office of a town planning department (neither of us ever discovered why). Has published only short stories; written for radio and television in Nigeria. Tireless collector of rejection slips and proud possessor of unpublished and unpublishable novels. Now works for the Ministry of Information, Northern Nigeria.'

SANSOM, WILLIAM, F.R.S.L. (1912). Educated Uppingham School, and variously in Europe. Has written regularly for literary periodicals in England; books translated into many foreign languages; awarded Travel Scholarship in 1946, literary bursary in 1947, by the Society of Authors. His published works include a number of novels and some volumes of short stories. *Among the Dahlias*, from which the selected tale is taken, appeared in 1957.

SHADBOLT, MAURICE FRANCIS RICHARD (1932). Born in Auckland, N.Z., and educated Te Kuiti High School, Avondale College, and Auckland University. Film director, New Zealand National Film Unit. His published works include *The New Zealanders* (a volume of stories), and *Summer Fires and Winter Country* (1963), from which the selected story is taken.

STIVENS, DAL (1911). A fifth-generation Australian who lives in Sydney. Spent the years 1949–57 in London. Awarded Commonwealth Literary Fellowships by the Australian Government in 1951 and 1962. His stories have been frequently broadcast by the B.B.C., and included in many anthologies, including collections in German, French, Yugoslav, and Czech. Author of two novels and five volumes of short stories. The selected story appeared in *The Scholarly Mouse* (1958) which is now out of print.

USTINOV, PETER ALEXANDER, F.R.S.A. (1921). Actor, dramatist, film director. Joint Director, Nottingham Playhouse, since 1963. Educated Westminster School. Has published many plays, a novel, and a collection of short stories, *Add a Dash of Pity* (1959), from which the selected story is taken.

WAIN, JOHN BARRINGTON (1925). Educated Newcastle under Lyme and St. John's College, Oxford. Fereday Fellow of St. John's College, Oxford, 1946–9; Lecturer in English Literature, University of Reading, 1947–55. Since 1955 has been a free-lance author and critic. Director of Poetry Book Society's festival, 'Poetry at The Mermaid', London, 1961. His publications include several novels, some volumes of criticism, and an autobiography. The selected story comes from his collection of short stories, *Nuncle and Other Stories* (1960).

WILSON, ANGUS FRANK JOHNSTONE, F.R.S.L. (1913). Educated Westminster School and Merton College, Oxford. Foreign Office, 1942–6; Deputy Superintendent of Reading Room, British Museum, 1949–55; Lecturer, School of English Studies, University of East Anglia, since 1963. One of the leading novelists of today, and has also written plays and collections of short stories. The selected story is taken from *A Bit Off the Map* (1957).

Reprinted offset in Great Britain by
The Camelot Press Ltd., London and Southampton